Dear Reader,

As an author, there are some stories that touch my heart in a special way. *Nowhere to Be Found* is one of those stories.

The Victorian house where Anne and the children live reminds me so much of the home where my great-grandmother lived in Iowa. If I close my eyes, I can still picture that big white house. It had a large front porch with round columns and a comfy porch swing. Inside the house was a wide staircase with intricate, hand-carved woodwork that led to a second floor with several bedrooms and a bathroom with a claw-foot tub.

The stories were the best part of visiting my great-grandmother's house. She was born in the 1870s and told me so many exciting stories about pioneer life. The house held stories as well, from the photographs on the walls to the decorative knick-knacks in the china cabinet and the vintage piano in the living room. I was given the antique piano stool from her home and will always treasure it.

In the series Secrets of the Blue Hill Library, Aunt Edie's home holds delightful memories for Anne, as well as some interesting secrets and many new adventures. It will be much fun to watch Anne and her children make the house their home *and* a town library. I can't wait to see what happens next!

Blessings,
Kristin Eckhardt
writing as Emily Thomas

Nowhere
to Be Found

Secrets of the
BLUE HILL LIBRARY

EMILY THOMAS

New York

Nowhere
to Be Found

CHAPTER ONE

A nne Gibson groaned inwardly as she stood with a workman in the front foyer of her great-aunt Edie's beautiful Queen Anne Victorian home, staring straight up to the third floor and out—at the clear blue sky overhead. A large hole in the ceiling hadn't been there when she left for lunch. Everything had been just as it should, with the sounds of energetic hammering ringing from various rooms of the old house, and puffs of construction dust occasionally pouring out an open window as part of a plaster wall came down to make way for new library shelves.

But in the short hour it had taken her to get Liddie and Ben down to the corner and feed them lunch, a section of the third-story roof about the size of an oriental rug had collapsed into the foyer. It now lay scattered in large chunks all over the wood floor, with bits of plaster trailing down the grand mahogany staircase.

Some of the plaster had even fallen into the old elevator that was located near the front door. The metal cage-style elevator had been there as long as Anne could remember and operated with a lever to close the doors and move it up and down. It went all the way to the third floor, and an elevator inspector had recently declared it safe for her family—and future library patrons—to use.

Liddie, her rambunctious five year old daughter, squinted up at the sky. "I need my sunglasses," she said.

Ben, Anne's nine-year-old son, quickly turned to his mother's purse, which still hung from Anne's shoulder. He hunted through it, found Liddie's white Minnie Mouse sunglasses, and gave them to her.

Anne rumpled Ben's hair. "Thank you, Ben," she said.

"You might call it a blessing in disguise, actually," the workman told her cheerfully. "Rot like that, it's gotta come down sometime. At least this way it didn't come down next month, with all the books here."

Anne pushed up her glasses, hoping that she seemed cool and in control. She tried desperately to think of an intelligent question to ask. She knew better than to voice any of the first ones that sprang to mind: *What am I doing here? What was I thinking, coming back home to start a library?*

Anne's husband, Eric, had passed away from a sudden heart attack three years ago, leaving her to raise their two small children alone in New York City. Moving back to Pennsylvania, to Anne's childhood home of Blue Hill, had seemed like a good idea, but now...

Liddie crouched and reached for one of the many chunks of plaster scattered at their feet. Just before she made contact, Anne scooped her up. "No, honey," she said gently. "Those aren't toys."

"It's a shooting star!" Liddie insisted.

Anne glanced back at the piece of plaster in question. Her five-year-old was right—the chunk did bear an eerie resemblance to the glow-in-the-dark shooting stars that graced the ceiling of Liddie's bedroom. Liddie squirmed in her arms. Anne put her down.

"Ben," she said "would you take Liddie around back and find Mrs. Pyle?"

He nodded and then reached for Liddie's hand. "Okay, Mom."

The town of Blue Hill was more than ready to have their new library. Anne hadn't even finished converting her great-aunt Edie's house, and not one shipment of the books she'd ordered had yet arrived, but one enterprising neighbor had already organized a library day camp. The first Anne had heard of it was a week ago, when an old wedding tent had appeared on Aunt Edie's shady back lawn. Less than an hour later, it had been filled with a couple of dozen kids. When Anne went out to investigate, Wendy Pyle, the mother of seven kids and the camp organizer, explained that the campers would be reading some of the children's books that had already been donated to the library by future patrons, along with participating in crafts and other reading activities. Then Wendy had introduced the three high school girls, including her fourteen-year-old daughter, who had volunteered to help supervise the younger children. Before Anne could even digest this information, Wendy had invited Ben and Liddie to join the camp.

Her children had been thrilled and, once Anne had cleared the camp with the contractor to make sure that no one was in any danger from the house construction, she'd given her permission. It wasn't how Anne would have gone about things, but having her two kids out from underfoot during this phase of construction was a godsend.

Anne turned back to the sizable hole over her head. The damage was substantial: It exposed the front hall, but it also seemed to gape wider into other rooms on the third floor. She was renovating the first floor and a portion of the second into the Blue Hill Library, following her beloved great-aunt's bequest to the letter. The third floor and the back half of the second contained the living space for Anne, Ben, and Liddie.

She glanced back at the workman, realization dawning. "It's not just this hall, is it?" she asked him. "We've got damage in the other upstairs rooms too."

For the first time, the workman seemed at a loss for words. He shifted from foot to foot, as if trying to decide how much to tell her.

"Where's Alex?" Anne asked.

"Up on the roof," the workman answered. "Inspecting the damage."

A shadow fell across the hall from high above. For a moment, Anne's mind raced, trying to understand where it had come from. Was the house still crumbling? Was it just a passing cloud? She looked up. Alex's familiar head was silhouetted against the noon sun, peeking over the edge of her damaged ceiling from his perch on the roof.

"Someone call me?" he said.

"How bad is it?" Anne asked. She tilted her head back but raised her hand to shield her eyes from the bright light.

"This?" Alex said. "This isn't a problem. It's all part of the reconstruction plan. We're actually ahead of time now with the ceiling tear-out."

Anne smiled. It was good to see him smile and joke around. She'd known Alex as long as she could remember. They'd grown up around the block from each other and had even dated in high school. But since she'd come home and hired him as contractor on the library renovation, he'd been so professional that she barely recognized him.

Anne pointed up at a chunk of ceiling that still swung gently from a cable in the afternoon breeze.

"I think you missed a piece," she told him.

"You're a tough boss, Anne," he said. "Hang on. There's something I want you to see."

He disappeared, leaving a view of clear sky.

The workman took this as his opportunity to offer her some comfort of his own. "You got nothing to worry about, lady," he told her. "I'm guessing all the rain we've had of late found a weak spot in your roof, and the rest is history. I've seen way worse than this. Once in Silver Lake, I watched a freak tornado throw a whole cottage in the water. Nothing left but the concrete slab it was sitting on. Compared to that, this is nothing."

Anne looked at the friendly man, at a loss for how to answer. He must have mistaken her silence for concern. "We don't get many tornadoes through here," he said reassuringly. "And even if we did, this place is built good. It's pretty, but it's solid."

Despite the gaping hole over her head, the workman's praise filled Anne's heart with warmth. She had always loved Aunt Edie's house—the white clapboard, the slate blue shingles, the shady porch with the delicate wooden detailing Aunt Edie painted so lovely every spring. Inside, it was full of mysterious nooks and crannies. As a girl, Anne had spent almost every day after school in this house while her parents worked. She had loved to sit in the window seat that looked over the side lawn, or pretend she was a lonely serving girl, living in the little garret that faced the backyard, or take the spiral staircase up the magical eight-sided room in the third-floor cupola. Aunt Edie's house hadn't been just a house to Anne—it was the stage for all her childhood dreams.

Through the front window, Anne glimpsed Alex climbing down the last rungs of the ladder. A moment later he was walking through the front door, sidestepping the chunks that had formerly been Aunt Edie's ceiling. Alex didn't stop to talk. Instead, he started picking up the debris that littered the grand staircase. A few moments later, he paused and turned around to see Anne staring at him. "You coming?" he asked.

Anne hadn't been able to resist that question since they were both six years old. She started after him, sliding her palm along the hand-carved mahogany banister as she climbed the steps.

When they reached the third-floor landing, Alex was turning around in a slow circle, his head slightly cocked, as if listening for a signal to tell him what to do next.

"Alex?" Anne asked.

Alex put up a finger for silence then started around the long sweep of banister that encircled the landing. All the rooms on the third floor led off of it. He ducked into the first room to the left. It had been Aunt Edie's art studio, where she practiced whatever craft had currently caught her fancy—drying flowers in white crystals, painting scenes on delicate china, weaving Easter baskets out of reeds and grasses. Now it was bare. Anne had packed up Aunt Edie's things and put them in the next room to protect them from construction damage. It might have been more efficient to store everything in the attic with Aunt Edie's other keepsakes, but the attic was already stuffed full. Anne wanted to use some of Aunt Edie's belongings to decorate the library, so people could feel like they had a connection with the woman who had donated the property. It was a good thing she'd boxed the delicate objects up. Part of the ceiling had collapsed in this room too, revealing a blinding flash of sky.

Alex worked his way along the interior wall of the room, tapping here and there. When he got to the other side, he seemed dissatisfied. He disappeared into the next room, a tiny sitting area. It had been Anne's favorite hiding place as a child. There was nothing in it but a small fainting couch, a little shelf of books, and a star quilt that covered one entire wall—the perfect place for a young girl to curl up and lose herself in one of her aunt's old novels.

Alex had ideas for transforming the sitting area as part of the restoration plan—breaking out walls to add the space to the craft room or Aunt Edie's bedroom next door. But Anne had refused. She wanted to leave this one corner of the house just the way it had been. The couch and the quilt were still there, crowded by boxes of items waiting to be unpacked when the other rooms were finished. She trailed Alex into the little room.

Now he was knocking on the cream-colored walls in earnest: rapping here, pausing to listen, then moving over a few inches and rapping again.

"Alex?" Anne said. "You're not telling me the walls are unsound now, are you?"

In answer, Alex pulled back a corner of the star quilt and rapped again. The sound was different there. Deeper. Somehow hollow.

"Yep," Alex said, talking to himself as if Anne weren't there.

"Yep what?" Anne asked.

Alex lifted a corner of the quilt gently then drew the whole thing back with a flourish.

Anne stared at it for a moment. "Is that a door?"

Alex nodded as he let the quilt fall back in place then reached over his head to lift it down, along with the display rod it hung from. The large square of wallpaper it had covered was a shade darker than the rest of the room, which was a rich cream, covered with pink flowers and vines. The pocket door was covered with the same wallpaper, making it blend in so well that Anne almost missed it.

"Does it open?" she asked.

"I don't know," Alex said. "This is the first time I've seen it. I could tell something was strange on the roof from the skylight and the way the rooms came together where the ceiling had fallen."

"What skylight?"

"The one on the roof that appears to be located just past this door. You can't see it from ground level, but it's up there." He nodded at the door. "You want to do the honors?"

Anne stood stock still for a moment as her mind grappled with this new discovery. She'd spent hours curled up just a few feet away and had never known this secret door was there. And what about Aunt Edie? She was one of the most open people Anne had ever known—warm, welcoming, talkative. Could she have kept this door a secret all these years? On the other hand, could Aunt Edie have lived in the house for so long without ever discovering it herself?

"Anne?" Alex said quietly.

His voice roused her from her thoughts. She took another step forward and placed her fingertips in the shallow brass pull on the door. She glanced at Alex then slid the door open.

Inside was a tiny triangular room with no furniture but a small writing desk and a simple chair. Light poured down on it from a strange skylight—a four-paned window, set into the ceiling.

Over the desk was a framed photograph of a young woman in a lacy white dress, with a bouquet of lilies and daisies so big that she had to hold it in both hands. Beside her stood a dark-haired young man who looked very uncomfortable in his ill-fitting suit. One broad hand rested on her great-aunt's forearm, the sleeve of his suit just a little too short. His mouth was blurred in a smile, but his clear eyes were in sharp focus.

Somehow Alex had followed her into the room without making a sound. He lifted the photograph gently from its nail.

"You recognize them?" he asked.

"That's Aunt Edie, when she was young," Anne said. "It looks like a wedding portrait." She narrowed her eyes at the grainy photograph. "But as far as I know, Aunt Edie never married."

CHAPTER TWO

It looks like you're wrong about that," Alex said, turning toward Anne. "Your aunt is wearing a wedding dress."

Anne stared at the photograph, her mind spinning. Aunt Edie looked about twenty years old and her groom only a couple of years older, at most. Her aunt had been born in 1930 and graduated from high school in 1948, which meant the photo must have been taken sometime in the late forties or early fifties. "Do you recognize the groom?"

Alex slowly shook his head as he studied the wedding portrait. "He doesn't look familiar. Although I'm sure he's changed a lot since that picture was taken."

"He must be in his eighties," Anne said, "if he's still alive." She glanced up to find Alex staring at her.

"You're really thrown by this, aren't you?" he said. "Are you sure Edie never said anything about a husband?"

"I'm absolutely positive," Anne said. "She told me so many things about her life." She gestured helplessly toward the wedding portrait. "How could she leave out something like this?" And what else had Aunt Edie hidden from her?

Alex glanced around the small room. "Looks like she had her secrets." He walked over to the door, examining the construction. "I'd say this door was installed at least forty years ago."

"And that quilt has been hanging on the wall for as long as I can remember." A sudden memory flashed through Anne's mind. "Aunt Edie always warned me not to play around that quilt, that it meant something very special to her." Her aunt had always had a mischievous streak, and she would delight in having a secret room all to herself. But a secret *groom* seemed too much—even for Aunt Edie.

Anne met Alex's gaze. "Now I'm wondering if it was the quilt that was special—or the room that it concealed?"

He shrugged. "I guess we'll never know." He reached for the door handle. "I'd better go find a temporary repair for that hole in your roof. There's a possibility of rain tonight."

Anne stifled a sigh as he walked out the door. Maybe she'd been wrong to move back to Blue Hill, following her heart instead of her head. She'd just always felt so safe here—and so loved. But now the hole in the roof and the hidden room made her doubt her judgment.

"Oh, Lord," she prayed softly, "give me strength." It was a prayer that she'd repeated often since Eric's death. The recent move to Blue Hill made her feel so far away from the life she'd built in New York with her late husband.

Anne looked around the room, noting the simple touches that reminded her of Aunt Edie. The faint scent of her aunt's lavender perfume still lingered in the air. One of Aunt Edie's many pairs of reading glasses lay on the writing desk. Wire-framed reading glasses lay on the writing desk. Anne walked over and picked up the glasses, smiling at the memory of them perched on her aunt's nose.

The memories gave her comfort, and her doubts started to melt away. Maybe Aunt Edie had left all of this here knowing that Anne would find the hidden room. They'd always loved reading mysteries together when Anne was a young girl. She looked at the desk, wondering if there were any clues that might help her discover the identity of the mystery groom in the photograph.

She opened the middle drawer and found several ink pens and pencils, along with a magnifying glass and some crisp, white pages of stationery adorned by a small cluster of embossed lilacs in the bottom right corner. Edie loved lilacs and had a row of purple lilac bushes bordering the large backyard.

Anne sat down in the chair, lightly brushing her hand over the top of the desk. Then her gaze fell on the wedding photograph, and she realized that Aunt Edie had placed the photograph directly in front of the chair. Had she spent hours looking at it? The placement of that photograph in such a prominent place in the room seemed to belie the possibility that Aunt Edie had suffered through a quick, failed marriage.

She leaned down to open another drawer. Inside, she found a small, black velvet box. Pulling it out, she lifted the lid and found a pair of gold cuff links inside. She gently removed one of the vintage cuff links, turning it over in her fingers. The cuff links were engraved with the initials J.R., along with a maker's mark.

Anne stared at the cuff links as she searched her memory for any man in her aunt's life who had the initials J.R. The cuff links were old, the sheen dull, as if they'd sat in the velvet box for decades. She plucked the magnifying glass from the middle drawer and walked over to the grainy photograph, leaning in for a closer look at the man's hand resting on great-aunt Edie's arm. His shirt sleeve peeked out of the groom's suit, and she could just glimpse a cuff link that appeared to be the same size and shape as the cuff link in her hand. She peered at it through the magnifying glass, noting that the filigree design on the cuff links looked very similar to the ones she'd found in the velvet box.

"Who is he, Aunt Edie?" Anne said out loud.

The sound of hammering started on the roof far above her. No doubt Alex had figured out how to seal the roof shut until he could make a more permanent repair. Even after all of these years, she trusted him to do the job right.

She turned her attention back to the photograph. The more she looked at it, the more curious she became. Had Anne's own parents known of Edie's marriage? Had it been a family scandal of some kind? Had that scandal driven Edie to this secret room where she could cherish this portrait and her memories in private?

Anne continued searching through the desk, hoping to find more answers. She placed the cuff links back into the velvet box and returned it to the drawer. Then she opened the drawer beneath it. There lay a thick sheaf of papers secured in the middle with a large rubber band.

She lifted it out, surprised to recognize Aunt Edie's flowing script on the lined, yellowed pages. Her gaze perused the first two paragraphs on the front page.

Ruth never believed in love at first sight—until she saw Harry walking down the lane that led to her father's house. She stood in the doorway, unable to move as he bounded up the steps in that easy way of his.

He introduced himself to her then told Ruth that he'd been hired to help harvest the family apple orchard. She didn't tell him that hired hands were supposed to arrive at the back of the house. Instead, she held out her hand, brazen as can be, and said, "I'm Ruth Chapman."

He reached out and shook her hand. "Hello, Ruth," he said with a smile, his eyes gazing into hers. They were a deep, rich blue with small flecks of gold. One smile was all it took. Ruth was in love.

Anne lowered the paper, her cheeks feeling a little flushed. She'd never imagined Aunt Edie as a romance writer, much less writing what appeared to be a love story. She fanned through the pages, noting that there were more than three hundred of them. She stopped at the last page. Under the words *The End* her aunt had signed her name, *Edie Summers*, along with the year *1954.*

She signed her maiden name, Anne thought to herself as she flipped back to the beginning to read more. Then she heard Ben's voice.

"Mom?" he called out. "Hey, Mom, where are you?"

She slipped the manuscript back into the drawer then hurried out of the hidden room, not wanting to let the children know about it until she'd had a chance to examine it further.

She closed the pocket door behind her then replaced the star quilt on the wall. By the time she finished, Ben was waiting for her at the top of the stairs.

"Hey, there," Anne said, noting the smudge of dirt on her son's nose. She reached over to rub it gently away. "What do you need?"

"Mrs. Pyle wants to know if we have any paper cups. We need them for a game."

"Let me take a look," Anne said, heading downstairs toward the old first-floor kitchen with Ben following behind her. She had stocked up on disposable plates and cups when they'd first moved, knowing it would take a while to unpack the dishes and glasses from home. She found an unopened package of cups and carried them over to her son. "Will these work?"

"Yep," he said, taking them from her. "Thanks, Mom." Then he turned around and bounded out the back door, letting the screen door bang shut behind him. She walked over to the window, pulling the curtain back far enough to see her son join the group of children waiting outside.

She leaned against the windowsill and watched them for a while, enjoying the warm August sun on her face. The daisies that bracketed the back door were in full bloom. Aunt Edie had been holding a bouquet of lilies and daisies in the wedding photograph. Had the daisies come from this yard?

Aunt Edie had moved here with her parents after they'd sold the family farm. She'd worked as a travel writer, penning articles for magazines and traveling frequently. When her parents grew frail with age, Edie stayed put in Blue Hill to care for them. They'd left this house to her in their will.

Anne began to wonder if all that traveling had been for Aunt Edie's magazine articles or to rendezvous with her secret husband.

She itched to get her hands back on the manuscript and find out more about the fictional romance that she believed was really the story of Aunt Edie and her mystery groom. But right now she wanted to put all her focus on her kids.

Tonight, after the kids were in bed, she planned to explore the secret room again and check out the progress Alex was making on the renovations. Then she'd read to her heart's content.

* * *

That evening, Anne stifled a yawn as she walked around the first and second floors of the house, turning off lights and picking up some of the clutter that the workmen had left behind. She enjoyed seeing the library come to life.

Anne loved walking through this house, still finding it hard to believe she'd be living here permanently. There were four rooms on the first floor, in addition to the foyer, that would be part of the library. More library rooms would be located in the front half of the second floor, with Alex remodeling the rooms in the back half into her family's private living room and kitchen. The living room was done, but the new kitchen was still under construction. Their bedrooms were on the third floor, along with Aunt Edie's old art room, the small sitting room, and the hidden room.

Now Anne just needed to decide what to do with all the library rooms she had available. Anne knew she wanted a fiction room, a nonfiction room, and a children's room, as well as an area for checking out books. That left three others rooms available for the library, perhaps rooms that could be dedicated to a certain subject or genre. She hadn't made any final decisions yet, but Alex would need some direction soon.

Her children were in bed, waiting for her to come up and hear their prayers. She smiled to herself, looking forward to her favorite part of the day. She and her late husband used to tuck the children in together, and sometimes she still felt him with her when she kissed each child good night. Anne knew Eric would be proud of her decision to pull up roots and move to Blue Hill. He'd always loved this house too, exploring the nooks and crannies with her the few times they'd visited Aunt Edie.

Only, they'd never found the hidden room behind the star quilt. Anne headed there now, eager to read more of the manuscript her aunt had left in the desk drawer. Her gaze moved to the wedding portrait, and she realized once more how happy her aunt looked in the picture. She'd been deeply in love, that much was obvious.

Anne retrieved the manuscript and then flipped off the lights. As she headed across the hallway, the glow of the moon shone through the white tarp that Alex had used to seal off the hole in the roof. Thunder rumbled in the distance, and she took comfort in Alex's assurance that no rain would find its way inside the house before he had a chance to make permanent repairs.

She headed to Ben's bedroom first, not surprised to find Liddie in the same bed as her brother.

"The thunder scared me," Liddie said before Anne even had a chance to comment on her bedroom switcheroo. "We were reading a story together."

"Well, that's nice," Anne said, setting the manuscript on the dresser then heading over to the bed. "Shall we say our prayers?"

Liddie climbed out of bed and knelt down on the floor, light brown hair falling on her face. She brushed it back then squeezed her brown eyes closed and folded her hands together on top of the log cabin quilt made by Anne's mother.

"Dear God," Liddie began, "thank You for not letting Justin Pyle squish that caterpillar today at library camp. I put it in one of the lilac bushes so it could turn into a butterfly. Please make sure it's safe in its cocoon. And please let us have oatmeal cookies tomorrow for our snack at camp, because I really like them. Amen." She opened her eyes again and started to stand up but quickly knelt once more. "But no raisins in the cookies, please. Amen."

Anne smiled as she watched her daughter climb back into bed. Then she leaned down to kiss Liddie's soft, freckled cheek, tucking the covers around her. She would move Liddie back to her own bed after she fell asleep, aware that her daughter still didn't feel quite at home in their new, big house.

Anne walked over to the other side of the bed as Ben knelt on the floor. "Dear God," he began, his voice very solemn, "thank You for everything. Please bless Mom and Liddie and Grandma and Grandpa Gibson and Grandma and Grandpa Summers, and Uncle Ted and Aunt Caroline and my cousin Oliver..."

As Ben went on to recite all the names of his family and friends, Anne reached out and gently brushed her fingers through his brown hair. Ever since Eric had passed away, Ben prayed for all of his loved ones every night. He was her brave little man, and he'd grown closer in his relationship with God—just as Anne had. They had all leaned on Him in their grief over Eric's death and had grown stronger these past three years.

"Thank You for letting me meet all the kids in library camp," he said, his voice faltering a little. "And if You could make them like me, that would be great. Amen."

Anne echoed his prayer in her mind. He'd been a bit lonely since their move from New York, and she longed for both of her children to make good friends in their new town. School was due to start in a couple of weeks, and she hoped and prayed they'd find new friends there.

After Anne tucked Ben into bed, she made her way to her own bedroom. It was the same room she'd had as a child whenever she stayed with Aunt Edie. Her family had lived in a house four blocks away, but her mother's job as a nurse and her father's accounting career often kept them working late, leaving Aunt Edie to take care of her. Anne still loved this room. On one side there was a large, leaded glass window that looked out over the valley. She could see Cooper's Pond in the distance, named for the family that had farmed the land a century ago. She loved to reminisce about the days she'd gone fishing at Cooper's Pond with her aunt. Someday soon, she'd take Ben and Liddie there for a picnic and a fishing lesson. She hoped they loved the idyllic spot as much as she did.

Anne prepared for bed and said her own prayers, thanking God for the wonderful blessings of her children and asking for His continuing guidance in her life. Even when doubts filled her mind, she knew that God was always with her.

She crawled into bed with Aunt Edie's manuscript, the glow of the bedside lamp lighting the pages in front of her. With a contented sigh, she began to read from where she'd left off.

Ruth had lived in Green Lake all her life. She'd never been tempted by the lure of the big city that had led some of her friends and family to move to Pittsburgh or even Philadelphia.

She loved life in this small town and loved the people in it. As a child, she and her brothers, Davey and Marvin, would head into town with their parents every Saturday night to watch a movie at the Green Lake Theater. The newsreels offered her an exciting glimpse of the major events around the world, but she'd always felt snug and safe in Green Lake.

Anne stopped reading for a moment, struck once again by the autobiographical nature of the story. Davey had been the name of Edie's older brother. Anne's grandfather, Marvin, had been the youngest of the family and would have been around seventeen years old in the setting of the story.

It was almost as if she were reading Aunt Edie's diary instead of a fictional romance. While the writing was somewhat simple, it was from the heart. Anne could almost hear her dear aunt's clear voice as she read. Anne snuggled down farther under the cozy, red-and-white quilt and kept reading until her eyelids grew heavy. She hoped to discover some clue to the secrets in Aunt Edie's life.

CHAPTER THREE

The next morning, Anne stood at the stove flipping pancakes while Ben and Liddie sat at the kitchen table. They were still using the original kitchen on the first floor until Alex finished the new private kitchen on the second floor. The night had passed without a rainstorm, despite the thunder that had rattled the windowpanes, causing Anne to toss and turn, her mind filled with unanswered questions about the wedding photograph.

"May I have more orange juice?" Liddie asked.

"Please," Anne reminded her.

"Please," Liddie echoed. She picked up her fork and ate one of the blueberries from her plate.

Anne had used different fruits to make faces on the pancakes. There were two sliced banana eyes, a strawberry nose, and a row of blueberries for the smile. Liddie had eaten almost all of the blueberries.

Anne walked over to the table to pour more juice into Liddie's glass. Then she turned to her son. "More orange juice?"

"Yes, please," Ben said, stabbing a pineapple ear on one side of his pancake.

Anne topped off his juice glass then returned to the stove to scoop up a pancake with her spatula and set it on the platter beside the stove.

She was about to pour more batter into the skillet when the front doorbell rang, echoing through the house. "Who could that be?" she murmured, cinching the belt on her yellow terry cloth robe. Alex and his crew weren't due for another hour, unless he'd decided to get an early start on the roof.

"I'll get it," Ben exclaimed, hopping out of his chair and bounding out of the kitchen, wearing his Spider-Man pajamas. She could hear his bare feet slapping against the wood floor as he ran through the rooms that led to the front door.

A few moments later, Anne heard Wendy Pyle's voice wafting from the foyer. Anne panicked for a moment, combing her fingers through her hair and wishing she'd dressed and applied a little makeup before breakfast. Dirty dishes from last night's supper were still stacked next to the sink, and there was a small dollop of pancake batter smeared on the counter. She quickly grabbed a dishcloth and wiped it away.

"Good morning," Wendy greeted her, following Ben into the kitchen. She carried two large shopping bags. "I hope you don't mind me barging in like this, but I have so much planned for camp today that I can hardly wait to get started."

"Not at all," Anne said, patting down her hair. "Sorry about the mess."

Wendy cheerfully brushed off the apology with a wave of her hand. "Oh, please, everything looks wonderful. I'd love to live in a house like this. With seven kids underfoot, my house always looks like it could be declared a natural disaster area." She laughed. "I'm letting their father cook them breakfast this morning before he brings them over here. This time he can clean up the disaster."

Anne couldn't help but laugh with her, charmed by Wendy's cheerful demeanor. "Would you like some pancakes?"

Wendy's blue eyes widened with delight. At forty-two, she was about eight years older than Anne, with chin-length black hair and an easy smile. "Well, maybe just one, if you have some extra. They look scrumptious."

"I have one ready to go right here," Anne said, adding some fruit to the pancake on the platter in front of her then setting it on the table. "How about some orange juice or a cup of coffee?"

"Coffee sounds great," Wendy said, taking a seat next to Liddie. She leaned over to the little girl as she arranged the fruit on the plate into a face on her pancake. "What shall I name him? How about Herman? He looks like a Herman to me."

Liddie snorted with amusement. "Not Herman. How about Fluffy?"

"Perfect," Wendy exclaimed, picking up the strawberry nose with her fingers and taking a bite. "You have a delicious nose, Fluffy."

Both Ben and Liddie laughed as Anne set a cup of coffee in front of Wendy.

"Oh, before I forget," Wendy said, picking up one of the shopping bags. "Do you have room in your fridge for some chocolate bars? We're making s'mores for our camp snack today, and I'm afraid the chocolate bars will all melt if I keep them outside."

"Sure, I can make room," Anne said as she walked over to the refrigerator. She'd gone grocery shopping the day before and had stocked the shelves almost full. She moved some packages around as Wendy approached her with the bags.

"I have some juice boxes too," Wendy said, pulling out three twelve-packs of fruit juice from the shopping bag.

Anne pushed her yogurt cups and deli meats and cheese as far back on the shelf as possible; then she began to cram in the juice boxes. "It's a little tight."

"I'm sure you can make it work," Wendy said, setting the boxes of chocolate bars on the counter next to the fridge. "Will you be around today?"

"I think so," Anne said, hoping that Wendy wasn't going to ask her to help out with the camp. Any other time she'd be thrilled to spend time with the children, but she still had so much work to do on the house. And there was still the lingering question of the wedding photograph.

Anne suddenly looked at Wendy. She'd been acquainted with Aunt Edie for the past five years or so. Was it possible she knew something?

Wendy cocked her head to one side, her mouth tipped up in a curious smile when she noticed Anne staring at her. "What is it?"

Anne hesitated, feeling a little uncertain now. "It's nothing really. I just was curious about something…"

Wendy's smile widened. "Well, now *I'm* curious, so you have to tell me."

"It's about my aunt," Anne explained, placing the first box of chocolate bars on top of an egg carton in the fridge. There was just enough room to squeeze in the rest of the boxes.

"Go on," Wendy encouraged her.

"Well, I found an old photograph of her." Anne closed the refrigerator door and turned around to face Wendy. "It was a wedding portrait."

"A wedding portrait?" Wendy gasped. "But Edie never married."

"I know," Anne said. "Or, at least, that's what I thought was true. But now I don't know what to think." She'd called her parents last night at their home in Florida and told them about the picture. They'd been as shocked as Anne at the possibility that Edie had ever been a bride.

Ben pushed his chair back, the wooden legs scraping against the floor. "I finished my pancakes. May I be excused?"

"Yes, you may," Anne said, glancing over at the table. Ben's plate was clean, but Liddie was making a new fruit face on the half pancake she had left on her plate. "How about you, Liddie?" Anne asked. "All done?"

Liddie popped a banana slice into her mouth then nodded as she slid out of her chair. The hem of her pink cotton nightgown brushed against her ankles.

"Okay," Anne told them, "why don't you two go brush your teeth and change into your camp clothes. Then you can help Mrs. Pyle set up today.

Anne glanced at Wendy as the two children scampered out of the room, realizing she might have spoken out of turn. "I hope that's all right."

"I'd love to have the help," Wendy said, slipping back into her chair. "Besides, they're so well-behaved; I'm hoping some of it rubs off on my kids." She poured a generous helping of maple syrup over the top of her pancake. "Now tell me more about this old wedding photograph."

Anne sat down across from her and began eating Liddie's leftovers. "Well, it looks like it was taken around 1950, when Aunt Edie was about twenty years old. The groom doesn't look much older, but I have no idea who he might be."

"Well, that is a mystery," Wendy said. "Why would Edie keep him a secret all this time?"

That was the question that kept plaguing Anne. She didn't tell Wendy about the hidden room behind the quilt or the manuscript and engraved cuff links she'd found there. She wasn't quite ready to share all of Aunt Edie's secrets.

Anne had made it to chapter three of the manuscript before she'd fallen asleep last night, but most of what she'd read had been flashbacks of Ruth's childhood, long before she'd met Harry. Flashbacks that had been all too similar to the stories Aunt Edie had told Anne about her own childhood. The Ruth and Harry characters had to be aliases for Edie and the mystery groom—a man with the initials J.R., since the engraved cuff links matched the ones in the photo.

"Wow, if she really got married," Wendy continued, "I wonder what happened. Maybe her husband died or they got divorced— she might not have said anything, since it would have been practically taboo back then. Or...oh dear! What if they got married and it didn't end?"

Anne opened her mouth to reply, but Wendy didn't stop for air.

"What if Edie has some mystery husband who's still out there?" Wendy said. "Imagine answering the door one day and having her husband say he's come to get their house back!"

Her words caused a slight chill to run through Anne's veins. Of all the possible scenarios she had considered last night, that hadn't been one of them. "Even if he were still alive, he must be in his eighties. Why would he want this house after all these years?"

Wendy shrugged. "I'm sure it's nothing to worry about, but *if* they never divorced and *if* he has nieces or nephews or other heirs, he might think he should get at least half the value of Edie's estate."

Anne took a sip of her coffee, her mind spinning. Aunt Edie's will had been quite clear. She'd bequeathed the house to Anne with the stipulation that it was to be converted, in part, into a library for the town of Blue Hill with Anne appointed to run it. The money from Aunt Edie's estate left enough to remodel the house and library, as well as a trust to pay Anne's salary. The town council members had agreed to enter into a fifty-year-term lease that allowed for public usage of the specified portions of the building for a nominal rental fee. All of the library-related contents were to become the official property of the town, and the library would eventually receive funding from the community for its upkeep.

The chance that Aunt Edie had a husband somewhere who might challenge the will had to be slim indeed. Still, stranger things had happened. She didn't want to live with that uncertainty, no matter how slight. The best way to feel secure in her new home was to find out the identity of the mystery groom in the wedding portrait and discover what had happened between him and her great-aunt.

"Well," Wendy said softly. "What are you thinking?"

Anne met her gaze. "I think I want to find out who he is. I'm just not sure where to start looking."

Wendy smiled. "That's fairly easy. I'd start with Reverend Tom. He knows just about everybody in this town."

Anne nodded then took another sip of her coffee, wondering if she should call the reverend today. The sooner she could identify the mystery groom, the better. "That's a good idea."

Wendy glanced at the clock on the stove. "Look at the time! I'd better start setting up for camp." She popped the last bite of pancake into her mouth then rose from her chair. "Thank you for breakfast. That was a wonderful way to begin my day."

"You're welcome," Anne said, following her down the stairs to the back door. "I may go out for a little while, so feel free to come in anytime and get your juice boxes and chocolate bars. Just watch out for the remodeling crew."

"Will do," Wendy promised then headed into the backyard. "And tell the kids to come outside and join me anytime. I've got plenty for them to do."

"I will." Anne quickly cleaned up the kitchen. Then she rounded up her children and made sure they were prepared for the day before sending them outside with Wendy. When she was alone once more, Anne picked up her cell phone and dialed the reverend's number.

"Hello, this is the Blue Hill Community Church, Reverend Tom speaking," he said, answering on the first ring.

"Hello, Reverend Tom," Anne began, trying to tamp down the flutter of excitement inside of her. "This is Anne Gibson. I was wondering if you had time to meet with me today."

"Of course," the reverend said without hesitation. "I'm leaving to visit a few folks in the hospital, but I could stop by your place on the way back."

Anne didn't want to try to have a conversation with the sound of noisy hammers raining down on the roof. "If you don't mind, I'll come to the church office. Will late morning work for you?"

"That sounds perfect," he said cordially. "I should be back from the hospital by eleven."

"Wonderful," Anne exclaimed. "I'll see you then." She hung up then headed to her bedroom to get dressed and prepare for the day ahead of her. The rumble of a pickup truck on the white gravel driveway announced Alex's arrival. Soon the hole in the roof would be fixed. Anne just hoped she could fill in some of the holes in the story surrounding that mysterious wedding portrait.

CHAPTER FOUR

L ater that morning, Anne walked out of Benkelman's Office Supply on Main Street. She'd taken the wedding photograph to the store and made a photocopy on one of the machines that Fred Benkelman made available to his customers. The copy had turned out well, looking almost exactly like the original. She placed it in her tote bag then returned to her car.

Anne took a few moments to carefully replace the original wedding photograph in its frame, wrap it in a quilt, and place it in the trunk of her silver Impala. Then she hopped into the driver's seat and made her way to the Blue Hill Community Church.

She'd grown up in this church, and it was like a second home to her. She could still remember giggling at the outrageous hats Aunt Edie used to wear on Easter morning. Her aunt had a stylish flair and would often inspire other women in the church to don Easter bonnets of their own, although usually much more modest than the hats Aunt Edie wore.

Anne and the children had found her aunt's collection of colorful Easter bonnets in a closet in one of the spare rooms. They were adorned with feathers and large bows, and one even had a large cascade of silk violets. Anne had modeled a few for the children, parading around the room until Liddie and Ben had both dissolved in laughter. But despite her aunt's fun with hats, she'd always honored the solemnity of the holy day; and her deep, abiding faith inspired the congregation even more than her hats.

Anne found herself smiling at the memories as she turned onto Church Street and pulled into the church parking lot. There was only one other vehicle there, a black vintage car polished to a high shine. Her husband had been a big fan of vintage cars, and she'd learned enough from him to identify this one as a Packard, probably somewhere around a 1948 model. She grabbed her tote bag as she climbed out of the car then walked over for a closer look. The front of the vintage car sported a heavy chrome grill. The smooth curves and the whitewall tires on the two-door sedan marked it as quite sporty for its day.

"Like her?" a voice called from the side door of the church.

Anne looked up to find Reverend Tom standing in the open doorway, a wide smile on his face. "She's beautiful. Is she yours?"

"She is," he confirmed. "My grandpa gave her to me when I was twenty years old. I've been taking care of her ever since."

"Excellent care, from the looks of it," Anne said, tempted to run her palm over the smooth-as-glass polished hood. She resisted the urge, remembering Eric's admonition that most vintage car owners preferred that admirers look rather than touch.

Reverend Tom joined her in the parking lot. He had a slim, lanky build and stood just under six feet tall. His hair was graying, but he still had a youthful twinkle in his kind brown eyes. "I don't usually drive Bessie to church, but I promised one of my parishioners that he could ride home in her when he got dismissed from the hospital."

"Bessie?" Anne said with a smile.

Reverend Tom chuckled. "My grandpa named her after my grandma and made it a stipulation of the gift that I didn't name the car anything else."

"What did your grandma think of that?"

"She always claimed that Grandpa talked to the car more than he did to her, but I think she was secretly pleased by it." Reverend Tom's eyes twinkled as he turned to Anne. "And I have Bessie to thank for my wife."

Anne lifted a brow. "Your grandma or your car?"

"Both, actually. Maggie was boarding with my grandparents while she was working as the new kindergarten teacher in town. Grandma suggested that I should ask her out on a date. Suggested it more than once, actually," Reverend Tom said with another chuckle. "I was pretty shy back then, but I finally worked up the courage to ask Maggie out for a drive in the country one Sunday afternoon."

She watched as Reverend Tom pulled a small microfiber cloth from his shirt pocket and polished a barely visible spot on the hood. He reminded her of her father, kind and gentle, with an easy way of talking that set her immediately at ease. She missed her parents. Her father had accepted his company's buyout offer for an early retirement and they'd moved to Florida five years ago. They'd wanted her and the kids to join them after Eric's death, but Anne had been determined to make it on her own. So far, she'd had no regrets and was comforted by the fact that her parents were only a phone call away if she ever needed their help or advice.

"Neither one of us said much on the drive," Reverend Tom said, continuing his story. "We were both shy back then, I guess, and I was starting to think our date was a big mistake, when something unexpected happened."

His smile was contagious, and Anne found herself smiling as she waited for him to tell her more.

"I ran out of gas," he said. "I can laugh about it now, but I was horrified at the time. I mean, some boys used to pull that kind of stunt on purpose—so I could only imagine what she must have thought of me. I apologized several times and then told her we'd have to walk back to town."

Anne hitched the tote bag higher on her shoulder. "Was she upset?"

"Not at all," he said, a note of wonder in his voice. "We walked three miles along country roads, and I'm not sure why, but our shyness seemed to fade away with every step. I talked more to Maggie on that one date than I'd ever talked to any girl in my life. By the time we reached home, I knew she was the girl I wanted to marry."

His story touched her deeply, and Anne suddenly sensed that she could trust this man as much as she could her own father. Any apprehension about showing him Aunt Edie's wedding photograph faded away. "So that's how Grandma Bessie and Bessie the Car both brought your wife into your life."

"That's how," he affirmed, giving the hood of the car a gentle pat. "We had our twenty-fifth wedding anniversary picture taken with the old girl." He chuckled. "I mean, the car, not Grandma. But I'm pretty sure she was smiling down on us from heaven." He stuffed the cloth back into his pocket. "Now I'm sure you didn't come here to hear the story of my life, so why don't we head into my office."

"All right," she said, following him into the church. It was a red brick building, constructed in the late nineteenth century with a huge stained glass window above the front entrance and narrow stained glass windows on both sides of the sanctuary. The original church bell still hung above the steeple. As a teenager, she and the other members of the youth group had taken turns ringing the bell before the worship service every Sunday. Someday, she thought to herself, Ben and Liddie would ring the bell.

Reverend Tom led her to the passageway that connected the church to the newly added fellowship hall. His office was located off that passageway and still had the aroma of new carpet.

"Please have a seat," Reverend Tom said, waving her toward the two padded chairs opposite his wide, oak desk. Two walls sported floor-to-ceiling bookshelves, and each shelf was crammed with books.

"This is impressive," she said, taking a glance at the bookshelf behind her. There were not only numerous theology books but books on history, philosophy, and science, as well as several volumes of fiction in a variety of genres. "You must like to read."

"I love it," he said, taking a seat behind his desk. "And I can't wait until you open the new library. How's it coming along?"

"We're getting there," she said with a wistful sigh, remembering the hole in the ceiling. "We seem to take two steps forward, then one step back."

He smiled. "I'm sure it will all be worth the trouble. Edie would be so pleased by your progress."

"I hope so," Anne said, wanting to do her aunt proud. "Aunt Edie is actually the reason I'm here."

Reverend Tom lifted a brow. "Oh?"

Anne reached into her tote bag and pulled out the photocopy of the wedding picture. She set it on the desk in front of him. "I found this in one of the rooms in Aunt Edie's house."

She left out the part about it being a hidden room, not ready to reveal that fact to anyone just yet. Maybe she never would. It could be a secret that she and Aunt Edie shared together—and Alex, of course. But something told her that Aunt Edie wouldn't mind him knowing about it.

He stared at it for a long moment. "Is that Edie?"

"It is."

"I never knew she was married," Reverend Tom said, looking at Anne in amazement.

"I never knew it either," Anne admitted, "not until I found this photograph. I still can't believe it's true."

Reverend Tom looked at the photograph again. "Who is the groom?"

"I was hoping you could tell me." She leaned forward in her chair for a closer look at the photo. "I don't recognize him, but I think there's a good chance he's from Blue Hill, or he at least lived here at some point. Aunt Edie lived here all her life, when she wasn't traveling."

Reverend Tom rolled his office chair back a few inches to open the middle drawer of his desk. He pulled out a magnifying glass then held it in front of the photograph. After several moments, he shook his head. "I wish I did recognize him, Anne, but he's not familiar to me at all." He looked up at her. "Of course, this photograph must have been taken about...sixty years ago?"

Anne nodded. "I think that's pretty close. It's probably about as old as your car out there."

A wry smile tipped up one corner of his mouth. "If only old Bessie could talk."

Anne nodded, not sure what to do next. Reverend Tom couldn't identify the mystery groom, but maybe he could tell her something about Aunt Edie that she didn't know. Something that would lead her in the right direction. "I hope you don't mind my asking, but did you and my aunt ever talk about...life?"

His smile widened. "All the time. Edie was a special woman, as I'm sure you know." He nodded toward his bookcase. "She borrowed many of my books here, and we had long discussions about history and philosophy—all kinds of subjects. I always valued her viewpoint and opinions."

"How about her personal life?" Anne asked. "Did she ever talk about marriage or children? Ever have regrets?"

He thought for a long moment and then shook his head. "I can't remember her ever saying anything like that to me. In fact, just the opposite. She lived her life to the fullest, enjoying the small moments as much as the big ones." He leaned forward, resting his forearms on his desk. "I remember I once asked her if she planned to celebrate her seventieth birthday. She looked at me like I was crazy and said, 'Of course! I celebrate my birth every day and thank the Lord for all my blessings.'"

Anne smiled, knowing that was Aunt Edie's style. She did celebrate life and had never shown much regret for anything.

"Regret is a waste of time," she'd said to Anne once. *"Instead of mourning the past, move toward the future. You never know what God has in store for you."*

As she remembered those words, Anne wondered if Aunt Edie had gained that philosophy through her own experience. Had she mourned her marriage before eventually learning to move forward and trust God in her life? Had that been the foundation of her deep faith? She might never know the answer.

Just like she might never know the name of the mystery groom.

"This troubles you, doesn't it?" Reverend Tom asked gently.

She nodded, nipping her lower lip between her teeth. "I guess it does. I've searched the Internet, especially the genealogy websites, for a marriage license or something to explain this, but there was nothing there." She took a deep breath. "Aunt Edie was so special to me and yet, I knew nothing about her marriage to this man. I almost feel like a part of my own life is missing."

"What do you plan to do now?" he asked.

"I want to find him, or at the very least, find out his identity." She met his gaze. "Do you want to help?"

He smiled, pointing to the bookshelf on his right. "Do you see all those mystery novels? There's nothing I'd like better than helping you solve a real-life mystery in Blue Hill."

She smiled. "I'm glad to hear it. I was hoping we might start with the church records."

He smiled. "Of course! I should have thought of that sooner."

"It's possible Aunt Edie's marriage was recorded there." He rose from his chair. "Let's go find out."

CHAPTER FIVE

A nne and Reverend Tom walked from the fellowship hall into the church and down the basement stairs. Anne had attended Sunday school in the church basement as a child, along with her best friend, Sallie Gifford. They'd lost touch shortly after high school, with Anne going off to college and Sallie heading overseas for a mission trip. Anne wondered if Sallie had ever come back to Blue Hill.

"Do you know Glen and Cindy Gifford?" Anne asked when they reached the basement. "They have a daughter, Sallie, who used to be a good friend of mine."

Reverend Tom turned to her. "I believe they moved away in 2000, the same year that Maggie and I arrived in Blue Hill. I remember hearing about them, but I'm not familiar with their daughter. I'm sorry."

"That's all right," she said, wishing she'd thought of looking up Sallie before now.

At the bottom of the stairs was a small foyer, along with a water fountain situated between two restrooms. Double wooden doors led into the large meeting hall that held a number of the Sunday school classrooms, partitioned off by folding doors, and an open area that served as a gathering place for funeral meals, potluck dinners, and circle meetings.

Beyond the hall was a kitchen, with swinging doors on either side. Most of the folding doors for the Sunday school rooms were open, their bulletin boards still decorated with colorful paper and animated cutouts of familiar Bible stories such as Noah's Ark and Jonah and the Whale.

"I haven't been down here for years," Anne said softly. "But it's just as I remember."

Reverend Tom looked around him. "It's humbling to think of the generations of families that have worshipped, mourned, and celebrated here. We may have moved some of the church activities to spiffier quarters, but the memories remain.

Anne nodded, cherishing all the memories she'd made in this place and praying that her own children would soon make wonderful memories of their own, both in this church and in Blue Hill.

"The church records are over here," Reverend Tom said, motioning toward one of the Sunday school rooms. The table that used to line the wall had been replaced by several metal filing cabinets.

A quick glance told Anne that the drawers were arranged in chronological order, starting with the 1880s. Reverend Tom quickly glanced over the drawer labels until he found the 1940s. "We'll start here," he said, "and work our way forward."

"We don't need to look before 1946," Anne told him. "That's the year Aunt Edie would have turned sixteen, and I'm certain she's older than that in the photograph."

He pulled out a record book and handed it to her. "These are church records from 1946 to 1950." Then he retrieved another book from the file drawer. "I'll check 1951 through 1955."

Anne carried her record book over to an empty table and sat down. Reverend Tom joined her there, taking a chair on the opposite side. Then she began to go through the book, looking specifically at the marriage records. She placed her index finger lightly on the yellowed page and carefully slid it down each row, looking for her aunt's name.

Halfway through the book, she glanced up to see Reverend Tom doing the same, his brow furrowed in concentration. She turned back to her record book, recognizing so many familiar surnames in her church family. The Kepples, the Benkelmans, the Ochses, and so many others. The records they were perusing, of weddings, baptisms, and deaths, gave a small snapshot into the lives of the church's members.

Anne stopped at a strange entry halfway down the page. "What does this mean?" she asked. "It says Deirdre Thompson married to Arthur Kingsbury. Then it has the words *Love Casualty* in parenthesis."

Reverend Tom smiled. "Yes, I've seen that before. It was one of my predecessor's ways of describing a church member who left here to join their spouse's church."

She laughed. "I guess that makes sense."

Several minutes later, Reverend Tom closed the record book in front of him. "There's nothing about Edie's marriage here."

"There's nothing in this book either," Anne said with a sigh of disappointment. "Although, I doubt it would have been a secret if she had married in this church."

"It's hard to keep secrets in a town the size of Blue Hill, but it happens."

Anne grew thoughtful, considering where to look next. "I'm sure you're right. I think I'll check the town records too, just in case Aunt Edie and her groom chose a civil ceremony." Such a thing was hard to imagine, considering her great-aunt's faith, but Anne had never imagined a secret marriage either.

"You need to cover all the bases," Reverend Tom agreed. "What about the original photograph? Is there a name of the photographer on the back? Or anything else that might be a clue?"

"No, it was blank. But it's entirely possible that the photographer was local or at least somewhere near Blue Hill. It's also possible that photographer or his descendents kept records of the business."

"You're right, but it seems like a long shot," Reverend Tom said. Then he snapped his fingers together, a spark lighting his brown eyes. "You know, there *is* someone who might be able to help. Her name is Mildred Farley. She and your aunt were very good friends."

"Yes, I know Mildred," Anne said. "We spoke briefly at the funeral." She rose from her chair, excitement building within her. She wouldn't have time to visit Mildred today, but she intended to make a visit to her soon. "Does she still live in the same house? The one on Laurel Lane?"

"She sure does." Reverend Tom returned the record books to the filing cabinet. "And she loves having visitors."

They made their way back to the church office. Anne retrieved her tote bag and thanked the reverend for all his help.

"Let me know if there's anything else I can do," he said, walking her to the side door and opening it for her.

"I will," she promised then headed for her car.

Despite the fact that she hadn't found any clues about the mystery groom, Anne considered the trip a success. She'd gotten to know Reverend Tom and looked forward to talking with him again. And he seemed like the perfect candidate to help her if she got stuck trying to solve this mystery.

As she drove home, she cracked the window and enjoyed the hot summer breeze that ruffled her hair. She cranked up the radio as it played one of her favorite tunes, and then turned onto Bluebell Lane and drove up the hill to her house.

Her house.

Sometimes she still wanted to pinch herself to make sure this was all real. She'd loved Aunt Edie's home for as long as she could remember, and now she'd been given the blessing of raising her own children here. There were times she still wasn't sure she'd made the right decision, but she trusted God to show her the way. *Thank You, Lord, for watching out for me and the kids. I'm so thankful You're always here for us.*

Anne parked her Impala in the driveway then headed for the front door. She could hear the whoops and hollers of children in the backyard.

As she approached the front door, she saw it open, and Ben slipped out.

He held up one hand, his eyes wide. "Mom, don't come in!"

"Why?" Anne asked, both amused and concerned by his reaction.

"Something bad happened."

Her amusement faded as she imagined the rest of the roof falling in. "Ben, what is it?"

He hesitated. "Okay, it's not that bad. I mean, we can fix it."

Anne appreciated the fact that he was trying to protect her, but she was beginning to imagine the worst. She moved beside him, giving him a warm squeeze. "It's okay, Ben, I can handle it."

"I hope so," he said as she reached for the doorknob.

Anne opened the door and tried not to gasp. Mud. Everywhere. All over her beautiful wood floor. The floor that had been refinished shortly before Aunt Edie's death. She stepped into the foyer, trying to avoid muddy footprints smeared across the floor and leading to the kitchen at the back of the house. "Ben, what happened?" Anne said at last.

He stood just behind her, and for the first time she noticed that he wasn't wearing shoes. The cuffs of his mud-spattered jeans were rolled almost to his knees. "Well, we had mud races in the dirt lot next door, and then it was snack time. Some of the kids ran to the front of the house before Mrs. Pyle could stop them."

At that moment, Wendy walked toward the front entrance from the back of the house, a bucket and mop in her hands. "Oh, hello, Anne. I was hoping to have this all cleaned up before you got home. I've got the high school girls supervising Liddie and the rest of the kids out back, but Ben insisted on staying in the house until you got home."

Anne didn't know what to say. She'd agreed to let Wendy have the library camp in her backyard and even appreciated the free time it gave her, but at what cost? Yesterday, the floor had been dotted with broken pieces of plaster from the fallen roof, and today it was covered in mud.

"I already cleaned up the kitchen," Wendy told her, setting the bucket of water on the floor and dipping the mop inside. "The mud came up pretty easy, but I had to dump the bucket three times."

"Wait!" Anne cried as Wendy wrung the mop out above the bucket. "You're not supposed to use water on a wood floor, are you?"

"Well, it can warp the wood," Wendy said, "but only if the water pools. That's why I'm only using a damp mop. I plan to be real careful and wipe up all the excess moisture."

The wood floor was so beautiful with its herringbone trim and the beautiful starburst in the center of the foyer. She couldn't bear to think of it warping.

"Here," Anne said, hurrying over to take the mop from her, "I'll clean it up. That way you can get back to the kids."

"Are you sure?" Wendy asked, surveying the mess. "With seven kids at home, I'm pretty good with a mop."

"I'm positive," Anne assured her, forcing a smile. "Ben, you can go outside too. I'll have this cleaned up in no time."

He smiled, obviously relieved that she hadn't been too upset at the mess. "Thanks, Mom."

She watched as Wendy and Ben headed toward the kitchen. A moment later, she heard the back door close. With a heavy sigh, she turned to the task at hand, not sure where to start. The mud was thick in places and starting to dry. Anne wondered if she should let it dry completely and then gently try to scrape it off or take action now while it was still wet enough to move easily.

Several moments later, she was still contemplating what to do when she heard the sound of footsteps behind her then a low whistle.

"Wow," Alex said, moving beside her and surveying the damage, "it looks like a mud bomb exploded in here."

He wore a pair of blue jeans and a chambray shirt, a leather carpenter's belt hanging around his waist. Long days working in the sun had turned his face and forearms a deep golden brown.

"Do you think the floor is ruined?" she asked, almost afraid to hear his answer.

He shook his head. "Hardwood is more durable than most people think, and this one has an excellent sealer on it. Do you have any rubber spatulas?"

She blinked, surprised by the question. "In the kitchen."

"We'll use them to pick up the clumps, and then we can clean up what's left with some damp rags. It may take a while, but your floor should be fine."

She appreciated his offer to help, but she knew he had work of his own to do. "I can handle this if you have something else to do."

"I have a lot to do," Alex said, "but the longer that mud stays on your floor, the harder it will be to clean up. We'll have the job finished twice as fast if we work together."

"I'll get the spatulas," Anne said. Then she hurried into the kitchen. When she returned to the foyer, she noticed two five-gallon plastic buckets that Alex had retrieved from one of the other rooms. He took a spatula from her, knelt on the floor, and began gently scraping up clumps of mud and dumping them in one of the buckets.

Anne followed his lead, starting on the other end of the foyer. Before long, her fingers were covered in mud as she scraped the clumps off the spatula and into the bucket. It was tedious work, but they slowly made progress until they met in the center of the foyer.

"I can finally see the starburst," Anne said, scraping one of the last clods of mud off the floor. "This might work." Then she looked at Alex. "You never asked me how all this mud got in here."

He glanced up at her, still peeling mud off the floor. "Seemed pretty obvious to me. Kids plus a dirt lot and a hose equals mud. I thought there might be trouble as soon as I saw those mud races, but Wendy usually has the kids under control."

Anne paused for a moment, rubbing the back of her muddy hand against her forehead to satisfy a small itch. "How well do you know Wendy?"

He gave a small shrug, peeling up the last of the thick mud. Only a thin layer remained that Anne wouldn't have much difficulty removing. "I've seen her around town a few times, and my Ryan is friends with one of her boys. Why?"

"I just wondered," Anne replied. The truth was that she was feeling a little put out by the way Wendy had seemed to take over the house and the yard. She was appreciative of Wendy's work with the library camp but also relieved that it would be over in three days.

Alex rose to his feet and reached for the bucket beside him. "I'll dump the mud outside. Can you handle the rest of the cleanup on your own?"

"Sure," Anne said, handing him her bucket. "Thanks so much for your help."

"No problem," he said. Then he headed out the front door.

It took Anne another hour to finish cleaning the floor, but by the time she was done, the wood was gleaming again. She washed up, removing every trace of mud from her hands and under her fingernails. When she was finally done, she retrieved the wedding photograph from the trunk of her car and carried it inside the house.

When she reached the third floor, she headed for the star quilt, slipped behind it, and then slid open the door leading to the hidden room. Once inside, she breathed a weary sigh, enjoying a respite from the noise outside. She hung the photograph back on the wall then stepped back to look at it. She wondered how often Aunt Edie had looked at it, seated at the writing desk where she had a perfect view. That alone told Anne that the man in the picture had been important to her aunt.

She sat down at the desk, opened a drawer, and retrieved a piece of notepaper and a pen. Now that the muddy mess had been cleaned up, she could turn her mind to the mystery groom once again. Writing down the clues she had so far—few though they might be—could help clear her mind so she could see something she might have missed.

She decided to start writing down the questions that were uppermost in her mind:

Why did Aunt Edie keep her marriage a secret?
Why did she have this secret room?
Who was the man in the photograph and what happened to him?
Would Aunt Edie's marriage have any effect on her will?

Anne paused as she looked at the last question. It wouldn't hurt to consult a lawyer just to be certain that Aunt Edie's groom or his heirs didn't have any rights to her estate.

A lawyer's answer would tell her how urgent it was to answer the other questions she'd just listed. She intended to visit Mildred Farley tomorrow, as well as make a stop at the town hall to peruse the marriage records. Then...

"Mommy? Mommy, where are you?"

Liddie's plaintive voice carried up the stairs. Anne put the list back into the drawer then hurried out of the hidden room. She met her daughter at the top of the stairs. "Here I am, sweetie."

"Where were you?" Liddie asked, a small scowl on her face. "I couldn't find you anywhere."

"I'm sorry," Anne said, leaning down to kiss the top of her head. "I was working on something." Then she noticed that Liddie was barefoot. "Where are your shoes?"

Liddie's scowl deepened. "They're all dirty."

"Mud?" Anne ventured, her heart sinking a little.

Liddie nodded. "Can you fix them for me, Mommy?"

As she and Liddie headed down the stairs to the first floor, a rainfall of hammers pounded on the roof, and a series of wild, boyish war whoops sounded from the backyard.

It was almost as if she were opening a zoo instead of a library. Then she heard the kitchen door bang open and the sound of running footsteps and childish laughter. "Lord, give me strength," she murmured to herself. She just hoped the kids had left the mud *outside* this time.

CHAPTER SIX

The next day, Anne knocked on Mildred Farley's front door. She'd wanted to call before going over, but Mildred wasn't listed in the Blue Hill phone directory. When no one answered the door, Anne stifled a yawn with her hand and then knocked again, louder this time. She'd stayed up late last night trying to wash all the mud out of Liddie's new pink shoes. By the time she was done, the shoes were wearable but not the same bright pink they'd been in the store. After the library camp ended yesterday, Wendy had apologized again for the muddy mess and promised to make it up to her.

Anne didn't want Wendy to feel bad. She just wanted the campers to stay outside. She told Wendy she was concerned that the kids might get underfoot of the construction workers and possibly be hurt. Wendy had assured her such a thing wouldn't happen, but Anne still worried. At least there were only two days of camp left. Hopefully, nothing disastrous would happen between now and then.

Anne leaned toward the door to see if she could hear the sound of footsteps coming toward her, but there was nothing. With a sigh of disappointment, she turned around and headed down the porch steps. She'd have to try and catch Mildred another time.

"Hello there!" sounded a voice from the next house.

She looked up to see a woman's gray head poking through the open screen door.

"Are you looking for Mildred?"

"Yes," Anne called back. "Do you know where I can find her?"

The woman waved her toward the house. "Over here."

Anne smiled to herself, happy that she'd be able to talk to Mildred today after all. The sooner she could put the puzzle of this mystery groom behind her, the sooner she could concentrate on the library renovations. She couldn't wait for the grand opening—the day that she'd make Aunt Edie's dream come true.

She hurried over to the neighbor's yard as a light rain began to fall. Although she'd seen the gray clouds gathering in the sky when she'd left the house earlier, she'd been an optimist, telling herself it wasn't going to rain. A few fat drops landed on her head before she arrived at the neighbor's covered porch.

"Just in time," Anne said with a smile as the woman opened the door wider to let her inside. "I left my umbrella at home."

"You can just sit here a spell until that rain stops," the older woman said cheerfully. "It'd be a shame to get that pretty brown hair all wet."

"That's very nice of you."

"Oh, it's my pleasure." Her green eyes twinkled behind a pair of thick glasses. "You're Edie's niece, aren't you? The one who moved into her house."

"Yes, I'm Anne Gibson." She looked around the small, cozy living room. There was a green velvet sofa and chair, a basket of yarn on the coffee table—but there was no Mildred.

"I'm Coraline Watson, and I can't wait until we have a library in town. It's such a wonderful gift. Edie was always so generous." She motioned toward a green velvet armchair. "Please have a seat, dear."

"Did you know my aunt well?" Anne asked as she sat down in the chair.

Coraline took a moment to consider the question. "I wouldn't call us best friends, but I did know her quite well. She was over at Mildred's all the time, the two of them chattering like magpies." She chuckled a little. "I'm a bird-watcher," she said, pointing to a pair of binoculars standing on the front windowsill. "It's amazing what you can see on a clear day."

They'd been talking for several minutes, but Mildred hadn't appeared. "So...is Mildred here?" Anne asked at last.

"I'm afraid not," the woman said. "That's why I called you over. She left for Tuscaloosa yesterday to visit her daughter and won't be home until next week."

"Oh," Anne said, trying to hide her disappointment.

"But the two of us can have a nice chat." Coraline reached over to pat her hand. "I'll just get us some nice hot tea."

"Oh, I don't want you to go to any trouble."

"It's no trouble, dear," Coraline said with a wide smile. "I put the tea kettle on as soon as I saw you pull up to Mildred's house." She disappeared into the kitchen, leaving Anne alone in the living room.

Anne looked around, wondering why, exactly, she was here. She was certain she'd find Mildred here when Coraline called her over. Instead, she was about to have tea with a perfect stranger.

Then she smiled to herself, realizing how long it had been since she'd lived in a small town. There were no strangers in Blue Hill. If you didn't know someone, you introduced yourself and talked about your family and friends until you found a common connection. Coraline was probably just interested in Edie's niece and the plans for the new library. Anne didn't remember meeting her when she was younger, but Coraline could have moved here in the intervening years. It certainly wouldn't hurt her to sip some hot tea, make a new acquaintance, and wait out the rain for a few minutes.

Coraline returned to the living room with a tea tray and set it on the coffee table. "As luck would have it, I just baked some chocolate chip cookies this morning."

"They look delicious," Anne said, her mouth watering at the plate of cookies on the tray. A pink rose-patterned teapot and two matching cups and saucers sat next to the plate. "And you have a lovely tea set."

"Thank you." Coraline picked up the teapot and poured them each a cup. "It belonged to my mother. She was a wonderful hostess."

"How long have you lived in Blue Hill?" Anne asked, taking the teacup from Coraline.

"Oh my, it must be twelve years now. My husband wanted to retire here. He loved the fishing in this area. Then he died six months after we moved."

"I'm so sorry," Anne told her. "That must have been difficult."

"It was," Coraline said, "but I found ways to keep myself busy. I enjoy knitting and bird-watching, among other things."

"Those sound like wonderful hobbies." She reached for a cookie from the plate and took a bite, finding them still warm from the oven.

"I enjoy them," Coraline said, settling herself in a chair next to the front window. "Now, tell me about you. I understand you also lost your husband."

"I did," Anne said softly. "Three years ago."

Coraline sighed and shook her head. "Such a tragedy, and with two little ones as well. How are they doing? You have a boy and little girl, right?"

"Yes, Ben and Liddie," Anne said, wondering how many other people in town knew about her family. "They're doing very well. We love Aunt Edie's house."

"Of course," Coraline agreed. "It's one of Blue Hill's lovely landmarks. I hear that Alex Ochs is in charge of the renovations."

"Yes, he's doing a wonderful job."

Coraline reached for a cookie. "That poor man has his hands full trying to keep his career going and take care of his sister's boy, Ryan Slater. You know, the poor little guy's parents were killed in a car accident." She shook her head. "I don't know how Alex does it."

For some reason, Anne felt a strange urge to stick up for him. "Alex is very competent."

"True," Coraline agreed, "but the poor boy losing his folks at such a young age can't be easy for him." She nibbled on her cookie. Suddenly, a screech of tires sounded outside.

"Oh dear," Coraline reached for the binoculars on the windowsill and held them up to her eyes, scanning the street outside. "It looks like Mr. Gunderson almost hit a squirrel. I've warned him again and again to drive more slowly on this street, but he never listens." She leaned closer to the window and then adjusted the lens on the binoculars. "And there's Wilson Huber, out for his morning walk. He had knee surgery a few months ago."

Anne smiled, sensing that Coraline did a lot more than bird-watching with those binoculars. She finished the last of her cookie then brushed the crumbs from her fingers. "Thank you so much for the tea and cookies. I really should be going."

"So soon?" Coraline asked, visibly disappointed. "It's still sprinkling a little. I don't want you to get drenched."

"I'll be fine," Anne said, rising from her chair. "Thank you again for your hospitality. I'm sure we'll see each other again soon."

"Oh, we will," Coraline assured her, walking her to the front door. "Especially when the library opens. I'm quite a voracious reader."

"I'm glad to hear it," Anne said then took her leave. She saw a man with a slight limp coming up the sidewalk. He looked up, saw Anne and Coraline standing on the front porch, and quickly turned around to head in the other direction.

"You take care now," Coraline called after her as Anne made her way back to the car.

Anne liked the woman, even if she was a bit of a gossip. She certainly seemed to know plenty about Anne's life—and the lives of others in Blue Hill, as well. For a brief moment during their tea, she'd thought about asking Coraline if she knew anything about the mystery groom. However, she feared her aunt's secret would be common knowledge in Blue Hill before the day was out.

As Anne pulled away from the curb, she turned on the windshield wipers. She started humming "Raindrops Keep Falling on My Head," a song that her great-aunt had loved to sing anytime it rained. It was a song she'd taught to her own children, and part of her wanted to turn the car toward home instead of driving to the Blue Hill town hall.

But with library camp ending in two days, she wouldn't have much time to track down clues on her own. So it was off to the town hall to search the marriage records.

* * *

An hour later, Anne stood in the archives room of the town hall and frowned down at the computer screen in front of her. All the public records were slowly being converted into digital form, and she'd already gone through a fruitless search of the paper records from 1946–1955. Now she was scrolling through the database on the computer, hoping to find something that would lead her to the mystery groom.

There had been so many marriages after World War II, and she could just imagine the joy of the soldiers coming home to marry their sweethearts. But Aunt Edie wasn't one of them, at least not among the marriages taking place in Blue Hill. She thought about making a trip to the towns surrounding Blue Hill, but that would take more time than she had available and might be just as fruitless. It was becoming obvious now that finding the mystery groom wasn't going to be easy. But she wasn't tempted to give up. She had to know why Aunt Edie had kept such a big secret all these years.

Anne turned off the computer then headed out of the archives room. She gave a wave to the town clerk, who, thankfully, hadn't asked her why she wanted to snoop through the marriage records. Anne wouldn't lie, but she didn't feel Aunt Edie's secret marriage was hers to share with everyone in town. Wendy, Alex, and Reverend Tom had already seen the photograph. And she might have to show it to more people to find the answers she sought, but she didn't want others speculating about Aunt Edie's romance or what might have happened to her groom.

Still, Anne thought to herself as she drove back to the house, Aunt Edie had to have known Anne would find the hidden room and see the photograph. And that she'd find the manuscript. She stayed up so late cleaning Liddie's shoes that she'd fallen asleep before she'd even had a chance to continue reading it.

Raindrops splattered on her windshield as she turned onto Bluebell Lane, and Anne feared that she'd find another muddy mess when she got home. That fear was magnified when she pulled up to the house and saw that the backyard was deserted.

Where were all the children?

She pulled into the driveway and hurried to the front door. Then she took a deep breath and opened it. To her surprise and relief, the wood floor was clean and gleaming. No mud. No children either.

She heard Ben's voice and followed the sound until she arrived in the kitchen. Her son and daughter sat at the table with Wendy and several of her children, a juice box in front of each one.

Wendy's youngest, four-year-old twins named Jacob and Ethan, shared a chair.

"Hello there!" Wendy greeted her. "Looks like you got caught in the rain."

"I did," Anne said, brushing her damp bangs off her forehead. "Where are the rest of the kids?"

"I sent them home early, right before the rain started," Wendy told her. "They were disappointed, but I think my big news made them feel better."

"Big news?" Anne echoed, laying her hand on Ben's shoulder.

"It's the best!" Ben exclaimed, looking up at Anne. "We get to have another week of library camp!"

Anne looked at Wendy. "Another...week?" The words came out a little rough, so she cleared her throat. "You're extending library camp?"

"I sure am," Wendy said with a grin. "We've been having so much fun, and I have so many activities and projects left for the kids to do. So I thought to myself, why not?"

Why not? Anne could think of plenty of reasons, the first of which was that Wendy hadn't even talked to her about it beforehand.

Wendy's kids and Liddie all started chattering to each other. Anne looked at Ben, who sipped his juice box and kept silent. Maybe another week of library camp wouldn't be so bad, she thought to herself. It might help Ben feel more comfortable with the other kids in town and open up to them. She knew he enjoyed their company, but he obviously didn't feel comfortable enough to join in yet.

"So what did you do this morning?" Wendy asked, as she began gathering up the empty juice boxes on the table.

"Oh, I had a few errands," she said. She could hear the sounds of men's voices and heard hammering on the floor overhead. The rain must have driven Alex's construction crew inside.

"Are you kids ready to go?" Wendy asked, rising out of her chair. "You've got chores to do at home."

The Pyle kids moaned and groaned, but they gradually followed their mother out the back door. Anne watched them pile into their red SUV, and then she waved as Wendy drove away.

"Now what are we going to do?" Liddie asked.

Anne wasn't one of those parents who thought children needed to be constantly entertained. She'd made her own fun as a child and trusted that her children could do the same. "Well, you have a bedroom full of toys. And there are games, books, and puzzles."

"I'm going to read," Ben said, rising from the table. "Charlie just found his golden ticket to the chocolate factory, and I want to see what happens next."

Liddie hopped out of her chair and bounded over to her brother. "I like chocolate. Will you read it to me?"

"Sure," Ben said, taking her hand as he headed for his room.

Anne watched them climb the stairs, thanking God that her son took such good, loving care of Liddie. She was so blessed. She wiped off the table then pushed all the chairs in. Faced with some free time this afternoon, she decided to do a little reading herself.

CHAPTER SEVEN

There was nothing Anne enjoyed more than the sound of rain pattering against the windowpane and settling in with a good book. She sat on the chaise lounge in the living room on the second floor, and snuggled under one of Aunt Edie's hand-sewn quilts. The workmen had gone home shortly after lunch. The rain had prevented them from completing some outside work that was necessary before they could continue on the interior of the house.

The kids were asleep in Ben's room, taking a long afternoon nap. Anne had tiptoed in there and gently removed *Charlie and Chocolate Factory* from Ben's grasp. She didn't want him to roll over on it and crumple the pages, aware that he'd be even more upset about it than she would be. He was an avid reader, just like his parents. She loved the fact that he could go on wild adventures and learn about so many things in the world just through the pages of a book.

Liddie enjoyed books too. She already recognized letters and some words, and she'd inherited her father's vivid imagination. Eric had been so good at telling the children a story before bedtime every night. If Anne closed her eyes, she could still hear his deep, gentle voice and found comfort in the memories.

Anne breathed a little sigh of contentment as she picked up Aunt Edie's manuscript and began to read where she'd left off.

Ruth pulled a pie out of the oven, carefully checking the flaky, golden crust for any defects. The blueberry filling bubbled out of the cutouts in the crust and filled the kitchen with its sweet aroma. She hoped Harry liked blueberry pie. Her mother had left to go with Marvin to the dentist and wouldn't be back until supper. She'd put Ruth in charge of taking lunch out to the men in the apple orchard. Ruth had spent the morning making fried chicken and biscuits, along with the pie and some succotash. They were her best dishes, and she hoped Harry was impressed. Davey didn't like succotash, but he was a picky eater, and she refused to cater to him like their mother did.

She'd always heard that the way to a man's heart was through his stomach. That morning, Ruth had gathered eggs and had seen Harry working hard, picking apples. He moved faster than Davey and even faster than her father. No doubt he'd been working up a big appetite.

Ruth reached for the picnic basket and began filling it with the food she'd prepared. The pie was still piping hot, but she didn't have time to let it cool. Her father expected his lunch by noon on the dot, or he'd complain to Mother. She packed up the pie as best she could. She expected it would be cool enough to eat by the time they were ready for dessert.

Anne smiled to herself as she turned to the next page of the manuscript, more convinced than ever that Aunt Edie was recounting her own budding romance with "Harry." Anne even heard Aunt Edie's voice in her head as she read.

Her father and Davey were sitting on a couple of tree stumps, ready for lunch, when she arrived with the picnic basket. Harry was still on a ladder picking apples and placing them in the bushel basket. She watched him for a moment, noting that he took great care not to bruise the apples that went into the basket.

"Are you planning to let us starve?" Davey complained, reaching for the picnic basket.

She moved it out of his reach. "Don't touch the food until you wash your hands. I brought wet cloths for all of you."

"A little dirt won't hurt anybody," Davey grumbled, but he took the wet cloth she offered him.

She handed another cloth to her father then whispered, "Shouldn't you call Harry for lunch?"

"He can see us," her father said briskly as he ran the cloth over his hands. "He'll come when he's ready."

Ruth spread the tablecloth on the ground then slowly placed the food on top of it along with the plates and silverware.

"What's the matter?" Davey asked. "You're as slow as molasses."

"Just hush," Ruth told him. She set the pie in the center of the tablecloth then knelt down and started to slice it into generous pieces. Steam rose up from the knife cuts, telling her that the pie was still too hot to eat.

"Is that a blueberry pie?" a deep voice asked.

She looked up to see Harry standing beside her, his broad shoulders almost blocking out the sun. "Yes, it is. Do you like blueberry pie?"

His smile made her heart flutter. "It's my favorite," he said, taking a seat on the ground beside her brother.

Ruth removed the largest slice of the pie and set it on a plate then handed it to Harry. "I hope you like it."

"I'm sure I will."

"As long as it's not apple, I'll be happy," Davey grumbled. "In fact, I'll be happy if I never see another apple as long as I live!"

Harry chuckled then took a bite of the pie before he even helped himself to the chicken or succotash.

"Be careful!" Ruth warned, but it was too late.

Harry's eyes grew wide as he chewed; then a moment later, he spit out the pie onto his plate. He grabbed the water jug next to him and took a long drink.

Davey began to laugh, and even her father chuckled a bit.

Ruth's cheeks flamed as she stared down at the tablecloth. She'd never been so embarrassed. He'd spit out her pie. So much for her plan to win his heart. She'd probably burned his tongue off!

"That's...hot," Harry said at last. "Good, but...hot."

"I'm sorry," Ruth said, wanting nothing more than to escape into the house and have a good cry. She'd worked so hard to make this lunch, and now everything was ruined.

"No, it's my fault," Harry said gallantly. "It just looked so good that I couldn't wait. That will teach me not to eat dessert first."

Davey was still rolling on the ground with laughter. "You should have seen your face," he said to Harry. "It looked like you were about to explode."

Ruth couldn't listen to any more. She picked up the water jug and said, "I'll go fill this up for you."

Then she practically ran to the water pump. As she primed the pump handle, her tears began to flow along with the well water. She'd tried to make a good impression on a young man and failed miserably. He'd been nice about it, but that hot pie had to be burning his mouth even now. She'd wanted him to remember her delicious food—not give him pain.

When she'd finished filling the jug, she picked it up and turned around, only to see her father standing behind her. He took the water jug from her. "I'll take it. You go back to the house."

"But—"

"I don't want you around that boy," he interjected, his voice firm. "Go back to the house."

"But—"

"Now," her father said, in a tone that made her quickly turn and head to the house.

She wiped her face as she walked, determined not to cry anymore. Crying wouldn't impress Harry. Neither would her blueberry pie. She'd have to find another way to win his heart.

"Oh, Aunt Edie," Anne murmured, as she read the last page in the chapter. Her heart went out to the young girl who had fallen in love with the farmhand. Had it been that way in real life? Had Edie's father forbidden her to see "Harry"? Had they run off and married in secret? She was more determined than ever to know the answer.

Anne placed the manuscript on the table beside her then drew the quilt up around her shoulders. The summer rain had cooled the house, and she enjoyed the warmth under the quilt. She closed her eyes, enjoying the lazy afternoon and the unusual peace and quiet. She had things to do, such as call a lawyer to make sure her legal rights to the house were covered, as well as write out a list for Alex about some of the renovations, but it felt so nice just to relax for a little while. As she drifted off to sleep, she wondered if she could find Aunt Edie's recipe for blueberry pie.

* * *

The next day, Anne helped Wendy set up the activities for that day's library camp and started her list for Alex. He and the men were back up on the roof, making permanent repairs so it didn't cave in again.

By noon, she'd called around and discovered that the lawyer who had handled Aunt Edie's will and estate was out of the country for an extended time. So she located another local attorney and set up an appointment for three o'clock, which left her enough time to stop by Kepple's Jewelry. She was hoping they'd be able to identify the mark on the gold cuff links she'd found in Aunt Edie's hidden room.

The jewelry store was located on Main Street and had been a fixture in Blue Hill since 1926. The current owner, Hank Kepple, one of her former high school classmates, was the fourth generation of his family to run the store. Hank's red hair and prominent freckles had made him easy to recognize in a crowd. He was a dominant football player and popular in school, known more for clowning around in class than making good grades.

Anne hadn't seen Hank since graduation, and she wondered if he'd changed much. As she parked in front of the red brick jewelry store, she noticed that it hadn't changed at all. It still had the two plate-glass display windows on either side of the original door with the brass door handle. Two white columns bordered the corners of the storefront, connected across the top by a narrow strip of leaded glass windowpanes.

She climbed out of her car and grabbed her purse then headed into the store. A chime sounded above the door as she opened it, and she saw a petite brunette standing behind the counter.

"Good morning," the woman greeted her. "Can I help you?"

"I'm looking for Hank," Anne told her, walking up to the counter. The inside of the store had definitely changed since she'd last visited. There were new display cases with glass countertops and accent lighting. Along with jewelry, there was also a case full of fine china and a row of grandfather clocks.

"He's in the back," she said with a smile. "I'm his wife, Heidi."

"Oh," Anne said with surprise, "I didn't realize Hank had married. I'm Anne Gibson. Hank and I graduated from Blue Hill High School together. Only, I was Anne Summers back then."

Heidi's smile widened. "I'm pleased to meet you." Then she leaned forward and whispered. "Do you have any good stories about Hank you can tell me? According to him, he was the king of Blue Hill High in his day."

Anne laughed, not surprised by her former classmate's opinion of himself. "Well, he was voted prom king, so I guess the name fits. But there was one time..."

"Hey, now," a man's voice sounded from an open doorway. "Don't you start telling stories about me, Anne Summers, or I'll have to retaliate with some stories of my own."

Anne laughed as Hank joined his wife behind the counter. His hair had receded quite a bit since high school, but it was just as red. His freckles had faded a little, but she still recognized that mischievous gleam in his green eyes. "There's nothing to tell about me. I was always the good one in school."

"I didn't say the stories would be true," he joked, circling an arm around his wife's waist. "I heard you moved back to town. And you've got a couple of kids now, right?"

"I do," she said, pulling out her cell phone and scrolling to the pictures of her children. "This is Ben, he's nine, and this is Liddie, she's five."

"They're adorable," Heidi gushed, studying the photos.

"Your little girl looks like you," Hank said, glancing up at Anne. "You son must take after his father." His smile faded. "I'm sorry about your loss, Anne."

"Thank you," she said softly, appreciating the sympathy. However, she didn't want to talk about Eric right now. "Do you two have children?"

"Twin boys," Heidi said, rolling her eyes. "They're nine years old, and they both take after their father, so as you can imagine, I have my hands full."

"We'll have to get them together with your boy sometime," Hank told her. "They'll probably be in the same class in school."

"Just how much do your sons take after you?" Anne asked, only half-joking. "As I remember it, you spent most of your elementary years in the principal's office."

"That's because I was her favorite student," Hank said with a grin.

Heidi glanced up her husband. "Your sons have already tried that excuse, remember? The goal this year is for them to spend more time in the classroom than in trouble."

"Got it," Hank agreed; then he leaned forward, resting his arms on the glass countertop. "Now, what brings you here today, Anne? Is there something you need?"

"I'm hoping you can help me solve a bit of a mystery," she said, drawing the small, black velvet box out of her purse. "I found a pair of vintage cuff links at Aunt Edie's house." She opened the box lid to show them.

"Oh my," Heidi breathed. "Those are lovely."

Anne looked at Hank. "Do you recognize the mark?"

Hank picked up one of the cuff links and examined it. "I sure do. That's my great-grandfather's mark. Your aunt must have purchased them here."

"Well, that's the mystery," Anne said. "I'm not sure if they belonged to Aunt Edie or if they belong to someone else in the family."

"Do you have someone with the initials J.R. in your family? That should narrow it down."

Heidi looked at her husband. "I'm sure she's thought of that already, Hank." Then she turned to Anne. "That's the mystery, isn't it? You want to identify J.R.?"

"I do," Anne confirmed, not wanting to reveal anymore. "I have reason to believe they were purchased in the late 1940s or early 1950s. Is there any chance you might have any store records from that time?"

Heidi laughed. "Hank, your family's pack-rat tendencies are finally going to pay off. We have records going back all the way to 1926!"

"Really?" Anne said, excitement rippling through her. For the first time, she felt close to identifying the mystery man. "May I look at them?"

"Of course," Hank said. "But you should know that my family may be pack rats, but that doesn't mean we're *organized* pack rats. If you don't mind digging through some boxes, I'll take you into the back room and you can search to your heart's content."

"I don't mind at all," Anne said with a smile. She placed the cuff links back into her purse then followed Hank and Heidi into the back room.

They led her to a rack of blue plastic totes, each one sealed with a plastic lid.

"These are copies of all the receipts from the store," Heidi told her. "When I first started working here, I got as far as sorting them by year."

"That's why I proposed to her," Hank joked, giving his wife a wink. "I figured anyone who likes to organize could have a lot of fun joining the Kepple family."

"It has been fun," she said, chuckling. "A little crazy but fun."

A chime sounded, signaling another customer coming through the door.

"I'll be fine here," Anne told them. "I don't want to keep you two from your work."

"Are you sure?" Hank said.

"Positive," Anne assured him then waited until Heidi and Hank returned to the front of the store before she dug into the first box.

CHAPTER EIGHT

An hour later, Anne knew Heidi hadn't been joking about the pack-rat tendencies of the Kepple family. The first tote box she'd opened had been full of carbon copies of sales receipts, with no rhyme or reason to them other than the year: 1948. She'd taken them all out of the box and sorted through them, one by one, looking for a name with the initials J.R. or the sale of a pair of gold cuff links. Then she'd done the same with the box from 1949.

She was now sorting through the receipts from 1950.

Thomas Hudson — gold and diamond ring
Stephen Hudson — platinum wedding band
Miss Myra Silverman — cameo brooch

Many of the surnames she recognized, although the individuals had made their purchases well before she was born.

Mrs. Grace Addington — silver cuff links. Engraved: T.A.
Howard Bell — diamond and ruby necklace — gift wrap
Miss Melanie Keen — opal necklace

Hank and Heidi had each checked on her a couple of times, offering to get her something to drink. She'd declined, not wanting to take the risk that she might accidentally spill a beverage on the receipts piled around her. Some of them were difficult to read, and her eyes were getting tired from squinting in the dim light of the back room.

Needing a break, Anne set down the pile in her hand and got up from her chair to stretch her stiff legs. J.R. was proving more difficult to find every day. She glanced at her watch, not wanting to miss her three o'clock meeting with the attorney. Jessica Myers was just one of a handful of attorneys listed in the Blue Hill phone directory. Anne knew nothing about her, but she felt her question was simple enough for someone with a law degree.

If that meeting went well and the attorney assured her that there was nothing to fear from the mystery groom or his heirs, Anne wondered if she should just give up the search. But the thought of not knowing the story behind Aunt Edie's secret marriage was like an itch that she needed to scratch. She wasn't sure she could let it go—not yet anyway.

She sat down in the chair and picked up the pile of receipts, feeling a new energy and determination flow through her.

Curtis Yance—gold cuff links—Engraved: C.Y.
Miss Layla Conley—emerald ring
Samuel Nevins—Silver and diamond cuff links

As she scanned each receipt, Anne reminded herself to look at both the name on the top of the ticket and the item purchased. Someone might have purchased the cuff links for J.R.—perhaps Aunt Edie herself. If that was the case, she'd be right back where she started.

She heard footsteps and looked up as Heidi entered the back room.

"Still hard at it, I see," Heidi said.

Anne nodded. "I can see why the Kepple family has been in business since 1926. They have a lot of customers."

Heidi laughed. "They do." Then she pulled up a chair. "Business is a little slow right now, though, so I'd be happy to help you. But you'll need to tell me what exactly you're looking for."

Anne hesitated for a moment then nodded. "I'd love some help. I'm looking for a receipt for the gold cuff links. I'm also setting aside any names with the initials J.R., just in case there's a connection."

"That sounds simple enough," Heidi said, grabbing a handful of loose receipts from the 1950 box sitting between them.

They sifted through the receipts in silence for several minutes. Then Heidi set the pile in her hand aside and reached for another cluster of receipts.

"So how do you like living in Blue Hill again?" Heidi asked, her eyes slowly scanning the receipt in front of her.

"I like it," Anne said. "It feels good to be back home, although it doesn't quite feel like home yet, if that makes any sense."

"It does," Heidi said with a smile. "I moved from Philadelphia to help take care of my grandmother and got a part-time job here. I certainly never planned on falling in love with Hank and staying here permanently. But Blue Hill is home to me now. I couldn't imagine living anywhere else."

Anne reached the end of the receipts in her lap, set them aside, and grabbed another handful from the box. "You two seem very happy."

"We are," Heidi affirmed. "And despite what we said about the twins, they really are good boys. I'm sure they'll be happy to meet your son."

"Moving here was tough on Ben," Anne confessed. "He had to leave his best friend behind. I know it bothers him more than he lets on. Ever since Eric passed away, he's tried to be so grown up."

"He sounds like a sweetheart," Heidi said, scanning another receipt. "I'm sure he'll make a lot of friends here."

Anne hoped it was true. She prayed that both Ben and Liddie would find friends here and truly consider Blue Hill their home. She knew it would take time; she prayed for patience for them and for herself.

She swallowed a small sigh and picked up another receipt.

Walter Ochs — one pair gold cuff links. Engraved: J.R.

Anne's heart skipped a beat as she read the receipt again. "I think I found it."

Heidi's eyes widened and she leaned over for a closer look. "The initials match, but who is Walter Ochs?"

"I don't know," Anne said. "But I might know someone who does."

* * *

Anne wanted to drive straight home and ask Alex if he was related to Walter Ochs. But she only had ten minutes until her meeting with the attorney, so she drove to Jessica Myers's office instead.

The law office was located just off of Main Street, in a small stone cottage that had been converted into an office space. The front yard was filled with flowers, including a trellis that arched over the front gate. Purple clematis in full bloom filled every inch of the trellis and made Anne feel she was walking into a garden party.

But inside the cottage, the décor was all business. There was a waiting room in the front of the office with a receptionist behind a stylish marble counter.

"Good afternoon," the young receptionist said, her dark hair pulled back into a loose bun. "You must be Mrs. Gibson."

"Yes," Anne replied. "I hope I'm not late."

"You're just on time. Jessica's running a little late, so if you could take a seat, it will just be a few minutes."

"That's fine," Anne said, walking over to one of the chairs set up along the wall.

"May I get you some coffee or tea?" the receptionist asked.

"No, I'm fine. Thank you."

Anne checked her cell phone for messages, hoping everything was going smoothly back at the house. Then she reached into her purse and pulled out the receipt she'd found at the jewelry store. Heidi had made a copy of it for her. Anne knew that it was possible this receipt might not have anything to do with the mystery groom in the photograph, but she could always return to the store and dig through more receipts.

Walter Ochs. The name sounded vaguely familiar, but she couldn't remember if she'd met him before. He had to be one of

Alex's relatives. There just weren't that many families named Ochs in Blue Hill.

A buzzing noise emanated from the receptionist's desk, and she smiled over at Anne. "Jessica's ready to see you now. I'll take you on back."

Anne followed her, suddenly feeling a little queasy. She hoped the attorney didn't think she was crazy for asking about the impact of a wedding photograph taken over sixty years ago.

There was a good chance she'd be in and out of this meeting in five minutes. But no matter what happened, it was worth it for her peace of mind. If there was the slightest chance that this mystery groom could cause trouble, she wanted to know about it.

The receptionist opened the door in front of her then waved Anne inside. The woman seated behind the desk rose as Anne entered.

"Hello there," she said, rounding her desk and holding out her hand. She was in her early forties, with shoulder-length, ash blonde hair and blue eyes that matched her blue silk suit. Her office was tastefully decorated, with a photograph of two young children the only personal item in the room.

"I'm Jessica Myers," the woman said, shaking Anne's hand. "And you must be Mrs. Gibson."

"Please call me Anne."

"I will, if you call me Jessica," the attorney said with a smile.

"It's a deal."

The receptionist closed the door, leaving the two of them alone.

"Please have a seat," Jessica said, returning to the chair behind her desk, "and tell me what brings you here today."

"It's a little unusual," Anne began, wanting to prepare her.

Jessica smiled. "Unusual cases are my favorite kind."

Anne reached for her purse and fished out the photocopy of the wedding photograph. "This is a picture of my aunt Edie Summers, taken sometime around 1950, I believe."

"I see." Jessica studied the photo for a long moment then looked at Anne. "And?"

"And I never knew she was married. I found this photograph in her house—the same house that she wants me to renovate into a library for the town of Blue Hill. I'm curious about the identity of her groom, of course, but I'm even more curious about what it might mean for me and my family's future."

Jessica set the photocopy on the desk in front of her. "So you didn't know she was married, and you don't know the identity of the groom?"

"That's right."

"So naturally, you wouldn't know how long they were married."

"I don't," Anne admitted. "For all I know, they were still married when my aunt died. That's why I wanted to meet with you. I've uprooted my family and moved to Blue Hill with every intention of fulfilling my aunt's last wishes. But what if her husband is still out there? Or his heirs? Could they try to take the house?"

"Did you bring a copy of your aunt's will with you?"

"I did," Anne said, digging in her purse once more. She pulled it out and handed it to Jessica. Then she waited silently for several minutes while the attorney read through the will.

"It appears to be fairly standard," Jessica said. "I know the attorney who drew it up, and he has a good reputation. There's no mention of a husband or any other heirs in the will, though. I'm sure he would have included them if—"

"If my aunt had mentioned that she was, or had been, married?" Anne interjected.

Jessica nodded, pursing her lips as she perused the will once more. "So she never mentioned anything about a husband? Nothing about a divorce or an annulment?"

"No, nothing."

"Interesting," Jessica mused. "Do you mind if I make a copy of this?"

"Not at all."

Anne waited while Jessica called the receptionist back into the office. She met her at the door and handed her Aunt Edie's will.

"I need one copy," Jessica told her. Then she turned back to Anne. "You were right, this case is unusual. If your aunt and her husband were still married at the time of her death, he may have rights to some or all of her property."

"And if they were divorced?" Anne asked.

"That would be much less complicated, unless there were children involved. Is there any chance of that?"

Anne blanched, not certain of the answer. "I can't imagine that she would have had a child and somehow kept that fact a secret for all these years."

"That would be much more difficult," Jessica agreed.

A moment later, someone tapped on the door.

"Come in," Jessica called out.

The receptionist entered, smiled at Anne, and then placed the original will and the photocopy on the desk.

"Thank you," Jessica said, handing the original back to Anne as the receptionist left the room once more.

"I guess what I need to know," Anne said slowly, "is how much risk is there that I might lose the house?"

"Well, I want to do a little research," Jessica said, perching on the corner of her desk, "but my best guess is that there's very little risk. If your aunt was born in 1930 and lived her entire life in Blue Hill, it's doubtful that she could be married for more than sixty years and no one would know about it."

"Her best friend might know," Anne said, thinking of Mildred, "but she's out of town at the moment."

Jessica nodded. "Any information you find will be helpful. Perhaps her groom died shortly after the wedding or they were quietly divorced."

Anne nodded, feeling a little better. "I'll keep looking. I just don't want someone showing up on my door and laying claim to Aunt Edie's house."

Jessica looked at her for a long moment. "I should warn you that it could still happen. Any heirs of the man in the photograph could sue the estate, claiming ownership."

Anne's relief quickly faded. "But would that stand up in court?"

"Doubtful. But just defending a case like that could cost the estate thousands of dollars." Jessica picked up the wedding picture from her desk and walked over to Anne. "I wish I could give you more definitive answers, but until we know all the facts, there's no way to know for certain." She held out the picture.

Anne took it from her then carefully placed it back in her purse. "So I need to keep looking until I can identify him — at least if I want any peace of mind."

"I think that's a good idea," Jessica said. "I'll do the research on my end, just to make sure that we've got all the bases covered, no matter what you find out." She gave Anne a reassuring smile. "And try not to worry. Most of the scenarios we talked about are long shots. Your aunt lived in this town for decades without a husband or his heirs showing up."

Anne nodded as she rose to her feet. She knew Jessica was right, but she still fought that little niggle of doubt deep inside of her. *Perhaps Aunt Edie kept the man a secret because he — or his family — was trouble.*

"Thank you so much for seeing me on short notice," Anne said, ready to take her leave. Now it seemed more important than ever to follow up the clue she'd found at the jewelry store. "I'll keep in touch and let you know what I find out."

"And I'll do the same," Jessica said, walking her to the door. "Information is our best weapon in this type of situation. The more we have, the more we'll know how to proceed."

Anne nodded and thanked her again, before heading for her car.

Weapon. The attorney almost made it sound as if they were in a battle. A battle with an unknown enemy. Then she thought of the way Aunt Edie wrote about "Harry" in the manuscript. He certainly didn't seem like her enemy. Yet, Edie's own father had warned her against him. Did Anne's great-grandfather know something about the man that made him wary, or was he just an overprotective father?

So many questions and not enough answers. Would she ever learn the truth about Harry?

CHAPTER NINE

Anne arrived home around four o'clock, eager to talk to Alex. She saw the kids seated under the white canopy tent in the backyard as Wendy stood in the center of the group and read from a book. Soon, two of the boys stood up and started dueling with each other using plastic swords. Anne smiled to herself, assuming they were acting out a part of the story. She'd have to ask the kids about it at supper tonight.

Anne climbed out of her cool car and into the summer heat, feeling sorry for the workmen toiling on the roof. She could only imagine how hot it was up there. As she walked toward the front door, she saw one of the workmen descending the ladder that was propped up against the front of the house.

She walked over to him, waiting until he reached the ground to speak to him.

"Hello," Anne said with a smile. "Do you know where I can find Alex?"

"He had to make a trip to the lumberyard," the workman said, "but he should be back soon."

"And how are you guys doing? Can I get you some water or lemonade?"

The workman wiped his damp brow with his sleeve then shook his head. "No, thank you, we've got plenty of water up there. It's a hot one today."

"It sure is," Anne said. She headed into the house and set her purse on a small table in the foyer.

She was met with the aroma of fresh paint and turned to the room on the left of the foyer. The sage green paint she'd chosen for the room had been applied to the walls and looked even better than she imagined. She turned slowly to survey each wall, trying to imagine how it would look when the white ceiling trim and floorboards were added.

That room led to another large room through an arched, open doorway that stretched about six feet wide. This second room hadn't been painted yet. Anne was still trying to decide if she should use the same sage green or a different color.

A double fireplace separated this room from a third room that she intended to use for checking out books. It had two doors, one leading into the foyer and one leading into the second room. August was too hot to use the fireplace, but she couldn't wait to have a cozy blaze in the hearth during the cold of winter and to decorate the mantle and the rest of the library rooms during the Christmas season. She closed her eyes, imagining all the festivities. Perhaps they'd go Christmas caroling with the neighbors and stop at the library afterward to enjoy cookies and hot cocoa.

"Daydreaming?" asked a voice behind her.

She turned to see Alex. He set a can of paint down on the floor beside him then moved closer to her. "You caught me," she said.

"I was thinking about winter. A little cold weather sounds refreshing on a day like this, but I'm sure I'll change my mind when it actually happens."

He hitched one thumb over his shoulder, toward the first room she'd seen. "What do you think of the paint?"

"It's wonderful. Just what I wanted."

"And what about this room?" he asked. "I just picked up some more primer, so we'll be ready for the color soon."

Anne nibbled her lower lip. "I'm just not sure yet. I've been looking over the different paint chip samples you gave me, but there are so many colors to choose from. I want to make the right decision."

"You have another day or two until you have to decide." He hiked up the tool belt around his waist and turned to leave. "Well, I'd better get back to work."

"Wait," Anne called after him. "I need to talk to you about something else."

He hesitated, looking back over his shoulder. "What is it?"

She moved next to him, wanting his full attention. "You remember that wedding picture we found in the hidden room?"

"Sure," he said.

"Well, I also found something else in that room." She took a deep breath. "A pair of vintage cuff links with the initials J.R. engraved on them."

"And?" he prodded.

"And I've been trying to identify the groom in the photograph, so I took the cuff links to Kepple's Jewelry. They still had the receipt from the purchase — all the way back in 1951."

He whistled low. "That's some good record-keeping. I didn't realize Hank was that organized."

She smiled. "I wouldn't exactly call his system organized, but the important thing is that they still had the receipt."

"So who's the guy in the picture?"

She hesitated, not sure where to start. "I still don't know his name," she said at last. "Just that his initials were J.R. and that the cuff links were purchased by a man named Walter Ochs."

He stared at her for a long moment. "Are you talking about *my* Uncle Walter?"

"So he is your uncle?"

"I don't know of any other guy named Walter Ochs from around here. And he's my great-uncle," Alex told her, slowly shaking his head. "You don't think he's the groom in that photo, do you?"

"Hold on," Anne told him. She hurried into the foyer and grabbed her purse. Walter's initials weren't J.R., but there had to be some reason those cuff links ended up in Aunt Edie's desk. When she returned to Alex, she drew the photocopy of the picture out of her purse and handed it to him. "Take another look. Does that man look like your great-uncle?"

Alex only studied it for a moment before shaking his head. "No, I'm sure that's not him." He handed the photocopy back to her. "I've seen old family pictures of Uncle Walter as a young man, and he looks nothing like this guy."

Anne nodded. "So if he's not the groom, my next step is figuring out why he bought the cuff links."

"I guess you'll have to ask him."

She blinked. "Ask him? You mean, he's still living?"

He chuckled at her reaction. "He sure is. In fact, he just moved into that new retirement complex on the south end of town."

Excitement bubbled within her, but she didn't want to spring herself on an elderly man. "Maybe you should talk to him," she said. "He might not be thrilled if I just show up out of nowhere."

"You don't know Uncle Walter," Alex said wryly. "He's ninety-three years old but still as much of a ladies' man as ever. He'd be happy to see you."

"Ninety-three?" she echoed. "Do you think he'll remember something that happened over sixty years ago?"

"That's hard for me to say," Alex replied with a slight shrug. "Uncle Walter's short-term memory can be a little spotty, but his long-term memory is excellent. Still, it's just a pair of cuff links."

A pair of cuff links that might hold the key to this mystery, Anne thought to herself.

Alex checked his watch. "I've got to get back to work now. Tell Uncle Walter I said hello."

He turned and left, leaving Anne alone in the room. As eager as she was to talk to Uncle Walter, she knew it was too late in the day to go on another fishing expedition. Library camp would be over soon, and the kids would be ready for supper. Then she needed to get them bathed and ready for another day of camp tomorrow. Uncle Walter would have to wait.

* * *

Later that evening, Anne sat at the kitchen table with Ben and Liddie, watching them dig into the butterscotch pudding she'd made for dessert. They'd dined on tuna fish sandwiches and sweet corn for supper, and the kids both asked for second helpings. The long days in the summer sun gave them big appetites, and she was happy to see them clean their plates.

"So tell me about library camp," Anne said. "What did you do today?"

"We had oatmeal cookies for snack," Liddie said, then scowled. "With raisins."

"I know you don't like raisins in your cookies," Anne said gently to her daughter, "but I hope you were polite and remembered to thank Mrs. Pyle for the treats."

"I did," Liddie replied, scooping up another spoonful of pudding.

"After I reminded her," Ben piped in. "She tried to hide her cookie in a bush, but I made her give it to me instead."

"It was for the caterpillar," Liddie protested, glaring at her brother. "He needs to eat too, and he probably likes raisins."

Ben sighed. "Caterpillars don't eat if they're in a cocoon, silly."

Liddie looked over at her mother. "Is that true?"

"I think so," Anne told her. "I don't really know that much about cocoons or caterpillars. Maybe we can read a book about it once the library is done." She stood up and started to gather the empty dinner plates. "I saw Mrs. Pyle reading a book to all of you and the two boys sword-fighting."

"She was reading Peter Pan," Ben told her.

"I wish I could fly like Wendy," Liddie interjected. "Have I ever flown in an airplane, Mommy?"

"Yes, sweetie," Anne replied, "but you were too little to remember it. We flew down to Florida to visit Grandma and Grandpa."

"I remember that," Ben said. He smiled at his sister. "You liked the airplane ride, Liddie. You were laughing a lot."

Liddie smiled then dug into her pudding once more.

"Anyway," Ben continued, "sometimes we get to act out scenes from the story that Mrs. Pyle reads to us. Justin Pyle and Ryan Slater were the lucky ones this time."

"Ryan Slater?" Anne echoed, remembering what Coraline had told her about Alex's nephew. "Is he about your age, Ben?"

Ben shrugged. "I guess so. We don't really talk."

"Why not?" Anne carried the dirty dishes over to the sink. When all the renovations were done to the house, there would be a brand-new kitchen on the second floor, but for now they were using the original kitchen on the first floor. "Don't you like him?"

Ben stared down at his pudding. "I don't know. He's all right, I guess."

"Have you ever tried to talk to him?"

"Mom," Ben grumbled, "I can't just go up to him and start talking. He'll think I'm a dweeb."

"Of course you can," Anne said, trying to encourage him to be a little more outgoing. "And you're certainly not a dweeb. I think you're a lot of fun."

"You have to think that," Ben said wryly, "'cause you're my mom."

Liddie reached for her glass of milk. "I *never* talk to the boys. They're icky."

"You talk to me," Ben reminded her.

"Yeah, because you're my brother," Liddie said. "It's all the other boys who are icky." She wrinkled her tiny nose. "I think Ethan Pyle ate a worm today." She paused. "Or maybe it was Jacob. I can't tell them apart." Anne smiled. "Oh, he was probably just teasing you. Maybe it was a candy worm."

"I hope so," Liddie said fervently. "Or maybe he was just hungry and didn't like the oatmeal raisin cookies either. I'm not sure which would be worse—a worm or raisins."

"Don't eat a worm, Liddie," Ben warned her. "I tried it once when I was little, and, believe me, you won't like it."

Anne returned to the table, still a little concerned about how Ben was getting along with the other boys. "If you don't play with Ryan, who do you play with?"

Ben shrugged again then pushed his half-eaten pudding away. "I don't know. It's different every day." He looked up at Anne with his big hazel eyes. "May I be excused, please?"

Anne didn't want to let him go, but she didn't want to push him either. "Of course, dear. You can play outside for a while, if you'd like, and then it will be time for a bath."

"Okay," he said, jumping up from the table and heading for the backyard.

"What did you do today, Mommy?" Liddie asked her. "I saw you leave in the car."

"I went to see an old friend," she told her daughter. "His name is Hank, and we went to school together."

Liddie's eyes widened. "Do I still have to go to school this year?"

The hint of fear behind her words made Anne sit down at the table next to her. "I thought you were excited about starting kindergarten."

"One of the girls told me that school is really hard in Blue Hill. They give you homework and everything. I don't even know how to read yet!"

Anne smiled then reached out to give her a hug. "Don't worry, honey, school won't be hard. Most of the kids in your class won't know how to read. And we've been practicing letters and sounds with your flash cards, remember? Those are the first steps to learning how to read."

Liddie scrambled off her chair. "Maybe I'd better go to my room and practice some more."

"Okay," Anne said. "But I don't want you to worry about school. You're going to love it, just like I did."

Later that evening, Anne gave the kids their baths then heard their prayers and tucked them into bed. She was still a little bothered by their dinner conversation. As a mother, she just wanted her children to be happy, and now she knew that Ben still hadn't made many friends and that Liddie was worried about starting school.

She used to have Eric to talk to whenever the kids had problems. Now she was on her own and so concerned about doing or saying the wrong thing. After she prepared for bed, she turned to God for His help, praying softly for several minutes.

She climbed into bed and reached for her Bible instead of Edie's manuscript. Reading some of her favorite passages always gave her comfort. Anne turned to the book of Colossians and began to read out loud from chapter three, starting at verse fifteen.

"Let the peace of Christ rule in your hearts, since as members of one body you were called to peace. And be thankful. Let the message of Christ dwell among you richly as you teach and admonish one another with all wisdom through psalms, hymns, and songs from the Spirit, singing to God with gratitude in your hearts. And whatever you do, whether in word or deed, do it all in the name of the Lord Jesus, giving thanks to God the Father through him" (Colossians 3:15-16, NIV).

A peace settled over her as she read the words again, knowing God had blessed her so richly, and comforted by the knowledge that He would never leave her.

CHAPTER TEN

Anne was just pulling out of her driveway on Friday morning when she spotted Wendy running toward her, waving her arms in the air. Alarmed, she put the car in park and climbed out just as Wendy caught up to her.

"What is it?"

Wendy held up one hand, trying to catch her breath. The smile on her face told Anne that there wasn't any reason for concern.

"My, I haven't run that hard in years," Wendy said at last, her chest still heaving. Then she chuckled. "We really should exchange cell phone numbers so we don't have to chase each other down."

"Of course," Anne said, pulling her cell phone out of her purse. "I can give you mine right now..."

"I'll have to get it later," Wendy said. "I left my cell phone back at the tent, and I'll never remember it if you try to tell me."

"Okay, you can give me yours," Anne said then punched in the number as Wendy recited for her. "Got it."

"I'm hoping there's something else you can get for me." Wendy brushed her black hair out of her eyes. "I forgot to buy graham crackers for our craft project today. We're reading *Hansel and Gretel,* and I want the kids to each make the candy house that Hansel and Gretel find in the woods. The graham crackers will be used to construct the house, using frosting to hold them together. Then we'll start adding candy."

Anne was impressed with her creativity — and her energy. "That sounds like fun. When do you need the graham crackers?"

"Not until this afternoon," Wendy said. "Do you have time to pick some up?"

"Sure. I can stop by the market after I run my errand, and I should be back around lunchtime."

"Great!" Wendy glanced over her shoulder at the kids gathering under the tent. "Oh, there was one more thing I wanted to ask you. Some of the kids want to put their sack lunches in your refrigerator. I've had a big cooler under the tent, but they're upset when their food gets smashed together. Do you mind?"

Anne hesitated but gave a reluctant nod. "That's fine. I just worry that the kids will get too close to the construction if they're in the house. I don't want anyone to get hurt."

Wendy waved away that concern. "Oh, I'll make sure they stay clear. They're pretty good kids." Then she chuckled. "Although, those Kepple twins sure keep me hopping. Almost as much as mine do."

"Yes, I've heard about them. I can't wait to actually meet them."

Wendy smiled. "I'll introduce you this afternoon. In fact, I could sure use an extra hand with the craft project if you have time."

A twinge of guilt shot through Anne. She should have been helping a lot more, but the work on the library renovations and her search for the mystery groom had kept her busy. "I'd love to help," she said. "How many graham crackers do you need?"

Wendy pursed her lips as she considered the question. "Let's get ten boxes. That should be enough to allow for a few broken crackers and a few for the kids to snack on." She reached into her pocket. "I've got some money."

"No, this will be my treat," Anne told her. "You've done so much already."

Wendy beamed. "I like to keep busy. I don't know what I'll do once the kids start school. My littlest ones, Ethan and Jacob, even start preschool this year, so I'll have a lot of time on my hands." Then she turned and gave her a wave. "I'd better get back to camp."

"See you later," Anne called after her.

Wendy is an interesting woman, Anne thought to herself as she climbed into her car. *If I had seven kids at home, I'd probably be counting the days until school started.* Wendy was not only disappointed that her kids would be going off to school soon, but she was running a library camp filled with even more kids! Anne shook her head, wondering where Wendy got her energy. The woman certainly had a strong personality, and Anne found it hard to say no to her requests. It seemed as though Wendy expected her to agree, without considering whether it might cause Anne any inconvenience.

Still, she appreciated Wendy's indomitable spirit and looked forward to helping with the craft project this afternoon. Hopefully she'd be able to see for herself if Ben was making new friends or still feeling like an outsider.

As she drove to the south end of town, Anne started to daydream about the children's room she wanted to design for the library. She loved children and looked forward to introducing them to books. There were so many books to choose from these days, and in all different forms. She wanted to offer not only hardbacks and paperbacks, but also audio books and even digital downloads that kids could borrow from the library to read on their computers or electronic reading devices.

Anne still remembered her favorite book as a child. Aunt Edie had given her *Where the Wild Things Are* by Maurice Sendak for her sixth birthday. After the party, they'd snuggled together on the living room sofa while Aunt Edie read the book to her. Soon Anne was reading it herself, over and over again. It was the first time she'd ever been transported by a book, and it was the most incredible feeling. Anne's mother had even made her a wolf costume like the one Max wore in the story.

Her copy had been lost after she'd moved away from home, but she'd noticed another copy of *Where the Wild Things Are* among a box of children's books that Aunt Edie had designated for the library. She knew the children of Blue Hill would enjoy it as much as she had.

Anne breathed a happy sigh at the memory, eager to give children in Blue Hill that same type of experience. She'd been perusing book catalogs and marking her selections, wanting a wide variety so she could find books that would appeal to children of all ages. For the adults, she'd ordered all the classics, along with some popular novels and all the literature award winners and nominees. Fortunately, Aunt Edie's estate had enough money to fill plenty of bookshelves and to add to them as new books were published.

When she reached the south end of town, she saw the new retirement complex. It was a lovely new building, three stories tall and made of brownstone. The building formed a U-shape, with the wings on both sides bordering a beautiful green space with a fountain in the middle.

Anne found an empty space in the parking lot and then made her way inside. There was a directory in the wide hallway, and she found Walter Ochs' name and unit number: 112. As she made her way through the building, Anne admired the open, airy feel and the way the bright sunlight streamed through the large windows.

She paused for a moment to get her bearings, and then she saw a sign that pointed to a hallway with the numbers 110–120. A bird began to coo in the aviary as she passed it in the hallway and several other birds joined in.

The retirement complex was laid out like an apartment building, offering independent living for seniors but providing a cozy, community feel. She saw a puzzle set up in a small alcove, and a group of men were drinking coffee at a card table.

A few minutes later, she reached apartment 112 and knocked on the door.

She heard the shuffling of feet on the other side, and a moment later the door opened. An elderly man with thick white hair and bright blue eyes stood on the other side. He was dressed in a gray suit with a narrow blue tie, and his black shoes had been polished to a high shine.

"Mr. Ochs?" Anne said, wanting to make sure she had the right apartment number.

"That's me," he said with a grin. "Although, I insist you call me Walter." He stepped into the hallway, closing the door behind him. "And you must be Anne. My nephew called earlier and said you might be stopping by today."

"I'm Anne Gibson," she told him, inhaling the scent of his aftershave. "I'd love to have a chance to chat with you, if you have the time."

He smiled, his eyes twinkling. "I've got all the time you need." He held out his arm. "Why don't we have our chat in the garden? Some of the women around here will start to gossip if they see a pretty young girl walk into my apartment."

She smiled as she took his arm. "The garden sounds perfect. It's a beautiful morning, although it's supposed to get hot again this afternoon."

"I know all about the hot summers in Pennsylvania. I used to hire out as a farmhand when I was a lad. We'd pick up hay bales or drive the cattle to pasture when it was well over one hundred degrees." They walked down the hallway, Anne's hand loosely grasping his elbow. "I've got it easy here," Walter continued. "We've got air conditioning and ceiling fans. They never want us getting too hot or too cold."

"Sounds like the management takes good care of its residents."

"They do all right," Walter agreed.

When they reached a set of French doors, Walter opened the door for her. "After you," he said gallantly.

Anne walked into the garden, the fountain bubbling merrily in the center. There were plenty of trees to provide shade and several patio sets and chairs placed beside the brick pavers. Two women seated at a small table glanced over at them and then put their heads together and started to whisper.

Walter led Anne to a table opposite the women and pulled a chair out for her. "I hope this spot suits you."

"It's lovely," Anne told him. He was such a kind man and so solicitous. She had a feeling that he'd dressed up just for her.

Walter took the chair beside her. "Now, tell me all about yourself. Alex told me that you grew up in Blue Hill and just moved back here to live in Edie Summers' place up on Bluebell Lane.

"That's right." Anne told him about the will and Aunt Edie's dream to turn the house into a library for the residents of Blue Hill.

"Well, that was nice of her," Walter said. "I never had much time to read anything but the newspaper, but I enjoy a book now and then."

Anne suddenly had an idea. "I'd be happy to bring you some books, once the library is up and going. Perhaps we could post a list here, in case other residents would like to borrow some too."

"Well now, that is a good idea. We have a small bookshelf in the activity room, but they've been read so many times that the pages are starting to fall out."

"You'll have to let me know what kind of books you enjoy," Anne told him, warming to the idea. This was exactly the kind of community outreach that she knew her Aunt Edie would love.

"I've always liked westerns myself," he said, chuckling a little. "When I was a boy, there was nothing better than going to the movie theater on Saturday afternoon and watching a western. I remember seeing *The Big Trail* with John Wayne and telling my folks that I was going to go out west to be a cowboy when I grew up."

"And did you?" Anne asked, curious about his life.

He laughed. "No, I found plenty to keep me busy here. My father passed away when I was fourteen, right in the middle of the Depression. I was the oldest of the bunch, so Mother depended on me to run the farm and help keep everybody fed. Those were hard times, but we all made it through and did it with a smile, most of the time."

He's charming, Anne thought to herself as she listened to his story. Alex had told her that Walter was a ladies' man, and she could see why. She might have fallen for him herself a few decades ago.

"But enough about me," Walter said. "Tell me what brings you here today."

"It's rather a strange story," Anne said, sensing that she could trust him with the details. She reached in her purse and pulled out the copy of the wedding picture. Then she laid it on the table between them. "This is a picture of my Aunt Edie. I don't know how well you knew her, but—"

"I knew her family," Walter interjected, studying the photograph. "But I only spoke to her once or twice. She was quite a bit younger than me. Now, I did know her brother David pretty well. We took a trip together to Philadelphia one time to pick up some farm equipment. He was a hard worker."

Walter slid the photograph closer to him. "That looks like Edie Summers all right, but I never knew she'd gotten married."

"Neither did I," Anne said. Then she told him about finding the picture. "I've been trying to identify her groom, but so far I've come up empty. One thing I did find was a pair of engraved cuff links. I believe they're the same cuff links that the groom is wearing in that picture."

"Oh?" Walter said, watching as Anne retrieved the black velvet box from her purse.

She opened the box to reveal the cuff links inside. "They're engraved with the initials J.R. I did a little digging and found out the cuff links were made and sold by Kepple's Jewelry."

Walter glanced over at the cuff links. "So what does J.R. stand for?"

Anne tried to tamp down her disappointment when he didn't recognize the cuff links. "I was hoping you might be able to tell me. The store still had a copy of the receipt." She pulled it from her purse and handed it to him. "It lists you as the buyer."

Walter's brow crinkled as he stared at it. "You're right. It does."

Anne took a deep breath. "Do you remember buying those cuff links?"

He didn't say anything for a long moment, still staring at the receipt. Then he snapped his fingers. "I do remember now. I was working on a harvest crew one year, and I had to borrow some money from one of the men. My wife needed to see a doctor and it couldn't wait." Walter got a far-off look in his eyes. "Must have been after the war, because the doctor had served with my brother in the Pacific."

"The receipt is dated 1950," Anne said, hoping that would help spark his memory.

Walter looked down at the receipt. "Well, so it does. 1950. Yes, that sounds about right."

"But what does the money you borrowed have to do with the cuff links?" Anne prodded.

Walter set the receipt on the table and picked up the open box of cuff links. "When harvest season was over, I finally had the money to pay the man. But he asked me to purchase a pair of cuff links for him instead, and he'd call it even. He even went with me to Kepple's and picked out the cuff links he wanted. They didn't cost as much as the loan he'd made to me, but he told me to buy a gift for my wife with the extra."

Anne could feel her heart pounding in her chest. "Do you remember his name?"

Walter's brow crinkled again. "Well, his first name must have started with a J...John, maybe? Or Joshua?" He shook his head. "I wish I could remember, but I'm drawing a blank."

She could see that he was almost more disappointed than she was. "That's okay," she said with a consoling smile. "It was a long time ago."

"I'll keep thinking on it," he promised. "If it comes to me, I'll give Alex a call and tell him." His eyes twinkled. "I'm glad that he's found such a nice lady."

"Oh, we're just friends," Anne said.

Walter nodded. "I see."

"Thank you so much for meeting with me," Anne said, reaching out to give his hand a warm squeeze, "and for telling me the story of the cuff links. That may help me more than you know."

They sat and chatted for another thirty minutes before Anne took her leave. Walter escorted her all the way to the parking lot and waved as she drove away.

She stopped at the market to pick up ten boxes of graham crackers then headed back to the house. As she drove up Bluebell Lane, she noticed a strange light flashing in the distance. When she crested the hill, Anne saw an ambulance parked right in front of her house.

CHAPTER ELEVEN

Fear rushed through Anne as she drove up to the house. All she could see was a cluster of children and workmen gathered around the base of the ladder. Her worst fear had come true—someone had been hurt during the renovations. "Dear Lord, please don't let it be Ben or Liddie," she prayed as she parked along the street. She felt so selfish in that moment, but Anne wasn't sure she could survive if she lost either one of her children. She took a moment to calm herself, feeling on the verge of panic. "Dear Lord, help us all," she prayed then climbed out of the car and hurried over to the house.

All she could see as she hurried toward the ladder was someone lying on the ground and being tended to by the paramedics. Her heart leapt into her throat when she realized that someone was a child.

She gently made her way through the throng of children, her knees wobbling as she recognized a pair of Ben's tennis shoes on the prostrate child. A cry tightened her throat, but she swallowed it back. Anne knew she couldn't fall apart now—she needed to be strong for him. Then she felt someone tug on her arm. She glanced back and saw her son behind her. It took her a moment to realize it was really Ben—all in one piece and looking perfectly healthy. She knelt down and wrapped him in a big hug, tears of joy and relief filling her eyes. Blinking them back, she finally forced herself to release him.

"Are you okay, Mom?" Ben asked, concern washing over his face.

"Yes," she said, the word sounding hoarse due to the tightness in her throat. "What happened? Who's hurt?"

"It's Ryan," Ben said softly.

Then Wendy was at her side, pulling her to her feet. "Oh, I'm so glad you're here. I wanted to call you right away, but the kids couldn't remember your cell phone number. I think they were in shock—we all were—when it happened. So I called the ambulance instead then tried to find Alex…"

"Wendy," Anne interjected gently. "What happened?"

"Ryan fell off the ladder," Wendy replied. "Alex told him to come to the house when it was time for lunch because Ryan had forgotten his sack lunch, so Alex was going to share his." Wendy stopped to take a breath. "Anyway, I guess he thought Alex was on the roof and decided to join him there."

Anne was almost afraid to ask the next question. "How badly is he hurt?"

"I don't know," Wendy said, concern etching in her face. "He was complaining about pain in his arm after he fell, but I wanted the paramedics to check him out before we tried to move him."

"That was smart," Anne said, seeing Alex now as the paramedics lifted Ryan onto a stretcher. She hurried over to him. "Alex, I'm so sorry. Is there anything I can do?"

He shook his head. "The paramedics think he might have broken his arm. They're going to take him to the hospital for an X-ray."

She closed her eyes, sorry the boy had to suffer the pain of a broken arm but relieved it was nothing much worse. When she opened them again, Alex was heading for his pickup truck. The children all watched as the ambulance pulled away, its siren sounding as it made its way down Bluebell Lane.

Wendy turned to Anne. "I thought about sending the kids home, but I think that might just upset them more. It sounds like Ryan isn't in serious condition."

Anne nodded. "They think it's just a broken arm, which is bad enough, but it could have been worse."

"Praise the Lord," Wendy said. "I've made more trips to the emergency room for broken bones with my kids than I care to count. It's not fun, but they've all healed without any problems."

"If you're going to continue with library camp, I think I'll go to the hospital," Anne told her, "just to make sure Ryan is okay."

"Good idea," Wendy said, pulling her cell phone out of her pocket. "And please give me your phone number before you go."

Anne gave her the number then fetched the graham crackers from the car and handed them to Wendy. "I don't know if I'll be back in time to help with crafts."

"Don't worry about it," Wendy assured her. "Ryan is more important."

Anne searched out Ben and Liddie before she left, wanting to make certain they weren't too upset by what had happened. Liddie was chattering happily with two little girls and just gave her a quick hug when Anne stopped to talk to her. Ben was sitting by himself under the tent, eating his lunch.

"Hey, Ben," Anne said, walking over to him. "You okay?"

"I'm fine, Mom," he replied, taking another bite of his peanut butter and jelly sandwich.

She knelt down beside him. "Can you tell me why Ryan was wearing your shoes?" Anne looked down at her son's feet, not recognizing the shoes on them. "And whose shoes are you wearing."

"Ryan wanted to trade with me," Ben said, still concentrating on his sandwich. "He said my shoes were better."

Anne studied his face. "Did you want to trade with him?"

Ben shrugged. "I didn't care."

More kids entered the tent with their sack lunches. Anne could tell she wasn't going to get more out of Ben, so she gave his arm an affectionate squeeze and told him she was off to the hospital.

"Okay, Mom," Ben told her. "I'll watch out for Liddie."

"Thanks," Anne replied, and she meant it. She was a little bothered that nobody had noticed Ryan climbing the ladder. With so many kids, it was probably difficult to keep track of them all, so she didn't blame Wendy or her teenage assistants for the accident. However, those few moments when she'd thought it was Ben lying on the ground still shook her to the core.

Anne made her way to the Deshler Community Hospital and parked outside of the emergency room. She found Alex in the waiting room inside.

"Where's Ryan?" she asked, taking a seat beside him. They were the only two people in the waiting room.

"They just took him down to X-ray," Alex replied. "The doctor checked him first and ruled out a concussion or any other serious injury." He rubbed a hand across his jaw. "I should have known he was going to do something like that. He's wanted to go up on the roof with me."

"Don't blame yourself," Anne said gently. "Accidents happen."

Alex nodded but didn't say anything.

"I called my insurance agent on the way over here," Anne told him. "He told me Ryan's medical costs would be covered by my policy..."

"Thanks, but that's not necessary," Alex said. "I've got good medical coverage for him."

"No, I insist. The accident happened on my property, and it's the least I can do. If I'd been helping with the library camp instead of out and about, this might not have happened."

He gave her a wry smile. "But think of how disappointed Uncle Walter would have been if you hadn't shown up today."

"Yes, I think he would have been," Anne admitted, relaxing a little. She could tell that Alex was still upset, but the shock seemed to be wearing off. "We had a very nice chat."

"And did he know J.R.?"

"I'm afraid he couldn't remember," Anne replied. "But I did learn why your Uncle Walter's name was on the receipt for the cuff links." She told Alex the story, wanting to distract him until Ryan returned from having his X-ray.

A few minutes later, the doctor appeared in the waiting room. "Mr. Ochs, your nephew will be back here shortly. The radiologist just called me and said that Ryan's arm is broken, but it's just a hairline fracture. We'll put a cast on it, but it should be as good as new in a few weeks."

Anne saw Alex's shoulders sag with relief, and she offered up a silent prayer of thanks to God.

"Thank you, Doctor," Alex said.

"I'll have the nurse give you instructions for his care," the doctor told him, "and we've given him a painkiller, so he'll probably be asleep for the rest of the day."

Alex nodded, combing his fingers through his hair. "Okay, I can handle that."

"I'll have the nurse call you into his room when he gets back from X-ray," the doctor said, nodding at Anne. He turned and disappeared through a swinging door.

"Thanks for stopping by, Anne," Alex said. "But you don't have to stay. It could still be awhile."

"Are you sure?" Anne said.

"Positive. It sounds like Ryan's going to be fine."

She smiled. "You don't know how relieved I am to hear it. Will you promise to let me know if there's anything I can do?"

"Sure," he said, but she sensed that Alex rarely asked other people for help. He had a lot on his shoulders, with running a business and raising his nephew on his own. She knew all too well the demands of being a single parent.

"Don't be in a hurry to come back to the house," she said, getting up to take her leave. "It can wait until Ryan is on the mend."

"Thanks," he said as the nurse appeared and motioned for Alex to follow her.

She watched him go, praying for both Ryan and Alex. Then she left the hospital. She was eager to get back to the house to help Wendy with the library camp crafts and to give each of her children a hug.

* * *

On Saturday afternoon, Anne took the kids shopping for school supplies. She'd called Alex that morning to check on Ryan, and the boy was already on the mend.

"He's bored," Alex told her over the phone. "And eating me out of house and home. Thanks for the graham-cracker house, by the way. He's devoured half of it already.

Yesterday evening, Wendy had dropped off a candy house that she and Anne had made for Ryan during library camp. It had been quite ornate, decorated with black and red licorice, butterscotch candies, and lots of chocolate drops. They had used frosting to adhere the candy to the graham crackers, and Anne had been quite pleased with the result. She even toyed with the idea of making a gingerbread house to display in the library at Christmas.

After the harrowing incident with the ambulance, Anne had enjoyed helping the library campers with their craft project. It had felt nice to just relax for a while and enjoy the summer sun. She'd had to impose a little discipline when the Kepple twins started putting frosting in the hair of some of the girls, but she'd quickly subdued the situation.

"Do you both have your list?" Anne asked as she parked the car in front of the drugstore. Last week, the school had mailed out school supply lists for each class. She'd put them on the refrigerator as a reminder that school was due to start soon.

"I've got my list," Ben replied, holding it up in the air.

"Me too," Liddie said.

Anne pressed the button to unlock the car doors. "Then let's go!"

The Thrifty Drugstore had been in business for as long as Anne could remember. It had a pharmacy, as well as beauty products, greeting cards, office supplies, and assorted odds and ends. It was located on the corner of Main Street and did a steady business. The old soda fountain was still in operation, although most people went there for coffee instead of ice cream sodas.

Anne let Ben and Liddie lead the way inside, hoping they'd really enjoy the shopping trip. This was a big event, especially for Liddie, and Anne wanted them to take their time.

Ben grabbed a cart and started down the aisle, with Liddie close at his heels. Anne followed them to the office-supply aisle, where many of their school supplies could be found.

"I need ten pencils," Ben said, reading from his list, "a spiral notebook, one blue ink pen and one red ink pen, a box of tissues, an eraser, and a pair of safety scissors."

"And don't forget a backpack," Anne told him. "Now that you're older, you're going to have homework."

"Can I get a backpack too?" Liddie asked.

"May I," Anne prompted, wanting to correct her grammar.

"Yes, you may," Liddie said with a smile. "Can I?"

Anne laughed, deciding to save the grammar lesson for later. "Yes, you *may*."

"Goody!" Liddie clapped her hands together.

"What's on your list?" Ben asked his sister.

"I don't know," she said, handing it over to him. "I can't read very much of it."

Ben looked at the list. "You need a box of crayons, a pencil, a pencil box, a pair of safety scissors, paste, a box of tissues, and a box of crackers or dried fruit for snack time." He sighed. "I wish we still got snack time in my class."

"You can have some of my crackers," Liddie told him. Then she looked at Anne. "What's dried fruit?"

"Well," she said, almost afraid to tell her, "it's fruit that's been dehydrated so that it doesn't spoil. You've had dried apricots before, remember? They were in one of your snack packs."

"Oh yeah," Liddie said. "Those were good!"

"And raisins are dried grapes," Ben told his little sister. "Right, Mom?"

"Right," Anne affirmed as Liddie made a face. "Maybe we should stick with the box of crackers."

"Good idea," Liddie said with an emphatic nod.

Anne helped the children pick out their school supplies. The selection of the backpacks took the longest, with Liddie trying to decide between a pink Barbie backpack and an orange one with horses on it. At last she picked the orange backpack and started naming the horses on the front of it.

Ben took less time selecting his backpack, choosing to go with a simple gray one with a Pittsburgh Steelers logo. Eric had been a big Steelers fan, and Ben used to watch the games with him.

Anne paid for their purchases at the cash register, feeling their shopping trip had ended too soon. Then she got an idea.

"Anyone want some ice cream?" she asked, turning to the kids.

"Me!" Ben and Liddie said in unison.

She led them back to the ice cream fountain, looking forward to a hot fudge sundae herself. When they got there, only three stools remained open.

"Looks like there's just enough room for us," Anne said, perching on a stool and setting the bags at her feet. Ben and Liddie each climbed on a stool and perused the menu board.

"I want a banana split," Ben said. "With extra whipped cream."

"That sounds delicious" Anne said, wondering if she should change her order. She hadn't eaten a banana split since college. Turning to her daughter, Anne, asked, "And how about you? Do you want a sundae or an ice-cream cone?"

"Do they have strawberry ice cream?" Liddie asked her.

Anne checked the menu board. "They sure do."

"Then I want a strawberry ice-cream cone, please." Liddie held up two fingers. "With two scoops."

"That's a lot of ice cream," Anne warned her.

Liddie nodded. "My stomach is feeling big today."

The women sitting beside them started to laugh, and Anne turned to look at them.

"Your daughter is adorable," the woman beside her leaned forward to smile at Liddie. "And your son is quite a handsome young man too."

"Thank you," Anne said. Then she noticed the woman sitting a few stools down, the one she hadn't seen until the lady next to her had leaned toward the counter.

It was Aunt Edie's best friend, Mildred Farley.

CHAPTER TWELVE

"Hello, Mildred," Anne said, standing behind Mildred's stool. She'd placed her order for a pint to go, and then left Ben and Liddie happily eating ice cream and chatting with the nice lady seated beside them.

Mildred turned from her brownie sundae and smiled when she recognized Anne. "Well, hello there." She swiveled on her stool to face her. "I've been meaning to stop by your place ever since you moved in, but I've been so busy."

Anne nodded. "I know what you mean. I actually stopped by your house the other day, but your neighbor told me you were in Tuscaloosa."

Mildred's smile widened. "Ah, so you met Coraline. She does her best to keep up with the comings and goings of everyone in our neighborhood."

"I had tea with her," Anne explained. "She told me you weren't coming back until next week."

Mildred brushed a few stray brownie crumbs from her navy blue pantsuit. The white lace swirls adorning the wide collar gave it a stylish flair that reminded Anne a little of her great-aunt. "Coraline must have misunderstood. I told her I wouldn't be able to visit with her until next week. I always like to take a few days to settle in after I return from a trip." Then she tilted her head to one side. "So how is everything going with the renovations? Not too many unwelcome surprises, I hope."

Anne laughed. "Spoken like someone who's been through a house renovation and lived to tell about it."

Mildred nodded. "I certainly have. They always take more time and money than planned. But I hope that doesn't mean you've run into trouble."

"Well, part of the roof fell in," Anne said, as Mildred's eyes widened in horror. "But Alex assures me that it was really a good thing. This way he can repair the weak spots in the roof before all the renovations are done on the inside of the house."

"That does make sense," Mildred said, "but I certainly hope things go more smoothly for you from now on."

"So do I." She glanced over at her children and noted they were starting to get a little restless. Now wasn't the time or place to ask Mildred about the wedding photograph, but she wanted to do it soon.

"How would you like a tour?" Anne asked. "I could use some advice about paint colors, and you could see our progress so far."

"I'd love a tour!" Mildred exclaimed.

"Does Monday afternoon work for you? Say around two o'clock?"

"I'll be there," Mildred confirmed. "Just promise me you won't go to any trouble trying to clean up the place. That's an impossible job when you're in the midst of renovations."

Anne thought about the mud that had plastered her floor a few days ago and knew that could easily happen again. "Okay, I promise. And I can't wait to hear your opinion."

"I'm sure I'll love it," Mildred said, beaming. "You're making Edie's dream come true, and that makes me so happy."

Anne smiled. "I'll see you on Monday," she said and turned to go.

"I'll be there," Mildred called after her.

When Anne returned to her seat, the man behind the counter handed her a covered container. "Here's your order — one pint of mocha almond fudge ice cream to go."

"Thank you," Anne said. She looked at the kids. "Are you two ready?"

Ben licked the last of the ice cream off his spoon. "I'm ready." He handed Liddie a napkin from the counter. "You've got some strawberry ice cream on the tip your nose."

"I'm saving it for later," Liddie told him.

"I don't think so," Anne said with a smile, taking the napkin and gently rubbing the smudge of pink ice cream off her daughter's nose. "There, that looks much better."

Liddie looked up at her. "But I bet it doesn't taste as good."

Anne leaned down to kiss the tip of her nose. "Nope, it tastes even better now."

Ben laughed, even as he shivered at the public display of affection. "Yuck."

"You'd better watch out," Anne teased, turning to her son. "You might be next."

That lit a fire under him and he was the first one to the car, with Liddie close on his heels. Anne loved spending time with her children and planned to play board games with them all afternoon. *"This is the day that the Lord hath made,"* Anne thought to herself, remembering one of Aunt Edie's favorite verses from her King James Bible, *"we will rejoice and be glad in it"* (Psalm 118:24).

* * *

On Sunday morning, Anne and her children sang the closing hymn with the rest of the congregation at Blue Hill Community Church. Liddie didn't know the words, but she raised her voice as well during the refrain:

> *"Lord of all, to Thee we raise*
> *this our joyful hymn of praise."*

As she sang, Anne glanced around at her fellow worshippers. She recognized more now than when she'd moved to Blue Hill a month ago. Some of them she'd known her whole life, of course, but others had moved to Blue Hill while she'd lived in New York City.

She saw Coraline in the front pew, with Mildred sitting beside her. Heidi Kepple was on the other side of the aisle, standing between her twin boys. She'd learned from Ben that their names were Kyler and Kevin.

Alex was here too, Anne observed, along with Ryan, who had a plaster cast on his left forearm. She was happy to see the young boy up and about. Hopefully his broken arm wouldn't slow him down too much and he'd be able to return to library camp tomorrow.

Her gaze moved to Reverend Tom, who stood at the pulpit, his deep, melodious voice sounding over the speaker system. His sermon today about accepting God's plan in our lives had touched her deeply. There had been times when she'd resisted God's plan or even rebelled against it. But through the years, she'd come to see that His plan did have purpose—even if she didn't always understand it.

His plan had been especially confusing to her three years ago when her husband died of a heart attack. It was the most difficult time of her life, and yet she'd found a strength inside of her that she didn't know she'd possessed. Now she knew that it was a God-given strength and that He'd been there for her to lean on when she'd needed Him. He'd helped her stay strong for Ben and Liddie during those first difficult days and months. That strength had bonded them together as a family, and they'd come out of the darkness and into the light. Their days were now filled with laughter and love. And her heart was filled with gratitude.

After the hymn, Reverend Tom gave the benediction then invited the congregation to join him in the fellowship hall for coffee and cookies.

Liddie tugged on the edge of Anne's white peasant blouse. "Can we stay for cookies? Please?"

Anne hesitated, glancing over at Ben. It might do them all good to spend some time with their fellow church members instead of leaving right after the service. That had been her habit for the last four weeks, overwhelmed by all the work at the house and reluctant to answer a lot of personal questions.

Now she realized that her reluctance might have caused Ben to shy away from new people too. Perhaps if he saw her mingling with the other church members and making some new acquaintances, he'd start to let down his guard a little.

"Yes, let's stay for cookies," Anne said at last, evoking a delighted squeal from her daughter.

She exchanged greetings with old friends and other church members as they slowly made their way to the fellowship hall. A large platter of cookies waited on the center table along with a coffee urn and a pitcher of lemonade.

Ben and Liddie stayed by her side as they waited until their turn at the refreshment table. Then Anne poured a glass of lemonade for the two of them and a cup of coffee for herself. "You may each have two cookies," she told them, certain they'd have a difficult time making a decision from the wide selection. There were some traditional favorites, such as chocolate chip, peanut butter, and oatmeal with Liddie's dreaded raisins. But there were also some thumbprint cookies with raspberry jam in the center, Russian teacakes, and Oreo truffles.

Anne found herself regretting the limit of two cookies that she'd set for herself and the children. She placed an Oreo truffle and a chocolate chip cookie on her napkin then moved aside to let other people through.

She took a bite of the truffle and almost melted through the floor at the creamy, chocolate goodness.

"What do you think?" Wendy asked. "I whipped up those truffles this morning and didn't get a chance to taste test them."

"They're delicious. I'd love to have the recipe."

"Oh, they're easy," she said with a laugh. "I'll email the recipe to you."

Anne took another bite, thinking it might be dangerous to make something this good. She'd be tempted to eat the entire batch in one sitting.

"I drizzled some white chocolate on the top of each one to just add a little pizzazz," Wendy continued. "I had to hide them from Chad and the kids or they would have been gone by the time we got to church this morning."

"I can see why," Anne said, licking some chocolate crumbs off her thumb. "But when do you find time to bake?"

"Oh, I make the time. With eight mouths to feed beside my own, I try to keep the kitchen well-stocked. I took a few classes in culinary school, but once Chad and I got married, I just couldn't find the time to go back."

Anne glanced over to see Ben and Liddie standing near a small table of children. Liddie was talking to one of the little girls, but Ben still lingered on the outside, paying attention to the conversations around him but not joining in much.

"I'd better go round up my crew," Wendy said, looking around the fellowship hall. "And I should probably start with finding my husband."

Anne hadn't met Chad Pyle yet, but she'd seen him standing next to Wendy in church. He was a tall, hefty man in his early forties with a thicket of dark brown hair and brown eyes. As far as Anne knew, neither he nor Wendy had been raised in Blue Hill, moving here a few years ago so Chad could take the job as the high school's math teacher and new football coach.

"Oh, I almost forgot," Wendy said. "I thought we might have a scavenger hunt at library camp tomorrow. We could divide the kids up into teams then give them a list of things to find in the yard and the house. Like a dandelion and a wooden spoon and an empty spool of thread." Her eyes sparkled with enthusiasm. "Doesn't that sound like fun?"

"It does," Anne agreed. "Maybe you could limit it to items they can find outside…"

"Oh, sure," Wendy said quickly. "I'll come up with some lists tonight. The kids will have a blast! And we can have prizes for all the teams when we finish."

"There's a wonderful book called *Remember Me to Harold Square* by Paula Danziger that's about kids going on a goofy scavenger hunt in New York City and…"

"Yes, I know that book!" Wendy exclaimed. "That's where I got the idea. I plan to read some excerpts of it during story time tomorrow morning, and then we can plan the scavenger hunt for tomorrow afternoon. I figure we'll need to divide the kids up into four teams. You can be in charge of two teams, and I'll be in charge of the other two. That way we make sure they stay out of trouble and definitely stay away from ladders!"

Anne wasn't sure the woman was ever going to take a breath. As soon as Wendy paused for air, Anne said, "I'm sorry, but I won't be able to help you tomorrow afternoon. I have a guest coming over."

"Oh, don't worry about it then," Wendy assured her. "I can keep track of the four teams myself, and it will make it easier if you're in the house when the hunt is happening. That way you can make sure they stay out of the construction areas."

Before Anne could reply, Wendy waved down her husband. "There's Chad. Now I just have to find the rest of them."

Anne watched her go, feeling a little bit like she'd just been flattened by a steamroller. She was still trying to figure out how to make it clear that a children's scavenger hunt and a construction site just didn't mix when Reverend Tom approached her.

"Hello, Anne," he said, his face lighting up in a smile. "How are you?"

"Very well," she said. "Thanks again for your help last Tuesday. It means so much just to have a listening ear."

He nodded. "Well, I'm eager to hear if you've made any progress in your search."

"A little," she confided then filled him in on the events so far, including her upcoming meeting with Mildred, her discovery at the jewelry store, and her chat with Walter Ochs.

"Walter is a wonderful man," Reverend Tom said after she'd finished her story. "He's a true gentleman, which, I'm afraid, is rather a rare breed these days."

"I enjoyed spending time with him," Anne replied. "And he promised to contact me if he remembers the name of the man who asked him to buy the cuff links."

Reverend Tom picked up an oatmeal cookie from the refreshment table. "And your meeting with Mildred may provide some answers too."

"I hope so." Then Anne took a deep breath. "I also have to consider the possibility that I may never discover the man's identity."

"It's possible," Reverend Tom agreed. "But you don't seem like the kind of woman who gives up easily."

She smiled. "Sometimes I'm not sure if that's a good thing."

He laughed. "I think it depends on the situation. In this case, I think it's a wonderful trait. And please come to me if you ever need to talk or brainstorm. I'm always happy to help."

"Thank you," Anne told him. "I will."

When Anne and the children left the church parking lot a half hour later, she realized how much she'd missed the fellowship from her former church in New York. There was a special bond within a church family, and Anne wanted her family to share that bond. Today was the first time they'd stayed for cookies and coffee after the worship service, but it certainly wouldn't be the last.

CHAPTER THIRTEEN

Later that evening, Anne sat in the second-floor living room, paging through one of the catalogs filled with library furniture. The children were finally asleep, kept awake long after bedtime by the howling wind outside. The house creaked and groaned under the assault by the strong gusts. The odd noises were new to all of them, and Anne reminded Ben and Liddie that their house in New York used to make noises too.

It had taken Liddie almost an hour to settle down and doze off. When she'd gone into Ben's room to turn off the light on his nightstand, she'd realized he was still awake too.

"I don't remember any noises in our old house," Ben had said, huddling under his covers.

"That's because we got used to them," Anne had replied, placing a reassuring hand on his shoulder. "Soon, we'll be used to the noises in this house too. Don't worry. We're safe. This house has been standing on the top of this hill since the late 1800s and survived much stronger winds than this."

Ben had looked up at her with doubt clouding his hazel eyes, but he gave a small nod. "Okay, Mom."

"And remember," Anne said gently, "You can always talk to God about your fears. He'll always listen."

"I've been trying," Ben said, his voice almost a whisper.

Anne leaned down and kissed his forehead. "Do you want me to stay here until you fall asleep?"

"No, that's okay." Ben pulled the covers higher around his neck. "I'm getting pretty sleepy now."

Anne moved toward the door. "Okay then. Good night, dear."

"'Night, Mom."

Anne lay back in the overstuffed chair, thinking about their conversation and wondering if he'd been talking about more than odd house noises when Ben said he'd been talking to God about his fears.

"Stop worrying so much," Anne scolded herself. The Bible said not to worry, in the sixth chapter of Matthew, verse twenty-seven: *Can anyone of you add a single hour to your life by worrying?* Anne paraphrased.

Only she wasn't worried about her life, she was worried about her son. But deep down, Anne knew the message was the same. Ben would be fine once he got acclimated to Blue Hill. Just like getting used to the strange noises in this house, it would take a while for them to adjust to the newness around them and feel comfortable again.

Aware that she'd been daydreaming long enough, Anne turned her attention back to the catalog in her lap. She needed bookshelves and tables and chairs as well as a nice, tall counter to check out books. Alex had told her he could make custom pieces for her but that it might be more economical to order ready-made furniture.

Anne flipped through the catalog, not sure where to start. There were so many options! Not only what style of furniture to use but what colors and type of wood for the bookshelves. Did she want the richness of dark cherry or the fresh feel of natural wood? Or the sturdy oak? Should she have wooden chairs or upholstered chairs? And how many tables did she need?

She reached for the spiral notebook she'd purchased for herself at the drugstore yesterday. With so many decisions to make, Anne decided it was time to get them down on paper. She could always cross them out later if she changed her mind. She picked up the pen on the table beside her and started listing the different rooms she planned to have in the library: *Fiction Room, Nonfiction Room, Children's Room…*

She tapped her pen against the notebook, deep in thought. There was still one room she hadn't named yet. It was the large one, to the left of the foyer with the large window looking toward the west. The natural light would make it a wonderful room for people to read or study. Anne planned to purchase a beautiful Oriental rug that would look perfect on the hardwood floor. And the room still had the original chandelier that had been installed when the house got electricity. *So much history…*

Anne sat up in her chair as an idea occurred to her. She could call it the History Room! It could be used mainly as a study but have local history books and old photographs in it, as well as any historical documents that people might want to donate. And perhaps she could display the works of local artists and photographers there also.

Excited by this new idea, Anne began looking through the catalog with a new vigor. Now that she'd decided on the theme of the History Room, she chose the dark cherry bookshelves and matching furniture, along with some chairs upholstered with fabric in rich, jewel colors.

She wrote the furniture items and page numbers down in the notebook, under the new category she'd added for the History Room. The renovations were coming along more quickly than Alex had projected, due in large part to his hard work. After seeing him in church that morning, she had no doubt that he'd be back on the job bright and early tomorrow morning.

For the next hour, Anne looked through the catalog, searching for library furniture for each of the different rooms. She decided to make them all unique in their own way. The walls of the Fiction Room would be painted in four coordinating colors and feature a book-of-the-month display in one corner. She could even change up the décor of the Fiction Room to match the theme of that particular book.

A host of ideas began to inspire her. She could adorn the room with palm trees and seashells for *Treasure Island* by Robert Louis Stevenson or display model trains and steamboats that were used in *Around the World in 80 Days* by Jules Verne. The possibilities were endless.

At last her eyes began to droop, so Anne put down the catalog and her notebook, now filled with new ideas. She stifled a yawn then padded down the hallway to peek in on Ben and Liddie. They were both still sound asleep in their beds.

Anne made her way to her bedroom. The wind rattled the windowpanes, making her shiver a little even though the room was warm. She quickly changed into her pajamas and then said her prayers before climbing into bed.

A night like this made her glad that Alex had reinforced the roof. All he had left to do up there was put on some new shingles; then he could give his full attention to the interior renovations.

She yawned again then picked up the manuscript on her nightstand, wanting to get a little reading in before sleep overtook her.

Ruth washed her face and dried her eyes before she returned to the orchard later that afternoon to gather the dirty lunch dishes. She hoped the men had moved out of sight of the picnic area so that she wouldn't have to see Harry again. He was probably nursing a burnt tongue right now and wishing he'd never tried her blueberry pie.

But when Ruth arrived at the picnic spot, she saw something that surprised her. It was a field daisy with perfect petals, and it was placed inside the now-empty pie pan. She bent down to pick it up, certain that neither her father nor Davey had put it there. It had to be Harry.

A thrill ran through her as she held the daisy closer and inhaled its fresh, sweet scent. Ruth tried to tell herself that it didn't mean anything. That it was just a token of Harry's appreciation for the lunch she'd made for them.

But no man had ever given her a flower before.

Then it occurred to her that Harry must have left it there when no one else was looking. No doubt her father would have tossed it away, not wanting the man to court his daughter. And Davey would have teased him endlessly—and her, as well. Which meant that Harry had stolen away from the apple-picking just long enough to pluck this perfect flower and leave it here for her to find.

Anne set down the page in her hand with a soft sigh then placed the manuscript back on the nightstand. She wanted to keep reading, but she could barely keep her eyes open.

She closed them now, turning on her side as the wind rattled the windows once more. Aunt Edie had loved to talk about the language of flowers. Anne drifted off with Aunt Edie's voice in her head. *"Bluebells symbolize humility; a white chrysanthemum means truth; and a daisy, well, my dear Anne, a daisy is a symbol of loyal love."*

* * *

The next day, Mildred arrived at the house at precisely two o'clock in the afternoon. The wind had finally died down, making it easier for Alex and his workman to nail the new shingles on the roof.

"I hope you don't mind the noise," Anne said, leading Mildred into the foyer as nail guns sounded three stories above them. "The roof should be finished today."

"I don't mind," Mildred said, looking around. "The foyer looks as lovely as it ever was. Are you planning to change anything here?"

"Not at the moment," Anne told her. "It's a beautiful entryway, and I adore the sunburst in the floor."

"Well, I'd love to see what you've done so far," Mildred said with an excited gleam in her blue eyes.

Anne turned to her left and led Mildred into the next room. "This is going to be the History Room," Anne told her. "I've just ordered the bookshelves and a study table this morning. I'll have a couple of armchairs in each corner for reading and four large desks against the south wall. And I'm planning to purchase an oriental rug to place under the table, right in the center of the room.

"The History Room," Mildred said, turning in a slow circle. "That sounds intriguing. Will it be full of history books?"

"It will," Anne confirmed, "especially the history of Blue Hill and the state of Pennsylvania. I can't wait to start filling up those bookshelves."

"And I can't wait to start learning more about my hometown and my state," Mildred told her. "A History Room is a wonderful idea. And it sounds as if it's going to be beautiful."

"I hope so." Anne led her through another doorway into the Fiction Room. "Alex hasn't started painting in here yet, but I've finally picked out the colors I want."

"Colors?" Mildred echoed.

"Yes, I've chosen a different color for each wall, with white molding lining each corner from floor to ceiling. I want the Fiction Room to be full of color and creativity." She told Mildred about her plan to feature a book-of-the-month and change the décor accordingly.

Mildred clapped her hands together. "Oh, I love that idea! And you know what would be wonderful? What if you let a library patron choose the book one month and decorate the room?"

"Perfect!" Anne exclaimed. "I want people in the community to feel like the library belongs to them, and that is a great way to do it. I could have a volunteer list available so patrons could sign up for whatever month they wanted."

Mildred smiled. "Well, I would definitely be on that list. I love to decorate, and how fun to be able to pick a theme from one of my favorite books!"

"You'll be at the top of the list," Anne promised her.

They continued the tour, with Anne showing Mildred the checkout area. Then she led her up the grand staircase to the second floor. "This will be the Children's Room," Anne said. "I've picked out a sunny yellow paint for three of the walls, but the fourth wall will be coated with chalkboard paint so the children can draw pictures on it whenever they want."

"So they can make use of their imaginations," Mildred chimed.

"That's right. I want them to think of the library as a fun place, just like I did when I was a child."

"Are you going to keep the wood floor or put carpet down?"

"I'm keeping the wood, but it will be almost completely covered with a rainbow of colorful throw rugs."

"I can picture it now," Mildred said with a happy sigh.

Anne had just placed a furniture order for the room this morning. "And the short bookcases will be all natural, with no wood stain on them, just a clear varnish. The child-size tables and chairs I've ordered will be the same."

"This is really something," Mildred said as Anne led her to the next room.

"Last but not least is the Nonfiction Room," Anne told her. "I'm planning to paint the walls a soft taupe color and use white accents on the floor and ceiling boards. And I've ordered some of those black vinyl letters that you can attach to a wall without damaging it. I plan to place quotes by a variety of different authors on each wall."

Mildred tilted her head to one side as she looked at Anne. "You've really thought this all through, haven't you?"

"Well, some if it anyway," Anne said modestly. "I still have other rooms that I want to use for the library, but I'm going to get started with these four first and go from there."

Mildred was silent for a long moment, her chin quivering a little. "Edie has given such a wonderful gift to this town—and you're part of that gift, Anne. You're making this place into something very special."

"I want this library to honor Aunt Edie," Anne said, her voice tight with emotion. "She meant so much to me—and gave me so much. Not just in material things but in the way she lived her faith, loved her family, and embraced the joy of life."

"She did, indeed," Mildred said, her eyes shimmering with tears. Then she took a deep breath. "I don't know about you, but I could use a cup of tea."

Anne smiled. "I've got some sun tea brewing on the back porch, or I could make you a cup of hot tea, if you prefer."

"Sun tea sounds just fine."

They made their way back down to the first floor, Anne describing the new kitchen that Alex was renovating for her on the second floor.

"I'm not sure what to do with this kitchen," Anne said as they entered it. "It's still in pretty good shape, but it's a little too far from our private living space to be convenient."

"Maybe a room for cookbooks or even a home-and-garden section," Mildred suggested, taking a seat at the table.

"Those are wonderful ideas." Anne retrieved the jar of sun tea from the back porch, hearing the shouts of the children from library camp. So far, no one had shown up at the door on a scavenger hunt, but she was keeping her ears open.

She poured them each a glass of tea then placed a plate of store-bought cookies on the table. "I'm sorry to say I haven't had much time to bake," she said, feeling a little embarrassed by her offering.

Mildred cheerfully waved off her apology. "I'm surprised you had time to make sun tea, to tell you the truth. You only moved here a month ago and have accomplished so much already. I'm not nearly as busy." She took a sip of her tea. "In fact, the next time I stop by for a visit, I'll bring the cookies. I have plenty of time on my hands."

Anne smiled. "I just may take you up on that offer."

They chatted for a little while longer, Anne waiting for the perfect time to bring up the subject of the photograph. Mildred had been Aunt Edie's best friend. If she didn't know about Edie's marriage, would she be hurt by the decades of secrecy?

"There's something I want to show you," Anne said at last, reaching for her bag on the counter. "It's a copy of a photograph I found here."

Curiosity lit Mildred's blue eyes. "Oh?"

Anne took a deep breath. Then she pulled the picture from the bag and set it in front of Mildred.

CHAPTER FOURTEEN

Mildred didn't move or speak as she looked at the photograph on the table in front of her.

Anne couldn't tell if the older woman was shocked more by the photograph itself or the fact that Anne had found it. "Have you seen this picture before?" Anne asked at last.

Mildred set the tips of her fingers on the bottom edge of the photograph and slid it away from her. "No."

Anne waited for her to elaborate. To ask questions. To wonder why her best friend of over sixty years had kept such a secret from her.

But Mildred's silence spoke volumes. She might not have seen the photograph before, but the marriage *hadn't* been a secret.

Anne slipped into the chair across from her, eager for answers. "I never knew that Aunt Edie had married, so you can imagine my surprise when I found that photograph. She looks so young. I assume she was around twenty years old."

Mildred glanced at the picture. "Yes, she looks about twenty," she replied, her voice flat. "Maybe closer to twenty-one or twenty-two. It's hard to tell."

"So that means the wedding portrait was taken around 1950?"

"Possibly."

The short, one-word answers and lack of emotion, so different from Mildred's cheery demeanor before she had seen the photo, made Anne wonder if there was something she was missing. *Had Mildred been unhappy about Aunt Edie's wedding? Had something tragic happened?*

Anne's years as an avid reader led her to consider all sorts of scenarios. Perhaps Mildred had been in love with the man herself? Had the marriage caused a rift between Mildred and Aunt Edie? A rift they'd obviously settled since they'd been best friends for as long as Anne could remember.

She mentally shook herself, aware it would do no good to go off on some wild tangent.

Mildred took a long sip of her tea. "Mÿ, it's getting late, isn't it? You probably need to start supper soon."

Anne told herself to slow down with the questions. She didn't want to scare Mildred off. "I'm afraid we're just having ham sandwiches and potato chips tonight. It's been so hot lately that I hate to turn on the oven."

"Yes, I'm looking forward to fall. It's my favorite season of the year." She smiled. "There's nothing I enjoy more than opening my windows and letting the cool fall breeze blow through the house, especially at night. I find it so comforting."

Anne nodded, searching for something else to say. "I've been dreaming of winter myself. I can't wait to decorate the house."

"Edie always had a flair for that kind of thing," Mildred said, chuckling a little. "I remember one year she hosted a Christmas party and dressed up as an elf, complete with green tights and a green elf hat on her head and a red jumper. She even made a pair of red felt shoes that curled up at the toes. Then she hung a little bell from each toe point so that she jingled when she walked."

Anne smiled, hearing only love and admiration in Mildred's voice and not one hint of resentment or anger. Her earlier conclusion that the marriage had hurt Mildred in some way was probably way off. So why the refusal to talk about the wedding picture?

"I bet she looked adorable," Anne said. "I missed her so much when I left for New York, even though we talked on the phone often." She looked down at the picture. "We talked about everything under the sun. That's why I find it so strange that she never mentioned the fact that she was married."

"Perhaps she had a reason."

Anne met Mildred's gaze. "Was she hurt in some way? Or trying to protect someone?"

"Anne," Mildred began, slightly shaking her head.

"Can you at least tell me the name of the man in the picture?" Anne interjected, feeling a little desperate.

"I really think the past is better left alone, dear," she said gently. Then she scooted her chair back and stood up. "Now I really must be going."

Anne rose to her feet, not wanting to end their visit on a cool note. She liked Mildred and felt a special connection to her because of the woman's long friendship with Aunt Edie. "Thank you so much for coming. And I hope you still want to help with the book-of-the-month in the Fiction Room."

Mildred smiled. "I'll be thrilled to help. Just let me know what month works best for you, and I'll start planning something special."

Anne walked her to the door. "Thank you again for stopping by. I hope we can do this again soon."

Mildred reached out and gently patted her arm. "So do I. You take care now."

"You too," Anne said as Mildred stepped outside and headed for her car.

Anne waved as she drove off, trying to ignore the wave of disappointment inside of her. Although Mildred may have given her good advice to leave the past alone, their conversation had the opposite effect on Anne. Now, more than ever, she wanted to know the identity of the groom and the story about their marriage. Mildred's silence and demeanor had made her even more curious.

Why the secrecy? Especially after more than sixty years. Anne had been so surprised at Mildred's reaction to the wedding picture that she hadn't even brought up the possibility that the mystery groom or his heirs might have some claim to Aunt Edie's estate. She wondered if that would move Mildred to talk about it or make her more determined to leave the past alone.

Anne walked back to the kitchen and cleared the glasses and plates off the table, her mind still spinning. A few minutes later, the back door opened and Ben and Liddie walked inside.

"Hello, there," Anne said, turning to greet them. "Is library camp over for the day?"

"Yep," Ben replied, moving to the refrigerator and opening the door. "What's for supper?"

"Ham sandwiches and potato chips," Anne replied, reaching over to give Liddie a hug. She still smelled like the coconut-scented sunscreen that Anne had applied to her arms and legs that morning. "Are you two hungry?"

"I'm starving," Liddie exclaimed, flopping into a chair at the table. "We ran around all afternoon."

"Ran around?" Anne gave Ben a quick hug as she reached into the refrigerator for the package of deli ham from the market. "Why were you running?"

Ben joined his sister at the table. "We played a game called Blind Man's Bluff. That's where one person is blindfolded with a handkerchief and tries to tag someone without being able to see them."

"I think Kyler Kepple could see through that hanky," Liddie said, sticking out her lower lip. "He tagged me right away."

Ben smiled. "But you tagged me right away and I know you didn't cheat."

Liddie brightened. "That's right, I did tag you right away!"

Anne looked over at her son, certain he'd let Liddie tag him. Ben was a fast runner and excelled at most games. "Who wants chocolate milk with their supper?" she asked, deciding it was time for a treat.

"Me!" the kids said in unison.

As Anne made the sandwiches and set the potato chips on the table, she remembered all the times Aunt Edie had planned some special surprise for no reason at all. She wanted to do the same with her own kids. To teach them that while it was important to study and work hard, that life could also be an adventure with fun surprises around the corner.

Anne made three tall glasses of chocolate milk then joined the kids at the kitchen table. "Who remembers where we're going tomorrow night?"

"The school open house," Ben said evenly, plucking a potato chip from his plate.

"That's right." Anne looked over at Liddie. "Are you excited?"

"Yes!" Liddie exclaimed, pumping her fist in the air.

Anne was excited too. She looked forward to meeting Ben's and Liddie's teachers, as well as some of the other parents. And once school began, the kids could get into a routine and start connecting with the kids in their class. The library camp was a great way for them to meet other children in town, but there was a wide range of ages, making it difficult for a kid like Ben to find a kindred spirit.

Anne truly believed her children would find good friends here—just as she believed that someday she'd discover the identity of Aunt Edie's husband.

* * *

On Tuesday morning, Anne was awakened by the loud rumble of a truck outside her house. She reached for her glasses on the nightstand then sat up, wondering if she was hearing things. The slam of a car door compelled her to climb out of bed and walk over to her window. When she pulled back the curtain, she saw a delivery truck parked in her driveway and the delivery man heading for the back door, where the private entrance was located.

She'd recently placed a sign out front stating that all deliveries should go to the back entrance, knowing she'd need to keep the front entrance clear for library patrons.

Anne quickly pulled on a pair of jeans and T-shirt before gathering her hair into a loose ponytail. Then she hurried down three flights of stairs in her bare feet, forgetting about the apartment-style buzzer at both the front and back doors that she could use to "buzz" visitors in. When she opened the back door, a stocky delivery man in a brown uniform stood on the other side.

"Good morning," he said, holding a clipboard. "I have a delivery for a Mrs. Anne Gibson at this address. Are you Mrs. Gibson?"

"I am," she replied, wondering what it might be. Then it hit her. *The books!* She'd ordered some starter books for the library two weeks ago, and they'd finally arrived. In an instant, she was wide awake and eager to get her order.

"Will you sign here, please?" the delivery man asked, holding out his electronic tablet. She picked up the attached stylus pen, gave the order form a quick once-over, and then signed on the dotted line.

The delivery man took the tablet from her and tapped a couple of buttons on it. "Looks like we're good to go. I'll get your order."

Feeling like a kid at Christmas, Anne stood in the open doorway and watched as the delivery man emerged from the back of the truck with a rolling hand cart stacked high with boxes. He pushed the cart up the walk and lifted it up the steps to the back door.

"Where do you want 'em?" he asked.

Anne hesitated, not sure what to tell him. "Let's just put them in the foyer for now," she said, leading the way. "I'll sort them out later."

"Will do," he said with a nod.

Dozens of boxes later, the delivery man drove off. Anne stood in the front foyer, looking at all the boxes stacked around her. She didn't even know where to start. Walking over to the first box, Anne popped the seal on the lid and opened the cardboard flaps. The sight that greeted her took her breath away.

A row of four hardbound books, front covers facing up, lined the top of the box. They were sleek and shiny and colorful. She drew one out, lightly grazing her hand over the smooth cover. "*A Lantern in Her Hand,*" she read out loud. Bess Streeter Aldrich was one of her favorite authors and wrote about pioneers. She'd felt like a pioneer herself lately, although she'd come home instead of leaving home. Still it was a big change from her life in New York. Just holding this familiar book made her smile.

Footsteps sounded on the porch steps. She looked up to see the front door open, but a stack of boxes blocked it.

"Anne?" Alex called out. "Are you there?"

"Come in," she replied, pushing the boxes out of the way.

He opened the door and walked into the foyer, his gaze moving over the boxes. "Looks like you got an early morning delivery."

"Isn't it wonderful? It looks like there are about twelve books to a box." She tried to lift the open box in front of her, groaning at the effort.

"Hey, put that down before you hurt yourself," Alex chided, taking the box out of her arms. "Just tell me where you want it."

"That box goes in the Fiction Room," she said, pointing the way. "I ordered about six hundred books to start. Two hundred fiction books, two hundred nonfiction books, and two hundred kids' books."

"Why don't you go ahead and open them here," he said, "then I'll carry them wherever they need to go."

"That sounds like a good deal," she said with a smile. "For me, anyway. We can use the elevator for the books that need to go on the second floor."

Alex smiled as he left the foyer with the box in his arms. While he was gone, Anne began opening the other boxes and checking out the books inside. She was just starting to separate the boxes according to category when Alex reappeared.

"I'll put the books that go in the Fiction Room here by the stairs," she said, sliding a box over to the banister. "The nonfiction books will be by the front door, and the boxes of children's books will be here in the center."

They worked quietly and efficiently, with Anne sorting the boxes into the right piles and Alex carrying each box to the designated room. Somehow her kids slept through it all.

It didn't ever occur to her until they were almost done that her hair hadn't been combed and she wasn't wearing a speck of makeup. She smiled to herself at her sudden self-awareness. The excitement of receiving the first books for the library had made her forget everything else—even her own appearance. And the condition of some of the rooms.

"Oh, I just thought of something," Anne said with a grimace. "We still need to paint all these rooms. Maybe we should put the boxes back in the foyer."

Alex shook his head and held up both hands. "I just carried twenty boxes out of here—and hauled a third of them up to the second floor. We're leaving the boxes where they are. We'll just put them in the center of the room when it's time to paint the walls and cover them with a thick tarp."

Anne nodded, although that meant she wouldn't get to start unloading right away.

"I just stopped by," he continued, "to see if you'd made any decisions about paint color."

"I did," Anne replied. "I've written the colors down in my notebook upstairs. Just hold on and I'll get it for you."

Before Alex could reply, she dashed up to the second floor. She tore out the list of paint colors from her notebook. Then she caught a glimpse of herself in the mirror. Startled by her disheveled appearance, she tucked in her T-shirt then paused just long enough to put a stray curl back into place.

"Here you go," Anne said when she returned to the foyer. She handed him the paint list. "I wrote the colors from the paint chip samples for each room."

"Thanks," he said, sticking the paper in his shirt pocket and heading for the door.

"You're welcome." Anne followed him to the door. "So are you and Ryan going to the open house at the school tonight?"

"I guess so," Alex said. "Are you?"

She nodded. "I want the kids to see the building and their classrooms before school starts next week. I'm not sure who's more nervous—them or me."

"They'll do fine," Alex said. Then he opened the door and stepped onto the front porch. "I'll see you later."

"Bye, and thanks for helping me with the boxes." Anne closed the door behind him then hurried into the Fiction Room. She might not be able to unpack all the books before the rooms were painted, but she could always take them out of the box just long enough to look at them. Aunt Edie's dream was coming to life.

CHAPTER FIFTEEN

Later that evening, Anne and her children arrived at the Blue Hill Elementary School. It was a tall, three-story brick building that was at least seventy years old. It used to house the high school as well but had been remodeled when the new high school was built a few years ago.

Liddie had wanted to wear her best church outfit, a blue and pink polka-dot silk dress with a wide pink sash, but Anne had finally convinced her that might be too dressy for an open house, so they'd finally decided on a black skirt with a matching red-and-black Minnie Mouse, short-sleeved top.

Like most boys, Ben hadn't worried about dressing up. He'd worn his pair of everyday blue jeans and a white Steelers T-shirt. But the way he kept fidgeting in his seat on the drive to the elementary school told Anne that he was more nervous than he let on.

Please, Lord, she prayed silently, *let this go well.*

She parked the Impala then turned to the kids with a wide smile. "Ready?"

"Yeah," Ben said, unhooking his seat belt and opening the door.

"Hand me your sunglasses, Liddie," Anne said. "I'll keep them in my purse until we leave."

"But I want to wear them," she countered. "They make me look cool."

"After the open house," Anne said with gentle firmness.

Liddie pulled the sunglasses off her face and handed them to Anne before climbing out of the car. The parking lot was almost full. She walked with the kids to the front entrance feeling a little nervous herself, then, patted down her hair, and pushed her glasses onto her nose.

They walked through the double doors and entered a long hallway. The building might be old, but it had been recently remodeled, so the interior of the school looked fresh and modern. On the right were the school cafeteria and the gym. On the left were the principal's office and a long row of classrooms on either side of the hallway.

"Hello," a woman said, walking up to greet them, "I'm Nina, the school secretary."

"Hi," Anne greeted her. "I'm Anne Gibson, and this is Ben and Liddie. We just moved to Blue Hill a month ago, so this is all new to us."

Nina smiled as she looked at the children. "Welcome to Blue Hill! I know you're going to love it here. Now, can you tell me what grade you're each going to be in?"

"I'll be in fourth grade," Ben told her, "and Liddie is starting kindergarten."

"Great," Nina replied. "I'll show you both classrooms, and you can decide which one to visit first."

Ben looked up at Anne. "We can visit Liddie's room first."

"Okay," she said softly as they followed Nina down the hallway.

Other parents and students passed them in the hall. Hank and Heidi waved to her, and she saw Wendy and Chad corralling their children near the water fountain. There were families she recognized from church as well, and she waved to a few of her old high school classmates who looked happy to see her.

Nina stopped in front of a door with a large orange ribbon tied on it. "Here's the kindergarten room." Then she turned and pointed. "The fourth-grade room is two doors down on the other side of the hallway. That door has a green ribbon."

"Thank you so much," Anne said.

"You're very welcome. And don't forget to stop by the cafeteria for some cookies and lemonade before you leave."

"We'll do that," Anne promised as she and the children headed into the kindergarten room.

Liddie stopped just a few steps into the doorway and looked around, her mouth gaping open. "This is kindergarten?

Anne couldn't tell if she was impressed or disappointed. Six small tables and chairs were set up in two rows in the center of the room. Along the perimeter of the room were different play stations, such as a mini-grocery store, a garden area with plastic vegetables and a miniature fruit tree, a small area with foam building blocks, and a large magnetic board on the wall with letters and numbers on it.

"What do you think?" Anne asked her.

"I think it might be fun," Liddie said as a young woman approached them.

"Hello, I'm Miss Reed, the kindergarten teacher." She leaned down to greet Liddie. "And what's your name?"

"My real name is Lydia Summers Gibson, but everyone calls me Liddie," Liddie replied. "Are you my teacher?"

"I sure am. We're going to have a wonderful class this year, and I'm so happy that you'll be here with us."

Liddie pointed to her shirt. "This is Minnie Mouse."

"I see that," Miss Reed said with a smile. Then she looked up at Anne. "Liddie is welcome to stay here while you and your son visit his classroom."

Anne appreciated the offer. She wanted Liddie to be comfortable here when the first day of school rolled around. "Is that okay with you, Liddie?"

She nodded quickly and made a beeline for the mini-grocery store station.

Anne laughed. "I think that means yes."

"Take your time," Miss Reed told them. "I'll keep a good eye on her."

Anne thanked her as she and Ben turned to leave the classroom. She liked Miss Reed and could tell that Liddie liked her too. It still seemed strange that her little girl would be going to school in a few days. Just the thought of sending her off to school caused a lump in her throat. Anne swallowed it back, well aware that Liddie would love school and that Anne would be free to devote her day to the library.

As they approached the door with the green ribbon, Ben slowed his step a little.

"Are you okay, buddy?" Anne asked him.

"Yeah," Ben said, straightening his shoulders and marching ahead of her through the doorway.

They were met by a man in his late twenties with short, dark hair and brown eyes. "Hello, I'm Mr. Layton, the fourth-grade teacher." He reached out to shake Ben's hand. "I don't think we've met before."

"I'm Ben," he said, shaking the teacher's hand. "Ben Gibson. We just moved here from New York."

"New York is a wonderful state," Mr. Layton said. "You can be our New York expert during social studies class, and soon you'll know just as much about Pennsylvania."

"My mom's building a library," Ben said, a note of pride in his voice. "She's already got more than a thousand books."

Mr. Layton emitted a low whistle. "That is a lot of books. Our class may have to take a field trip there."

"I'm not actually building it," Anne said with a smile, reaching out to tousle Ben's hair. "My great-aunt left the house to the town of Blue Hill so that it could be converted into a library. I'm just helping fulfill that dream."

"What a wonderful service," Mr. Layton said. "Perhaps you could come and talk to my class sometime about what it takes to put a library together."

"Well, I'm still learning that myself," Anne said, chuckling. "But I may be ready someday down the road."

Mr. Layton nodded then turned back to Ben. "Would you like to see your desk?"

"Sure," Ben said.

While Mr. Layton took Ben to his desk, Anne walked around the room, looking at the displays and making small talk with some of the other parents. Ben had never had a male teacher before, but she was glad he would have one now. Now that Eric was gone, Ben needed some good male role models in his life.

As she turned to look at the bulletin board, she saw Alex walking up to her.

"Hello," she greeted him. "Is Ryan in this class too?"

Alex nodded. "Yes, although he's a little older than the other kids." He hesitated for a moment then said in a low voice, "His folks passed away when he was in first grade. That was a tough year for him with a lot of changes, so the teacher thought it best if he repeated that grade."

"That's certainly understandable," Anne said, her heart going out to the boy. "How is his arm?"

"Healing well, according to the doctor. He should have the cast off in about three weeks."

Ryan walked over to them and stood beside his uncle. "I'm ready to go now."

"Okay," Alex said, "but have you met Mrs. Gibson?"

Ryan looked up at her with his big brown eyes. "We have library camp at her house."

"That's right," Anne said. "But I haven't really had a chance to talk to you before now. Are you looking forward to fourth grade?"

The boy wrinkled his nose. "Not really. I don't like math. Or English. Or science."

Alex chuckled. "That leaves recess and gym and lunch."

Ryan looked up at him. "*And* social studies. I like social studies."

"Okay," Alex said with a smile, draping his arm around the boy's shoulder. The affection between them was sweet and endearing. "We'd better get going."

Anne watched them leave and then looked around the room for Ben, who stood by the world map with Mr. Layton. She was halfway to him when Wendy intercepted her.

"Oh, here you are," Wendy said. "I should have guessed. I just wanted to catch you and let you know about an idea I had for library camp. There are only a few days left, and I want to do something big for the finale, so I thought we could have a costume party with different characters from the books we've been reading."

"That sounds fun," Anne said.

"Doesn't it?" Wendy's eyes sparkled with excitement. "I've already purchased all the materials and printed off the patterns from the Internet. I figured that if you make half of them and I make half, we'll have them done in a jiffy."

Anne blinked, surprised by her plan. "I don't..."

"Oh, it won't take any time at all," Wendy said. "There's not a lot of sewing involved. Most of the costumes are held together by Velcro and glue. I'll just leave the supplies on your kitchen table tomorrow."

Anne's head was spinning. She didn't have time to make costumes. Not when she had a library to put together and a mystery to solve. "I really am stretched too thin right now and..."

"Oh, I'll give you a hand if you run out of time," Wendy said and then craned her neck toward the door. "There's Chad. I'd better go. Just give me a shout if you have any questions about the costume patterns."

The next moment, Wendy was out the door. Anne stared after her, feeling as if she'd just been caught in a whirlwind. It had always been difficult for her to say no to people. Eric used to tease her that she was a people-pleaser, even at the expense of her own needs. Anne knew he was right, but Wendy had done so much for the library camp. Maybe the costumes wouldn't take too much time...

"I'm ready to go, Mom," Ben said, moving beside her.

"Okay, dear." She was still playing the conversation with Wendy over in her mind as they walked to the kindergarten class, trying to remember if she'd actually said the word *no*.

They picked up Liddie, who chattered all the way to the cafeteria about her new class and new teacher. Ben talked about Mr. Layton too and the fun projects the class was going to undertake this year. Anne put her conversation with Wendy behind her, so relieved that Ben and Liddie liked their teachers and seemed excited about school. She'd been praying for that to happen every night since they moved back to Blue Hill.

When they reached the cafeteria, Ben and Liddie headed straight toward the cookie platters while Anne made a point to say hello to one of her old classmates.

"This certainly isn't anything like our old cafeteria," Anne told Lisa Morelli. "We didn't have a salad bar."

"Or a frozen yogurt machine," Lisa said. "And if they don't like the main dish for the day, they get to have a slice of pizza instead."

Anne smiled. "I have a feeling my son will be eating pizza every day. I used to love hamburger and french fry day at the old cafeteria."

"I think that was everybody's favorite day." Lisa chuckled. "There was even a picture in our high school yearbook of Hank Kepple with his mouth stuffed full of french fries, remember?"

Anne nodded, realizing she hadn't looked at her old yearbook for years. It would be fun to page through it again. Back when the high school was in this building, there used to be a rack of framed senior class photographs in the old cafeteria.

"What happened to the pictures?" Anne asked suddenly, looking at Lisa. "Remember the ones that were each in a large frame and held decades of senior class pictures from Blue Hill High?"

"Oh, those," Lisa said with a nod. "I think they were moved to the new high school when it was built. Remember how we used to laugh at some of the old-fashioned hairstyles in those pictures?"

"I do," Anne said wryly. "And now kids are probably laughing at us."

Lisa grinned. "There's no 'probably' about it, I'm *certain* they're laughing at us."

Anne laughed and said her farewell then went to gather up Ben and Liddie. But instead of driving home, she headed to the high school, which was also holding an open house that evening.

"Why are we going here?" Ben asked her as they pulled into the high-school parking lot.

"I just want to look at something," she explained. "It shouldn't take too long."

Ben and Liddie followed her into the one-story building. "I've never seen the new high school," she told them. Anne took a moment to look around and orient herself and then made a beeline for the cafeteria, which was also serving as a reception area for visiting parents and students.

"You may both have one more cookie," Anne said; then she pointed to the rack with the large frames on it. "I'll be right over there."

"Come on, Liddie," Ben said, grabbing his sister's hand. "Let's go get in line."

She watched the children head toward the reception table, and then she moved to the picture rack. It was set up so that each frame held two class photos, one in the front, and one in the back. The frames were attached to the wall and were able to be flipped back and forth like the pages in a spiral notebook.

Anne was tempted to start at the beginning, with the sepia portrait of eight students from the 1890 senior class. But she decided to wait until another time, not wanting the kids to get restless waiting for her. She flipped through the frames until she reached the year 1949. Then she stopped and studied the faces and names of the students pictured there. Each student's portrait was set in a small circle on the photo mat, with their name written in ink underneath. Aunt Edie had graduated in the 1948 class. Anne's gaze moved to her great-aunt's black-and-white photo first. She looked so young, but her smile was exactly the same. Then Anne started to look for any young man with the initials J.R.

There were over forty students in Aunt Edie's class, with about twenty boys. But none of them had the initials J.R., and none of them looked the least bit like the mystery groom.

Then again, the mystery groom had looked a little older in that wedding portrait. She flipped a couple of frames back to the 1947 class. At a quick glance, only one of the boys slightly resembled the mystery groom in the photograph. Then she looked at his name, and her heart skipped a beat. *James Roland.*

She dug into her purse and pulled out a piece of scrap paper and pen, jotting his name down. There was one other boy in that class with the initials J.R., although Jack Rasmussen didn't look like the groom. And there was a John Rink in the 1946 class, although he didn't look much like the groom either.

She checked the 1945 class and even the 1949 and 1950 classes, but there were no boys there with the initials J.R. or anyone who resembled the photograph.

Three names, Anne thought to herself as she placed the paper and pen back in her purse. Now she just had to track them down.

Chapter Sixteen

Anne sat in Reverend Tom's church office the next day and read him the list of names she'd found at the high school.

"James Roland, Jack Rasmussen, and John Rink," she said and then looked up at him. "Aunt Edie graduated in 1948. James and Jack were in the 1947 senior class, and John graduated in 1946."

Reverend Tom leaned back in his chair, his chin perched on his fingertips. "The groom does look a little older than Edie in the picture, so that fits."

"I believe James Roland is the most likely one at this time, since he resembles the groom in the photograph. I conducted an Internet search on all three names but didn't find anything helpful."

"Well, I've met both Jack Rasmussen and John Rink," Reverend Tom said. "They both passed away a few years ago, but nothing about them or their pasts tells me that they might have married your aunt."

Anne leaned forward in her chair, intrigued. "Will you tell me about them?"

"Well, John Rink was a fine fellow," Reverend Tom said. "He joined the army the day after graduation and left for Germany. He came home about four years later with a German wife."

Anne nodded. "So that probably rules him out. And what about Jack Rasmussen?"

"He's another interesting fellow," Reverend Tom said. "We had some wonderful conversations about religion and philosophy. He was a Catholic priest."

"Oh," Anne said, surprised to hear it. But that didn't necessarily rule him out. "I suppose he and Aunt Edie could have had a romance before he entered the seminary."

"It's possible," Reverend Tom told her. "Although, I attended a reception in celebration of his fifty years in the priesthood. Now, that reception was shortly after I arrived in Blue Hill in 2000, and, according to what Jack told me, it took about four years to go through seminary…"

Anne quickly did the math in her head. "So if his fiftieth anniversary was in 2000, that meant that he probably graduated from seminary in 1950. Subtract four years and it appears that he entered the seminary right after graduation. That meant he didn't have time for a romance."

"I think you're right," Reverend Tom agreed.

Anne crossed both John Rink and Jack Rasmussen off her list. "That leaves James Roland, who resembles the groom."

"And that's someone I have never met," Reverend Tom said.

Anne pondered the name for a long moment. "I sure don't remember any Rolands when I was growing up in Blue Hill. Do you know any?"

He shook his head. "Not offhand. But that doesn't mean they're not out there."

Anne nodded. He was right. She finally had a name that might go with the face in the photograph. It was time to do some digging. She chatted with Reverend Tom for a few more minutes and then took her leave.

As she sat down in her car, she considered what to do next. She was tempted to call Mildred and ask about James Roland, but after their last conversation, she wasn't convinced Mildred would tell her anything, even if she knew the man. Then Anne thought about Mildred's neighbor, Coraline. She seemed to have her finger on the pulse of this community. But the woman was also a bit nosy, and Anne didn't want to explain why she was looking for a man she'd never met.

"I guess you're on your own," Anne said to herself as she started the engine. Then she put the car into reverse. She made her way to the newspaper office, hoping they'd have some old editions from that time period.

As she entered the office, Anne was met by a pretty blonde woman in her late twenties or early thirties. Her skin was so flawless that Anne wanted to ask her what skin creams she used, but that probably wasn't the best way to make a good first impression.

"Hello," Anne said. "I'm hoping you can help me."

"Well, I'll do my best," the woman replied with a smile, "but I'm just the editor. The receptionist is out today." She held out her hand. "I'm Grace Hawkins."

"Nice to meet you," Anne said. "I'm Anne Gibson."

Grace's blue eyes widened in recognition. "You're the woman who's putting the library together."

Anne smiled. "That's me."

"We did a story about your great-aunt leaving her house to the town for a library. I'd love to do a follow-up with pictures."

"That sounds fine," Anne replied then added a caveat. "*After* the renovations are all done."

Grace laughed. "Of course. I'm thrilled about the new library, and I can't wait to see it. Now, how can I help you today?"

Anne hesitated, aware that her request sounded a little unusual. "Do you have a newspaper archive?"

"We do," Grace affirmed. "Is there a particular issue that interests you?"

"More than one, actually. I was hoping to take a look at the issues from May 1946 through 1951, if they're available."

Grace chuckled. "That is a lot of newspapers, but at least they're weekly and not dailies. You're welcome to check them out as long as you leave your name, address, and phone number."

Anne stared at her. "You mean I can just take them with me?" Something like that would be unheard of in New York. Then she reminded herself that she was in Blue Hill and that life was different here.

"Sure," Grace said. "We've got copies of all the issues on microfiche, but our machine is broken and I'm not sure when—or if—it will be repaired. So I'll just go grab the paper editions that you want and be right back."

Anne waited in the reception area, thrilled that she'd be able to take the papers home with her and peruse them at her leisure. Especially since she would have over two hundred papers to scan for any information about James Roland.

A short time later, Grace reappeared carrying a large plastic crate. "Here you go," she said, setting the crate on the floor. Then she rounded the reception desk and pulled a piece of paper out of a drawer. She handed it to Anne, along with a pencil. "If you'll just put your contact information on there, you can be on your way."

"Great," Anne said, writing down her name, address, and phone number. "Do you need them back by a certain date?"

"No," Grace replied, taking the form from her. "And if something comes up, we know where to find you. Now, do you need any help getting them to your car?"

"No, I've got it." Anne bent down and lifted the crate filled with newspapers. It looked as if each year was in a separate, clear plastic bag. "Thanks for your help."

"Any time," Grace said as Anne made her way outside.

When she arrived home, Anne set the box in the foyer then made her way to the kitchen to grab a glass of iced tea. She was eager to spend the rest of the afternoon looking through the newspapers. But when she walked into the kitchen, she saw something on the kitchen table that made her groan.

It was a large shopping bag, and inside were all the patterns and supplies to make costumes, along with a short note from Wendy.

Here you go, Anne! I think you'll love how easily these costumes go together. I know you're busy, so I only gave you enough supplies to make five costumes. I'll put together the other fifteen. Have fun with it and don't be afraid to be creative!! —Wendy

"Lord, give me strength," Anne murmured, wondering how she'd ever find time to make five costumes. It would probably take her most of the night just to go through all the newspapers.

Anne poured herself a glass of tea. Then she grabbed the bag of costume materials and hauled it up the back spiral staircase to her third-floor bedroom. She'd just set the bag on her bed when she heard a strange banging noise.

That sound was immediately followed by the whoops of children and something that sounded like a herd of elephants stampeding through the house.

"Oh no!" she cried, remembering the crate of newspapers in the foyer. She'd feel awful if anything happened to them.

Anne rushed down the hallway toward the grand staircase as a large boom of thunder sounded overhead. The kids below screamed, some in fear and some in delight. Anne took the steps two at a time until she reached the crowded foyer.

Children milled about, many of them with muddy shoes and damp hair. Wendy was nowhere in sight, but her three teenage assistants were trying to subdue the children. Alex and his crew were at another job site until the rest of the paint she'd ordered came in.

"Everybody settle down," Anne said, raising her voice loud enough to hear above the din. She didn't see Ben or Liddie, but she could hear the sound of children in the other rooms on the first floor.

Anne made her way to where the crate stood, hoping all the newspapers would still be in one piece. Another boom of thunder evoked screams from the children.

"You're all safe here," she called out, wanting to reassure them. Although, she could see smiles among many of the faces and realized that sometimes it was just fun to have an excuse to scream. Maybe she'd do the same at the next thunderclap.

Anne gently moved a little boy out of her path and saw the crate. It was still in one piece, and though the top bag of newspapers was slightly mud-spattered, it appeared that the mud had stayed on the outside of the bag. The old newspapers were safe.

She picked up the crate then turned her attention back to the children. "Everybody, please follow me upstairs." Anne called out, hoping they could all hear her.

Then she turned toward the staircase. She intended to take them to a large, empty room to sit out the storm. A room that hadn't just been recently painted or renovated. She climbed the stairs to the second floor, glancing over her shoulder often to make sure that there were still children behind her. The line of children streamed down the stairs and into the foyer.

She could only hope that there wasn't any real damage from the muddy shoes and dirty fingers. Anne marched the line of library campers down the second-floor hallway to the empty room across the hall from the Fiction Room. She led them inside, standing by the door, with the crate in her hands, as she counted heads. There were eight kids missing.

"Where are your mom and the other kids?" Anne asked Wendy's fourteen-year-old daughter, Hannah. She was tall and had a serenity about her that Anne found comforting in all the chaos.

"Some of the kids just started running when the rain started," Hannah explained. "Mom tried to get everybody under the tent, but when she saw a flash of lightning, she ordered everyone to the house."

Anne nodded, knowing she would have done the same. "So she went after the other kids?"

"Yes," Hannah said. "I hope they're all right."

Anne knew she couldn't just stand there when children might be in danger from the storm. "Hannah, do you mind if I leave you in charge while I go help your mom?"

"No, that's fine. I babysit all the time."

Anne smiled. "Thank you. I'll be back as soon as I can. Please try to keep the children in this room. There's a restroom down the hall if anyone needs it."

"Okay," Hannah said with a nod.

Anne scanned the room once more and saw Ben and Liddie clustered around the window with some other children watching the rainstorm. Then she headed out the door, carrying the crate upstairs to her bedroom before grabbing an umbrella and going down the back stairs to the kitchen. She walked over to the back door and looked outside. It was pouring rain, and she could see the flaps of the white tent blowing in the breeze, but there was no sign of Wendy or any kids.

"Dear Lord, please keep us safe," she prayed. Squaring her shoulders, she walked outside. She stood under the back porch awning just long enough to open her umbrella. Then she headed down the steps to the backyard.

Her shoes squished with each step on the rain-soaked lawn, and a strong gust of wind tried to grab her umbrella out of her hands. She held on tight and headed farther into the backyard. It was hard to see with the wind whipping raindrops into her face. She heard a noise and turned to see Wendy running toward the house with a small gaggle of children.

"Thank You, Lord," Anne breathed, heading in their direction.

Wendy herded the children to the front porch then held the door open as they ran inside. Anne quickly followed as a bolt of lightning lit the sky. She closed the door behind her then hung her wind-crumpled umbrella on the antique coat tree.

"My goodness, that is quite a storm," Wendy said, brushing her wet, bedraggled hair from her face. "It certainly caught us by surprise. One moment we were reading *Skippyjon Jones* and the next, buckets of rain just fell from the sky."

"The thunder scared me," a little girl said, her body shaking either from fear or her cold, wet skin.

Anne took her jacket off and wrapped it around the little girl. "Here you go." Then she looked at Sarah Pyle, Wendy's twelve-year-old daughter. "Why don't you take these kids upstairs while your Mom and I dig up some snacks in the kitchen? The other children are already up there."

"Okay," Sarah said. She motioned to the other children. "Everybody follow me."

After the kids were gone, Wendy turned to Anne. "I'm thinking we should invest in a mop factory. These floors are taking a beating."

Anne sighed at the muddy shoe prints all over her beautiful foyer. It certainly wasn't the kids' fault, but she already had so much to do. "I think I should invest in some rugs instead. This is happening much too often."

"Oh well," Wendy said with a smile, "it will clean up. And the kids sound like they're having fun upstairs."

The rising crescendo of noise and thumps on the ceiling told Anne that they'd been left alone long enough. "I'll start cleaning up if you'll take charge upstairs. There should be a couple of boxes of cookies on the counter if you want to hand them out."

"You think of everything," Wendy said cheerfully. "Isn't this fun? I wish library camp could last all month!"

Anne opened her mouth then closed it again, not wanting to snap at a neighbor. This was all getting to be too much. The costumes, the mud, and Ryan's broken arm. "About those costumes...," she began.

"Oh dear," Wendy interjected, craning her neck toward the stairs. "I think I hear someone crying. Looks like it's time for some Wendy 911." She hurried toward the stairs. "Will you bring those cookies up when you have a chance?"

"Sure," Anne said wearily, staring at the mess surrounding her.

The roof falling a week ago was starting to look good in comparison. She stood alone in the foyer, not sure what to do next. At this rate, she'd never identify the mystery groom. Then she pushed up her sleeves and went in search of a mop, determined not to let a little mud or a whirlwind named Wendy stop her.

She'd find James Roland, no matter how long it took.

CHAPTER SEVENTEEN

It was almost midnight when Anne finally climbed into bed. She'd been cleaning ever since library camp had ended for the day. She'd even fed Ben and Liddie sandwiches for supper again, hoping to buy enough time to wipe up all the mud before it dried on the floor. Thunder still rumbled in the distance, but the rain had finally stopped.

She'd set the crate of newspapers by her bed, determined to look through them until she couldn't keep her eyes open any longer. She grabbed the stack from 1946 first, hoping to find some news about the high school seniors who had graduated that year.

Sitting up in bed with the pillow propped against her back, Anne started reading through the May 1946 issues of the *Blue Hill Gazette*. Most of the stories were about local news and issues, with a few feature articles thrown in. She smiled to herself as she read the society column.

Mr. & Mrs. Otis Watkins entertained family for a Mother's Day dinner on Sunday, May 12. A good time was had by all.

"Only in a small town," Anne murmured to herself as she turned the page. The newspaper only had six pages, so she made quick work of the first two issues. Unfortunately, there were no articles about James Roland or anyone with the surname Roland, for that matter.

She picked up the issue for the third week of May, and her pulse quickened when she saw a front page story about the commencement ceremony at Blue Hill High School. But a quick scan of the article only revealed the graduates' names, followed by a detailed description of the graduation speeches, the number in attendance, and the musical performance of the high school choir.

Anne's eyelids began to droop as she turned the pages, realizing that it might take her days to get through all the newspapers at this rate. *Maybe I should develop some kind of system,* she thought to herself, *where I read three newspapers in the morning with my coffee and three at night before I go to bed.*

"One more," Anne told herself as she picked up the last newspaper published in May of 1946. She began to page through it, nodding off once on page three. Then as she turned the last page of the paper, she gasped. There, in black and white, were pictures of each senior, along with their names and their plans for life after high school.

The newspaper had obviously stopped that practice sometime before she graduated, because there had been no back page tribute to her senior class.

She zeroed in on James Roland. His senior picture was the same one she'd seen in the high school. Then her gaze moved to his plans after high school.

James has chosen to join the army and will leave for basic training in Biloxi, Mississippi, on June 3 of this year.

Another clue, Anne thought to herself. The army might even have a current record of his whereabouts, even after all these years. Excited by this discovery, she stayed awake long enough to look through the June and July editions of the *Gazette*. But there was no more news about James.

Anne put the newspapers aside and settled into bed with a happy sigh. As she lay there, she wondered if he'd signed up for a four-year commitment to the army. If so, he would have been discharged in time to work with Walter Ochs during the harvest season in 1950.

She closed her eyes, telling herself to go to sleep or she'd be dragging all day tomorrow. Lightning flashed just outside her window, lighting up both the sky and her room. It was followed by a loud clap of thunder.

A few moments later, she heard the sound of footsteps. She sat up in bed just as her bedroom door flew open and Ben and Liddie ran inside.

"Liddie was scared," Ben said, crawling onto the bed.

"I don't like thunder," Liddie said, as another flash lit up the window. She huddled next to Anne, sliding her feet under the covers.

Anne slid over to the middle of the bed to make room for both of them, one on either side.

Anne slid her left arm around Liddie's shoulders and her right arm around Ben's shoulders and then pulled them closer. "We can just keep each other company until the storm passes."

After she said the words, she realized they'd done it before. As a family, they'd weathered the emotional storms of Eric's death and leaving their home in New York. But she knew they hadn't done it alone. The Lord had been with them all the way.

"Your dad loved storms," Anne said as rain began gently tapping against the windowpane. "He'd watch them for hours and take pictures of lightning."

"I remember that," Ben said. "He let me take a picture once."

"I remember too," Liddie said.

Anne smiled as she gave her daughter an extra squeeze. Liddie had only been two years old when Eric passed away, but she'd heard so many stories about him from Anne and Ben that their memories became her own—and maybe that was a good thing.

"Dad said there was thunder and lightning when Moses went up on the mountain," Ben said.

"That's right," Anne murmured, surprised that Ben would remember. "It reminds us of God's power. He can do anything."

"Can He make it stop raining now?" Liddie asked, laying her head against Anne's shoulder. "I'm tired."

"You can pray and ask Him to stop the rain," Anne said gently. "You can ask Him anything. But also remember that the rain helps plants grow and provides fresh water for all the animals in the forest. Rain is a very good thing."

She glanced at her daughter, who was now fast asleep on her shoulder. Then she looked over at Ben, whose eyelids were drooping. When another clap of thunder sounded, he snuggled under the covers then turned on his side and let out a soft, sleepy sigh.

In that moment, she knew that their love for each other, and God's love and tender care would help them weather any storms in their future. On that comforting thought, Anne closed her eyes and fell asleep with her children by her side.

* * *

On Thursday, Anne made sure everything was running smoothly at the library camp before she left to look for more clues about James Roland. She needed to find military records for this part of the state. She needed a library. But her library wouldn't be ready for another two to three weeks, so she decided to take the twenty-minute trip to Deshler, located south of Blue Hill.

Deshler was slightly larger than Blue Hill, and its shopping mall was the main attraction for the many small towns around it. But Anne wasn't interested in shopping today. She headed for the library just off Main Street. She'd looked up the address before leaving home and still knew the town well enough to find her way around.

The library was in the same place it had always been and looked the same to her too. It was a two-story building constructed of gray stone blocks. The first floor contained nonfiction and a children's room, while the second floor featured the adult fiction, periodicals, and an impressive collection of audio books.

Anne walked through the glass door and straight ahead to the long checkout counter. A woman in her midfifties stood in front of a computer terminal, pecking at the keys. Her salt-and-pepper hair hung in ringlets down to her shoulder and was pulled back from her face with a powder blue headband that matched her blouse. She looked up when she saw Anne approach.

"May I help you?"

"I hope so," Anne said. She'd been planning to introduce herself to the Deshler librarian sometime in the future, hoping they could share the tips and trials of running a library. "I'm Anne Gibson, and I'm putting together a library for Blue Hill."

The woman's green eyes twinkled when she smiled. "I've heard all about you! What a wonderful project for your town! How are the renovations coming?"

"We're almost there," Anne said. "I'm hoping to open the library in the next week or two—if the bookshelves and other furniture arrive in time. I've got a good start on my book collection, but I need a lot more."

"I have some catalogs you can have," the woman said. "I'm Kim, by the way, Kim Olivett. I've been the library director here for the last twenty years."

Anne smiled. "How wonderful to have someone with experience so close by! I hope you don't mind if I come to you for advice once in a while. I have a master's in library science, and I worked at a small branch in New York, but I've never run a library by myself before."

"You'll love it," Kim said without hesitation. "And you'll discover something new every day. That's one of the things I like the best about this job. There's rarely a dull moment." She grinned. "And if there is, you can just grab a book and start reading."

Anne chuckled. "You're a woman after my own heart."

"Let me get those catalogs for you," Kim said. "In fact, come around the counter and I'll show you some of our inner workings."

Curious, Anne followed her into the staff room that was located between the checkout desk and the children's library, with a door leading to each area. Kim showed her some of their organizational tools and their methods for handling overdue or lost books. Then she gave her a general tour of the library.

Anne soaked it all in. This tour, plus her own education and experience as a librarian, made her confident that she could handle the job at Aunt Edie's house. But she wanted to do more than handle it—she wanted to excel.

"Here's our reference area," Kim told her. "With the advent of the World Wide Web, it doesn't get near the use that it did in the past, but we keep it close to the front counter in case our patrons have any questions. These books aren't available for checkout, of course."

"What's that room over there?" Anne asked, pointing to a door with a small, square window.

"That's our soundproof room. We have a wonderful collection of old record albums, thanks to a generous bequest by a former patron. Those aren't available for checkout either, although people are welcome to take them into that room and play them on the record player."

Anne listened to all the services available at the Deshler Public Library and tucked them away in her memory. She'd write them down when she got home and keep a running list of new ideas. Her goal was to serve the best interests of the people of Blue Hill and to discover what they wanted and needed in a library.

"What about large-print books?" Anne asked her. "Is there a big demand here?"

Kim nodded. "We have a large population of senior patrons, and some of them prefer the large-print editions. Our collection is growing, but I'm hoping to expand it even further in the next year."

Anne wanted to add some large-print books to her collection too. Then she asked Kim the question that had brought her here today: "Do you have any county or state records, such as military service?"

Kim arched a dark brow. "Are you looking for something specific?"

"Some*one*," Anne clarified. "I'm doing some family research and was hoping to find some information on his military career."

Kim winced. "I'm not sure we can help you with that. There are some local books that may contain some information, but there's not a comprehensive list that I know about. You could check with the national archives, but in my experience, that could take a while."

Anne nodded, filing away that information in case she wanted to go that route later. She hadn't found J.R. here, but at least she'd met Kim and enjoyed the library tour. "I guess I'll just have to keep looking."

Kim smiled. "Well, good luck. And call or stop by anytime. I'd love to hear how you're doing."

"Thanks," Anne told her. "I'll do that."

She left Deshler, driving along the highway with big band music playing on the radio. She was back to square one and wasn't sure where to look next. All her clues about the identity of the mystery groom seemed to lead to a dead end.

There was still the manuscript, she thought to herself, as the song "In the Mood" came on the radio. She'd been reading Aunt

Edie's story whenever she had the chance. So far, she hadn't found any hints about the groom's identity, but she enjoyed seeing Aunt Edie's romance unfold. The only drawback was that she was almost certain it wouldn't have a happy ending. She intended to read more of it tonight and see if the answer lay between the pages.

When Anne arrived in Blue Hill, she headed for the market. Poor Ben and Liddie had eaten sandwiches for supper too many nights in a row. This evening, she intended to go all out with fried chicken and green beans, along with some mashed potatoes and gravy. Thanks to the storms yesterday, the day was cooler than it had been in a long time, so it was the perfect opportunity to warm up the kitchen with some good home cooking.

Anne parked the car, then she walked into the market and grabbed a shopping cart. She started down the outside aisle, picking up a package of romaine for a salad. As she examined the cucumbers on sale, she heard a voice behind her.

"Hello, Anne."

Anne turned to see Mildred Farley standing beside her cart. "Oh, hello, Mildred. How are you?"

"I'm just fine. It's nice to see you again."

"You too." She remembered their last meeting, when the subject of Aunt Edie's marriage had elicited such a strange response from Mildred.

But there was no harm in trying again.

CHAPTER EIGHTEEN

"Mildred, I feel like our last conversation upset you," Anne began. It was an awkward beginning, but she couldn't tiptoe around the subject. "And I'm afraid I just can't let it go."

The older woman's smiled faded. "I wasn't upset, Anne. Please don't think that. I only want the best for you and your family."

Another customer walked by and reached for a head of cabbage. Anne didn't say anything until the woman was out of earshot.

"I appreciate that," Anne told her. "And it means so much to me that you and Aunt Edie were such close friends. Perhaps she made you promise to keep her secret—"

"Anne," Mildred said, trying to interject.

But Anne used Wendy's example and kept right on talking, determined to convince Mildred to reveal the secret of Aunt Edie's marriage or, at the very least, the identity of the groom. "But I'm concerned that her marriage, as long ago as it was, might have some unintended consequences even now. I've talked to a lawyer and—"

"A lawyer?" Mildred gasped. "Whatever for?"

Anne lowered her voice another notch as more customers passed by them. "To make sure that Aunt Edie's estate is protected.

I don't know if her husband is still alive and may have marital rights to her properties. Or even if he is deceased or an ex-husband, he could have family who might want to claim part of her estate."

Mildred paled. "That can't really happen, can it?"

The older woman's reaction just made Anne more curious. Mildred *did* know something so why was she so reluctant to tell her?

"I've done everything I can to find this mystery man. I've even sacrificed time that I should be using to get the library up and running, but this is too important for me to let go."

"Oh dear," Mildred fretted. She started to say something else before closing her mouth again.

Please just tell me, Anne pleaded silently. The unknown was becoming worse than the most awful truth. "I've looked everywhere," she continued, "but he's just nowhere to be found."

Before Mildred could reply, one of the store clerks walked over to them. He was a lanky teenager with peach fuzz above his upper lip and shaggy brown hair.

"Hey," he said, greeting them. "Do you ladies need any help here?"

Anne turned to him. "No, thank you. We're just chatting."

"Okay, well, the cucumbers are on sale," he said. "And we've got a special on fresh turkey legs. They're great on the grill."

Mildred reached out to pat his arm. "Thank you, Michael. I'll take a look at those turkey legs when I get to the meat department."

"Okay," Michael said. He turned and made his way to the back of the store.

Then Mildred faced her. "Please don't think I'm doing this to torture you. It's simply not my story to tell."

Both her tone and the expression on her face told Anne that it would do no good to push her any further. If she was looking for answers, she wouldn't find them with Mildred.

"I'm sorry, dear," Mildred said, placing a hand on her arm. "I hope you're not too upset with me."

Anne patted her hand. "I'm not upset with you at all. I know you loved Aunt Edie as much as I did. I plan to keep looking for him, though. I hope you understand."

Mildred sighed. "I do. I just wish it didn't have to be this way."

Anne wanted to ask her what she meant, but a young mother and her four children walked into the store at that moment and started down the produce aisle.

"I'd better get going," Anne said, "or the kids will raid the refrigerator for leftovers again. It's time they had a nutritious meal."

"How's the new kitchen on the second floor coming along?" Mildred asked her, moving to a more pleasant subject.

"Very well. Alex installed the cupboards yesterday. Now all I have to do is wait for the electrician to hook up the stove and dishwasher and it will be ready to go."

"That's wonderful. I'm sure the kids are excited too."

Anne chuckled. "I think they'll be more excited that I'm actually going to cook for them tonight. I haven't made a big meal since we moved."

"You've had your hands full," Mildred said, her voice full of empathy. "Once school starts and the library opens, you'll all fall into a nice routine and have more time for cooking and other hobbies."

"I hope you're right."

They chatted a few more minutes and then parted company. Anne picked up the ingredients for supper, along with a carton of chocolate almond ice cream to take home for dessert. As she stood in the checkout line, she saw Mildred chatting with some other shoppers.

Did anyone else know about Aunt Edie's marriage? The thought had crossed her mind before, but she'd assumed the word would be out if others knew. Now she wasn't so sure. If Mildred had kept the secret for so long, perhaps others had too. The problem was that she had no idea who else Aunt Edie might have confided in.

That brought her back to James Roland.

He had to be somewhere. She'd already looked in the phone directory, but there was no one by the name of Roland listed. Then she thought about the pile of old *Blue Hill Gazette* newspapers still sitting in her room, and she got an idea.

* * *

When Anne arrived home, she carried the groceries into the kitchen.

That's when she saw the blood.

Drops of blood spotted the tile floor, each one about a foot apart. The sink had a little blood in it too. Or maybe it was food coloring, Anne told herself, trying not to think the worst. Or dye. Or red paint. Wendy probably had the library campers making a craft project that needed red paint.

Only it didn't look like paint. Or dye. Or food coloring. It looked like blood. She put the chicken in the refrigerator then left the rest of the groceries on the kitchen table as she went in search of Wendy. She checked the backyard first, but all the kids were gone. Then she looked at her watch, surprised to see that it was already five o'clock.

Voices sounded from the other room, so Anne turned and headed toward the door leading to the front of the house. When she opened it, she saw Wendy seated in a folding chair with Ryan on her lap. He was holding a bloody tissue up to his nose.

Ben and Liddie sat on the floor a few feet away, neither of them saying anything. They looked up when Anne walked into the room.

"Mommy!" Liddie cried, jumping off the floor and running over to her. She wrapped her arms around Anne's legs. "I'm so glad you're here!"

"My goodness, what happened?" Anne said, looking over at Ryan. She took Liddie's hand then walked over to where Wendy sat. "Are you all right, Ryan?"

"He will be," Wendy said, gently patting the boy's back. "He's got a bloody nose, but I'm pretty sure it's not broken."

"What happened to you?" Anne asked, looking at his face. The poor kid still had a cast on his arm from the fall off the ladder. She never imagined that library camp could be so dangerous.

"Ben hit me," Ryan accused.

Anne blinked then turned around, aghast. "Ben?" she said. "Is that true?"

Ben scowled but didn't say anything.

"I'm afraid it is," Wendy said at last. "He said Ryan provoked him, but I didn't hear it. I just saw Ben punch him in the nose."

Anne took a deep breath, trying to stay calm. Ben was not a fighter or a bully. There had to be a reason he'd hit Ryan, even though there was no excuse for it. "Ben, come here, please."

Ben slowly rose from the floor and walked over to Anne. She placed one arm around his shoulders. "I'd like you to tell me what happened."

Ben licked his lips, glancing over at Ryan for a moment, then met Anne's gaze. "I punched him."

She waited, but he didn't elaborate. "Why did you punch him?"

"Because he made me mad."

Anne and Wendy exchanged glances. Then Anne turned back to her son. "Okay, tell me how he made you mad."

Ben pressed his mouth together, his gaze moving to the floor. After a long moment, he spoke. "Because when I told him that you were making fried chicken for supper tonight, he told me that his mom made the best fried chicken in the whole world and that *your* chicken stinks."

Anne glanced over at Ryan. His cheeks were flushed and he couldn't meet her gaze. Her heart went out to him, and she didn't take offense at the fried chicken insult. Everybody wanted to think the best of their parents, especially when they weren't around anymore. Just like Ben and Liddie adored their dad.

"Ben," she said evenly, "I want you to apologize for hitting Ryan."

Her son started to sputter, his face indignant. "But he said..."

"It doesn't matter what he said," Anne explained. "Hitting never solves any problems. It was wrong and it hurt him. I want you to apologize."

Ben kicked the floor with his foot. "Sorry," he mumbled.

Anne leaned down and whispered in his ear. "You can do better than that, young man."

Ben lifted his gaze and took a deep breath. "I'm sorry I hit you, Ryan. I hope it doesn't hurt too bad."

Before Ryan could reply, Anne heard Alex's voice from the other side of the room. "I think Ryan owes Ben an apology too."

They all turned around to see Alex standing in the open doorway between the Fiction Room and the History Room.

"How long have you been standing there?" Wendy asked, as Ryan slid off her lap and rushed to Alex's side.

"Long enough." Alex ruffled the boy's hair then tipped up his chin with one finger. "Let's take a look," he said, slowly removing the tissue. The bleeding had stopped, but the nose was still a little red. "Not too bad."

"It hurts," Ryan told him.

"I know," Alex replied. "And I agree with Anne that Ben shouldn't have hit you. But you shouldn't have insulted his mother's cooking either. And I think you owe both Ben and Mrs. Gibson an apology."

Anne started to object, since Ryan was really the only injured party, but the expression on Alex's face kept her quiet.

"I'm sorry I was mean," Ryan said, as his flush deepened.

Liddie walked over to him and reached for his hand. "It's okay, Ryan. You just don't know how good my mommy's chicken tastes. Why don't you stay for supper and find out?"

Wendy rose from her chair. "Now that sounds like a wonderful idea. I'd stay myself if I didn't have eight hungry mouths to feed at home." She walked toward the kitchen. "I'll just go out the back door. See you all tomorrow."

"Bye," Anne called after her then turned back to Alex. "You and Ryan should stay for supper," she said, trying to smooth over the awkward moment. "I have plenty of food."

Alex hesitated. "Are you sure?"

She smiled. "Positive. I'll go start the chicken and you can play referee."

"I'll help you, Mommy," Liddie said, coming up behind her as she walked toward the kitchen. Then Liddie glanced over her shoulder at the two boys. "No more fighting," she warned them, "or you might not get dessert!"

* * *

Two hours later, Alex and Anne sat at the kitchen table drinking coffee while the kids enjoyed their ice cream. Liddie's warning had worked. The boys hadn't come to blows, but they hadn't spoken much to each other either.

She swallowed a sigh, worried about Ben and still startled by the fact that he'd hit another boy.

"You'll have to take a look at the Children's Room and the Nonfiction Room," Alex told her. "We finished painting up there today. Now we just have to wait for the bookshelves to arrive and we'll be finished here."

Anne picked up her coffee cup. "Really? I can't wait to see the rooms. Did you leave one wall unpainted in the Children's Room?"

"I did," he said with a nod. "The chalkboard paint is up there, so you can add it anytime you want."

"Wonderful." She took a sip of her coffee. She had wanted to add some of the final creative touches to this room herself, but now she wondered when she would ever find the time. She still had to put those costumes together, although now that she'd looked at the patterns, she realized that they really wouldn't take too long. Library camp would be over tomorrow and then school started on Tuesday. Only a few more days with her kids at home.

Alex drained his coffee cup and rose to his feet. "Finish up that last bite," he told Ryan. "It's time to go home."

Ryan swallowed his last spoonful of ice cream and then got up from the table.

"What do you say to Mrs. Gibson?" Alex asked him.

Ryan looked at her. "Thank you for the fried chicken. It was almost as good as my mom's."

Anne smiled, walking over to give him a hug. "That's a wonderful compliment. Thank you."

She walked them to the door. "Will you be working here tomorrow?"

"For a little while at least," Alex said. "I want to finish up some odds and ends. Then I'll do cleanup on Monday and won't be back until the bookshelves arrive."

"I hope they come soon," Anne said as they reached the foyer.

"You should probably enjoy the peace and quiet in the house while you can," Alex said, opening the door. "Once the library opens, you'll be sharing it with the entire town."

Anne smiled as she watched them leave. Then she waved as they drove away. She wouldn't exactly call these last few weeks peaceful or quiet. Especially after what had happened tonight.

She closed the door and turned around, surprised to find Ben standing behind her.

"I really am sorry, Mom," he said, his chin quivering.

It was times like this when she missed Eric the most. A son needed a father, especially when it came to learning how to be a man. But Eric wasn't here, so she'd have to do the best that she could. *Lord, help me say the right words.*

Anne reached out to give him a long hug. "Sometimes when we're mad, we do things on impulse," she said, holding him in her arms. "But it's important to take time to stop and think. And to always remember the Golden Rule."

"Do unto others as you would have them do unto you," Ben recited as he stepped out of the hug. "But it's just *so* hard sometimes."

"I know," Anne said. "If it were easy, we wouldn't need a rule."

That brought a small smile to his face. "I guess so."

"You know, Ryan doesn't have his mom around anymore, so remembering special things about her, like her great fried chicken, probably makes him feel close to her. Just like when you remember things about your dad."

"I didn't think of that," Ben said, his voice quiet.

"Well, it's something to remember if he ever says anything to make you mad again." Anne looked down at her son, her heart so full of love for him. "Remember when you two traded shoes?" she asked him, although she was fairly certain the trade wasn't voluntary on Ben's part.

"Yeah," he replied.

"Well, sometimes it's helpful to put yourself in someone else's shoes for a while. To think about what their life is like and why they may act in a certain way. It doesn't excuse bad behavior," she added, "but when we understand someone, it usually makes it much easier to talk to them."

Ben nodded, his face pensive.

She kissed his forehead then headed for the kitchen. "You've got kitchen duties for a week, Ben. I'll wash tonight, and you can dry."

"What about Liddie?" he protested.

"Liddie didn't get in trouble today," Anne replied, waiting for him to catch up as she entered the kitchen. "But if you ask her nicely, she might sing for you."

"Oh no," Ben said with a groan.

But it was too late. Liddie had heard them and now began to sing the "Alphabet Song" at the top of her voice.

Anne laughed and joined in and soon Ben was singing too. She just prayed that her talk with him had sunk in.

CHAPTER NINETEEN

That evening, Anne sent the kids to bed early. They were both exhausted from the long day, and she wanted them to be ready for the last day of library camp tomorrow.

When they were asleep, she set up her sewing table in Aunt Edie's art room on the third floor and spent the next two hours working on the costumes for the library camp play. Her hard work came to a sudden halt when Wendy called her with a change of plans. Now the costumes were out. Instead, Wendy had hired a storyteller to come and entertain the children.

"She's wonderful," Wendy gushed over the phone. "She's been an artist-in-residence at several schools, and the teachers just rave about her. I think the kids will have a blast."

Anne agreed with her but had one question. "What do you want me to do with these costumes?" Three of them are finished, and I have fabric already cut out for the other two."

"Why don't you keep them?" Wendy said. "You can use them in your library. Children love to dress up. Just think how fun it would be for them to have a trunk full of costumes in the Children's Room."

Anne stared at the finished costumes on her sewing table, barely registering Wendy's suggestion. She didn't know whether to be frustrated that she'd wasted the last two hours or relieved that she now had the rest of her evening to do whatever she wanted.

"So you don't need any costumes for tomorrow?" Anne said, just wanting to make sure she was clear about Wendy's decision.

"The only person in costume will be the storyteller," Wendy assured her. "Do you have any room in your attic? Maybe we could save all the costume supplies for library camp next year?"

"I don't have much room," she said, thinking of all of Aunt Edie's furnishings up there. It was packed from the floor to the rafters.

"Well, we'll find a way to fit them in," Wendy said, then rang off.

Anne replaced the cordless phone on the table, relishing her sudden freedom. She cleared her sewing table and placed the costume materials in a bag. Then she turned off the light and headed for her bedroom.

She couldn't wait to dig into Aunt Edie's manuscript again. After preparing for bed, Anne said her prayers and then climbed under the covers, eager to do some reading. The lamp on her nightstand illuminated the pages as Anne read about Harry and Ruth's secret courtship. It had started with the daisy and then moved on to secret notes passed between them, left in a romantic spot by the brook, which served as their "mailbox."

Ruth held the love letter from Harry in her hands. He wanted her to meet him under the moonlight, next to the barn. It wouldn't be their first secret meeting nor, she prayed, their last. Harry had been a perfect gentleman, although Ruth had been bold enough to kiss his cheek the last time they'd met.

Ruth knew that harvest season would be over soon, and Harry would need to move on to find work. Oh, how she wished he could stay! He was such a hard worker and was sure to make something of himself one day. If only her family could see him as she did.

Ruth feared that her mother suspected something between them. Did her mother know about her meetings with Harry? Ruth was certain that her father did not, or Harry wouldn't be working for him anymore. Ruth hated keeping secrets from her parents, but she simply couldn't risk losing the love of her life.

Anne breathed a soft sigh as she read Aunt Edie's words. She sounded so young—and so in love. Anne wondered if that fantasy had evaporated after their marriage and the sometimes harsh realities of life set in, or if Harry had died, leaving Aunt Edie a widow with the memories of a perfect love. If the answer was in the manuscript, she needed to keep reading it to find out.

"You're late," Harry whispered, when Ruth reached the barn. "I thought you might not be coming."

"Mother was up later than usual," Ruth told him. "I couldn't leave until she went to bed. I'm sorry you had to wait."

He grasped both of her hands in his own and stared into her eyes. "I'd wait forever for you. I love you so much, Ruth."

"Oh, Harry," she cried, never realizing she could be this happy. "You know I love you too."

"I asked your father for permission to court you," he said.

Just like that Ruth's happiness turned to dread. "You what? He'll never agree. He—"

"I know," Harry said, his voice dejected as he dropped her hands. "He's ordered me to leave his farm and never return."

Ruth felt dizzy and reached out to grab him for support. His strong arms encircled her waist, giving her strength until she could stand on her own two feet again.

"I'm sorry, Ruth," Harry said. "I have to go."

She looked up into his gorgeous blue eyes and knew she could not live without him. "Then take me with you."

* * *

Anne was still thinking about the story the next day as she made her way up to the attic. She'd read late into the night. Harry had proposed to Ruth when he'd realized that she wouldn't let him leave town without her.

The young couple had planned the day and time of their departure, both of them fearing that her family would find out and keep her from leaving with him. Right before Anne had dozed off for the night, she'd read that Ruth was preparing to write a letter to her mother and fearing that she might never be reunited with her family again.

Anne had been so tempted to continue reading the story this morning, but other duties had called. She'd had to get the kids ready for the last day of library camp and then play hostess to the storyteller, who had arrived one hour before Wendy showed up.

The woman had proved delightful, and Anne was certain the children would be entertained by her. Wendy had brought over the bags of costumes that she'd already made and asked to store them in Anne's attic.

So now here she was, lugging up both her bag of costume materials and Wendy's bag of completed costumes to the attic, hoping to find some little nook or cranny to squeeze them in. She unlocked the attic door and switched on the overhead light. The small windows in the attic provided some natural light but not enough to see well.

Aunt Edie's furnishings made a narrow, winding maze throughout the attic room. Anne had a few pieces picked out to use in the library and planned to ask Alex and his workmen to carry them down as soon as the other furniture arrived. She wasn't exactly sure how much space she'd have until she saw the bookshelves in place in each room. Anne continued along the narrow path, looking for the best spot for the bags. There were so many boxes already piled on top of one another that she was afraid they might all topple over if she added more.

Someday she'd go through everything up here, Anne promised herself. And that would take a while, because it looked as if Aunt Edie's entire life was stored in this attic. There were dolls from her childhood, textbooks from her years in school, a collection of travel magazines that had published her articles, and so many other items.

Some of them were in full view and others were hidden away in boxes or chests or bureau drawers.

Her entire life.

Anne stopped in her tracks, realizing she might not have looked in the one place that could tell Aunt Edie's life story. There was no way she could go through it all now, she thought to herself, looking around the crowded attic. But there might be something — some hint of her life with the mysterious "Harry" that would give Anne the answers she so desperately wanted.

She set the bags inside on the narrow strip of bare floor behind her. Then she went in search of something — anything — that would lead her to the mystery groom. For the next two hours, Anne paged through old photo albums and faded hatboxes filled with old papers. Most of the letters were written by family and friends while she was away on her travels. There were a few receipts from Kaufmann's department store. Aunt Edie had always loved to shop, and that had been one of her favorite stores in Pittsburgh. Anne thumbed through the rest of the papers in the hatbox, noting a few travel brochures and some old postcards. She read each postcard but saw nothing that caught her eye.

Anne replaced the lid on the hatbox and moved on to the next box. When she was just about ready to give up, she found it. A small wooden trunk with brass trim and a leather strap for a handle. On the lid of that trunk, someone had written the initials J.R. in black ink. It looked like Aunt Edie's handwriting, but Anne couldn't be sure.

She reached for the brass fastener on the lid but hesitated a moment, wondering what she might find inside. The thick layer of dust on the trunk told her it had been up here for years, probably decades. But Aunt Edie had kept it for a reason, just like she'd kept everything else. Perhaps she'd even meant for Anne to find it here.

Unable to wait any longer, Anne slowly lifted the lid. Her breath caught in her throat when she saw what lay inside. It was a bridal gown—the same gown that Aunt Edie had worn in the wedding portrait. It had been lovingly folded with tissue paper between the layers of lace and silk. A lavender sachet was tucked between the silk lining of the lid and the gown. The scent was faint now, but it evoked images of a simpler time.

Or not so simple, if you were a young girl in love and your father forbade the young man from seeing you. Edie had been ready to leave her family behind—perhaps forever—for the man in the photograph.

She slowly lifted the dress out of the trunk, the delicate gown falling open at the movement. The tissue paper fluttered to the floor as Anne held the dress in front of her. The waist was so narrow and the neckline so modest. Just like in the photograph. It was the same wedding dress. This meant that she'd been on the right track with the initials J.R. Aunt Edie had kept the gown in his trunk because both had been special to her.

"Mom?"

Ben's voice sounded from far below, carrying through the air registers to the attic. She was surprised that library camp had ended this early, especially after hearing about all the wonderful stories the storyteller planned to perform.

Anne carefully folded the dress back into the trunk, promising herself she'd come back for it another day. She wanted to have it properly preserved—a keepsake of a special time in Aunt Edie's life. A special time that she'd kept completely secret. And Anne still didn't know why.

"Anne?" Wendy's voice sounded near the attic door. There was a frantic note in her tone that made Anne quickly close the trunk lid then hurry toward the attic door. She almost tripped over the bags of costumes she'd left in her path and quickly shoved them out of the way. A stack of boxes wobbled precariously at the impact but somehow stayed upright.

When she finally opened the door, Anne saw Ben and Wendy hurrying toward her.

"There you are," Wendy said, her tone a blend of relief and apprehension.

Anne could tell just by looking at their faces that something was wrong. "What is it?"

"It's Liddie," Ben blurted out. "She's gone!"

CHAPTER TWENTY

Anne spun on her heels to look at Wendy. "What does he mean? Where is Liddie?"

"I'm not sure," Wendy told her. "One minute she was listening to the storyteller with the rest of the kids in the tent, and the next minute she was gone."

Fingers of panic were starting to grip Anne's heart and it began to race in her chest. Her daughter couldn't disappear — not from library camp in Blue Hill. She had to be somewhere close.

"Did you check the restroom?" Anne asked. "Or look in her bedroom? She likes to play in there. What about the kitchen? Maybe she got hungry and wanted a snack."

"I've checked all those places," Wendy said. "I've got the older kids searching the yard for her, and I thought one of us could search the woods."

The woods. There was a small copse of trees just outside the backyard. Their leaves were verdant green in the summer and a blaze of yellow and orange glory in the fall. Anne had loved to play there as a child and had discovered so much about nature.

But she'd been older than Liddie when Aunt Edie let her explore the woods — much older. And she'd always had a friend with her. Her daughter wouldn't know what to do if she got lost. She'd be scared and alone.

Dear God, please keep my little one safe.

Then she turned to Wendy. "Why weren't you watching her?" Fear made the words sharp. "I've tried so hard to just go along with whatever you've wanted, but now you've lost my daughter!"

Wendy drew back, surprised by the accusation, and then tears filled her blue eyes.

Anne felt a stab of regret at her words, but she was too distraught about Liddie to do anything but hurry down the stairs in search of her little girl.

Ben followed close on her heels. "She couldn't have gone very far, Mom. She's just little."

"I know," Anne told him, wanting to reassure her son and herself. "Did anyone check her room?"

"I did," Ben told her, as they reached the third floor. "She wasn't there. Neither was Cleopatra."

Cleopatra was the name of Liddie's favorite doll, a gift from Eric after one of his rare business trips out of town. She always kept Cleopatra on her pillow when she wasn't playing with her.

"She must have come into the house if she took Cleopatra," Anne said. She hurried to Liddie's room, hoping to find some other clues.

But when she walked inside, her heart ached at the sight of the pink, ruffled bedspread and the small, blue nightgown laid out on top of it. Movement outside the window drew Anne there, and she could see Wendy looking under bushes and up at the trees in the backyard.

At what point should I call the police?

Just the question made her feel sick inside.

Then a small noise sounded behind her. She turned to look at Ben. "Did you say something?"

"It wasn't me," Ben told her, looking around the room. "But I heard it too."

"*Sh*," Anne said, holding up one hand.

A moment later, it happened again. This time the sound was so faint that she barely heard it, but it sounded like a soft snore.

"Liddie?" Anne called out, following the sound. It led her to the bed—but the bed was empty. She even tore off the ruffled blanket just to make certain.

Then Anne knelt down and looked under the bed. There, to her surprise and utmost relief, slept Liddie with Cleopatra wrapped in her arms.

"She's here," Anne said, still shaking a little from the scare.

Ben scowled. "You mean she's been hiding under her bed all this time?"

"She may have started out hiding," Anne said, as she gently stretched one hand out to shake Liddie's shoulder, "but she's sleeping now."

Liddie's eyes opened. "Mommy?"

"Hi, sweetie. I'm going to help you out from under your bed, okay?"

"But I like it here," Liddie told her. "There aren't any trolls."

"Trolls?" Anne echoed, confused. Then it hit her. "Did you hear a story about a troll today?"

"Yes," Liddie said, slowly moving toward Anne. "Trolls are green and they drool and they like to scare people."

Ben shook his head. "But trolls aren't real, Liddie. They're just pretend."

"Well, I still don't like them," Liddie proclaimed, scooting herself out far enough for Anne to pick her up. "So I came up to my room to tell Cleopatra, and then I heard a noise up there." She pointed at the ceiling. "And I thought it might be a troll, so I hid under my bed."

It was me, Anne thought to herself, giving her daughter a big hug. Liddie had heard her sliding the trunk over the floor and thought it was a troll. That's what had made her go into hiding and sent the library camp into an uproar.

"Come on," Anne said, taking her daughter by the hand. "We have some explaining to do."

And Anne needed to take Wendy aside and apologize to her. She winced as she remembered the things she'd said to the woman—and the way she'd said them. *Lord, forgive me.* She just hoped that Wendy would forgive her too.

* * *

On Saturday morning, Anne received the phone call she'd been waiting for—the library furniture would arrive today! She was so excited that she sent Alex a phone text to let him know. A moment later, her cell phone rang and she saw Alex's name appear on the caller ID screen. "Hello?"

"Hey, Anne, did they tell you what time the furniture would be here?"

"Sometime in the next hour or so."

"Okay, I'm going to head over and start taking off some of the doors so there's plenty of room for them to bring the furniture through."

"Okay, that's great," she said, relieved to have another adult to help her supervise the delivery.

"Do you mind if I bring Ryan along?" Alex asked her. "I know he and Ben have had some trouble, but I've talked to him about it and I think he'll be fine."

"Of course you can bring him," Anne said, feeling a little bad that Alex felt he even had to ask. "Ryan is always welcome here."

"Thanks. We'll see you soon."

Anne hung up the phone then walked into the kitchen where Ben and Liddie were eating a late breakfast. They'd all stayed up late last night to watch the movie *Shrek*. The main character was an ogre, not a troll, but she thought there were enough similarities that it would show Liddie not to be afraid of a fictional character.

Anne had made a big bowl of buttered popcorn and strawberry ice cream shakes for their movie last night. She couldn't remember the last time they'd had so much fun since the move from New York. Now that library camp was over and the major renovations to the house were mostly complete, they finally had some time to relax.

She still felt bad about snapping at Wendy yesterday. Shortly after Liddie had been found, Wendy had ended library camp and taken her leave before Anne had a chance to apologize fully for her harsh words. She'd tried to call her earlier this morning, but there had been no answer.

Feeling that an apology should be made in person rather than recorded on a voice mail, Anne hadn't left a message. She would try to call her again later. She was determined to clear the air between them. Despite Wendy's tendency to act first and ask permission later, Anne did appreciate the time they'd spent together and all the hard work she'd done with the library camp.

"Time to finish up," Anne told the children, as she picked up the milk carton from the table and set it in the refrigerator. "Alex and Ryan will be here soon to help with the new furniture."

Ben groaned. "Why does Ryan have to be here?"

Anne turned to him. "Because Alex asked to bring him and I said yes. Besides, you two need to bury the hatchet. Alex said he talked to Ryan, just like I talked to you. I think you boys can get along for just a few hours."

"I'll play with Ryan," Liddie offered. "Do you think he likes dolls?"

"I don't know, honey," Anne said with smile. "I guess you'll have to ask him."

"Maybe I'll just stay in my room," Ben said.

Anne reached over him to pick up his empty cereal bowl; then she carried it to the sink. "That would be rude, Ben. Sometimes there are people who rub us the wrong way, but it's still important to be polite."

"Okay," he mumbled.

She walked over to the table and gently combed her fingertips through his brown hair. "Why don't you two go upstairs and get dressed while I wash these dishes?"

"Race you!" Liddie challenged her brother, then slid off her chair and ran for the open doorway.

"Hey, wait," Ben said, chasing after her, "you started before me."

"No running," Anne called after them but knew it was probably fruitless. Their footsteps pounded on the stairs, and she could hear them racing across the third floor hallway above her.

Twenty minutes later, Alex and Ryan arrived. Alex was dressed to work, with his tool belt strapped around his waist. "Any sign of the furniture truck yet?" he asked her.

"Not yet."

"Good, that will give me time to get this front door off. It's an original, so I don't want to leave it for the delivery men to handle." He turned to his nephew, who was clad in blue jeans, a green T-shirt, and a Pittsburgh Steelers ball cap. "Why don't you find Ben and Liddie?"

"Can I help you instead?" Ryan asked him.

"Sure," Alex said as he began to take a screwdriver to the vintage hinges on the front door. "You can hold these screws after I take the hinges off. It's very important not to lose them."

"Okay," Ryan said solemnly, cupping his hands together and holding them out in front of him. A few minutes later, Ben and Liddie made their way downstairs.

Ben moved beside Anne, his gaze fixed on Alex. "Can I help too?"

"I can always use an extra hand," Alex said, waving him toward the door. "These hinges have been on here for over a hundred years, so they might be stuck, especially since they've been painted over a few times. So I will probably need to use two hands to loosen the hinge plates. When I do that, you'll need to hold the screwdriver for me."

Ben nodded. "That's easy."

Alex turned his head to look at Liddie, who sat with her doll on the bottom step of the grand staircase. "Do you want to help too?"

"No, thanks," she said. "Cleopatra and I will just watch."

Anne watched as well, cringing a little as Alex struggled to loosen the hinge plates from the door. She was certain the wood doorframe would crack from the pressure he applied to it. She was amazed when he finally removed the hinge plates without any damage.

Then Alex carried the door, with the hinges still attached, through the house until he reached the first-floor kitchen. He set the door gently on the kitchen rug so it would be out of the way of the delivery men.

"That's one down," Alex said as he returned from the foyer. "Now let's go do the same thing to some of the doors on the second floor. We want to leave plenty of room for the furniture to fit through."

Ben and Ryan raced up the stairs ahead of Alex, and then Liddie followed behind them. Anne stayed downstairs to watch for the arrival of the delivery truck. She kept walking back and forth between the History Room and the Fiction Room, trying to imagine how different they would look with the new furniture. She hoped that she'd made the right choices with colors and styles. It was difficult to make those decisions just by looking at some photos in a catalog.

It was so important to Anne to make Aunt Edie's dream of a town library come true. She wanted everything to be just right.

A few minutes later, she heard the faint rumble of a motor outside and moved toward the window. She pulled the lace curtain back far enough to see outside. A long-bed delivery truck puttered up the hill toward the house.

Anne dropped the curtain and spun around, hurrying toward the staircase. Then she shouted up the stairs. "The furniture is here!"

CHAPTER TWENTY-ONE

The furniture looked even better than she'd imagined. Anne stood in the History Room, running one hand along the top of the smooth, dark cherry wood table. The matching bookshelves were tall and ornate, with intricate, hand-carved scrollwork along the top of the shelf. Alex had directed the delivery men to position the bookshelves so that they were accessible from either side. They were heavy enough that they didn't need to be bolted to the floor, which would be handy if she ever decided to rearrange the room in the future.

She walked into the Fiction Room, where she'd chosen beautiful golden oak furniture. The color of the wood was the perfect complement to the four walls, each one painted a different color from the seascape-themed paint samples. Blues, greens, corals, and a sandy taupe. Overstuffed chairs filled two corners, each upholstered in a beautiful turquoise blue fabric. The book-of-the-month display table sat in the third corner, made of that same golden oak. When she closed her eyes, she could envision the cozy room coming to life, the wood gleaming in the glow of the fireplace.

"Wow, this looks so different," Liddie said, walking into the Fiction Room. "Can we put the books on the shelves?"

"Sure," Anne said, anxious to see how they looked. She'd worry about placing them in alphabetical order later.

"Where are Alex and the boys?"

Liddie set Cleopatra on the display table and then headed toward the boxes of books that had been set next to the brick hearth. "They're upstairs helping Alex put the doors back on."

Anne couldn't wait to see how the Children's Room looked, but first she helped Liddie place the fiction books on the shelves. Another big order of books was due to be delivered in a few days. The library renovation was almost finished.

When all the fiction books were on the shelves, Anne stepped back to look. "Wow, is right! This looks amazing."

Liddie walked over and gave her a hug. "I like our library, Mommy."

"So do I." Anne gave her a warm squeeze, unable to stop smiling. "Why don't we take up some snacks to the boys? They're probably ready for a break."

Liddie heaved a weary sigh. "Cleopatra and I need a break too. Can we have a snack?"

"Yes," Anne said, gently tickling her ribs.

Liddie snorted with laughter as they made their way into the kitchen. Anne retrieved a tray from the cupboard and set it on the table. She washed some grapes and put them in a bowl, while she directed Liddie to pour the box of cheese crackers into the basket. Then they added five juice boxes to the tray and headed to find the guys.

Alex stood just outside the Children's Room, turning the last of the screws into the door's bottom hinge plate.

"There we go," Alex said, swinging the door back and forth to make sure it swung freely. "That was the last one."

"Where are the boys?" Anne said as she and Liddie walked up to him with the tray. She hoped they hadn't clashed again. "I thought they were supposed to be helping you."

"So did I," Alex said wryly, "but then Ben noticed Ryan's cap and asked him if the Steelers were his favorite football team. When Ryan said yes, Ben told him he had an autographed picture of Ben Roethlisberger in his room. The next thing I knew, they were gone."

Anne was about to reply when she heard hoots of boyish laughter emanating from the room above them. Could it be possible? Were the boys actually becoming friends? She didn't want to get her hopes up, but she couldn't help smiling. "Well, it looks like you were able to finish up without their help. The doors look just as good as before."

He nodded. "And the delivery men did a good job with the furniture. There aren't any new dings or scratches in the walls that I can see. Having them use the elevator for some of the pieces made the job a lot easier."

Liddie nudged between Anne and Alex. "Maybe we should have our snack now."

Anne smiled then looked up at Alex. "I thought we could all use a break. I'll set the tray in here if you want to get the boys."

"Sounds good," Alex said then headed toward the stairs on his way to Ben's room.

Anne and Liddie walked into the Children's Room, which looked so fresh and cheerful with its sunny yellow paint on three walls and the new bookshelves and small tables and chairs. The natural wood finish fit perfectly in the room. All she had left to do was apply the chalkboard paint to the fourth wall and a few creative touches here and there this room would be ready to go.

She set the tray down on one of the tables and then examined all the new furniture until Ben and Ryan walked into the room, followed by Alex.

"Can we take our snack into my room?" Ben asked. "I'm showing Ryan how to make a Steelers' helmet with my Legos, and I'm only halfway done."

Anne smiled. "Yes, you may. Just put the food you want into one of the plastic bowls and be careful not to spill your juice."

"We'll be careful," Ryan promised as Ben handed him a box of juice. Then they each filled a paper plate with cheese crackers and a few grapes before heading off to Ben's room once more.

When Alex sat down in one of the small chairs, Liddie giggled. "That makes you look like a giant."

"It makes me feel like a giant too," he said, his long legs stretched out under the table. Liddie and Anne joined him there, fitting a little better on the chairs than Alex.

They each helped themselves to the snack tray and a juice box. Then Liddie stood up again. "I want to take my snack to Ben's room too."

"Go ahead," Anne said. "Just be careful not to spill in there."

Liddie nodded as she carried her juice box and paper plate out of the Children's Room.

Anne turned back to Alex. "I'm glad to see the boys getting along so well. I guess they bonded over their love for the Steelers." Then she smiled. "It must be a guy thing."

"We like our football," Alex agreed, popping a grape into his mouth. "I hope you don't mind, but I told Ryan about Ben and Liddie losing their dad. That seemed to change something for him—probably because he'd lost his own parents."

Anne took a sip of her juice. "I guess they do have more in common than the Steelers."

"Ryan needs a friend," Alex said bluntly. "He keeps to himself a lot, and the other kids don't always include him. I've been trying to tell him to just join in, but he just feels awkward about it, I guess."

"Ben can be the same way—at least until he feels comfortable," Anne replied. "I've been a little worried about him."

Alex sighed. "That seems to come with the territory."

Anne thought of how difficult it must have been for Alex to be thrust into the parent role after Ryan's parents died. "It looks to me like you've done a terrific job."

He chuckled. "I don't know about that. My goal is just to keep him clean, fed, and out of trouble until he graduates from high school."

The love in his voice belied the words, and Anne sensed that Alex shared every parent's dream of wanting the child in their care to be happy. "Sometimes keeping my kids fed well seems to be the hardest part. I've been so busy trying to find the mystery groom in that photograph that I haven't done a lot of home cooking lately."

Alex reached for a cracker. "How's the search coming?"

She sighed. "I'm at a dead end." Then she filled him in on her search for James Roland and the newspaper article that reported his plan to enlist in the army."

"Did you say Roland?" Alex asked.

She leaned forward. "Yes, do you know him?"

"No, but I know a Red Roland. He lives on a small farm near Deshler."

She almost dropped her juice box. "I can't believe it. I've been looking for someone with the name Roland for days. Do you think this Red Roland might be related to James?"

Alex shrugged. "I don't know, but it sounds like it's worth checking out."

"Do you happen to have his phone number? I didn't find anyone by the name of Roland in the local phonebook. I even searched the White Pages on the Internet but didn't find anyone by that name in this area."

Alex shook his head. "Red doesn't have a phone. And I should warn you that he's a bit of a hermit. Harmless, though. I did some construction work on his farm a few years ago. He's a nice guy, but he rarely leaves the place. I think he prefers spending time with his pigs rather than people."

"Do you think he'd mind if I just stopped by?"

"Probably not." Alex pulled a scrap of paper and a stubby pencil from his shirt pocket. "I'll write down the directions to his place for you."

A rush of excitement shot through her. Could she actually be coming close to finding Aunt Edie's groom? "Would he mind if I took the kids?"

"I wouldn't recommend it. There are so many school fundraisers around here that he'll probably think you're selling something and refuse to answer the door. But I'm coming back here on Monday afternoon to finish up a few odds and ends. The kids can stay here with me while you run out to his farm. It will be their last day of freedom since school starts on Tuesday."

"It's a deal," Anne said, "as long as you bring Ryan with you."

"Okay," he said. He drained his juice box and stood up. "I've got a few things to clean up here and then we'll be on our way."

More boyish laughter drifted from the room above them. This was turning out to be her best day in Blue Hill yet. The library furniture had arrived and looked wonderful; Ben had made a friend; and she just might have found the one person who could tell her everything she wanted to know about the mystery groom in the photograph.

CHAPTER TWENTY-TWO

On Sunday night, Anne lay in bed with the manuscript open in front of her. She and the children had attended the cookies-and-coffee fellowship after the worship service that morning then enjoyed a lazy Sunday afternoon at home. Anne had used that time to come up with a list of questions for Red Roland. She just hoped he'd let her in the door.

With a contented sigh, she settled into her pillow and began to read.

Ruth paced back and forth across the braided rug in her room, waiting for the rest of the house to fall asleep. It occurred to her that she might never walk these old floors again. Or smell her mother's banana bread baking in her oven, or hear her brother Davey laugh at a joke or watch Marvin tinker on his jalopy. At this moment, she was so tempted to walk upstairs and knock on her parents' bedroom door. She'd tell them that she was in love and about to elope with Harry, with or without their blessing.

Ruth tried to imagine them reacting with joy and welcoming Harry into the family, but she knew that was an impossible dream.

Her father would never allow it. Her mother would tell her reasons why Harry was all wrong for her. He didn't have money or property and no family to speak of either. How would he support Ruth and any children they might have together? What if he took her away from Green Lake and the only people she'd ever known?

The last question had already been answered. He was taking her away from Green Lake. It was their only option if they wanted to be together. And she did love him — with all of her heart. Now all she had to do was convince her head that she was really making the right decision.

The grandfather clock in the hallway began to chime. It was midnight. Harry would be out there waiting for her. Now was the time for her to decide if she should stay or go.

Anne set the manuscript on the bed beside her and yawned. She already knew what Ruth had decided. Aunt Edie's wedding portrait revealed the answer. Unless Aunt Edie's manuscript had a different ending — one that explained why Aunt Edie had lived most of her life in Blue Hill and had never spoken of having a husband — at least not to Anne.

She'd keep reading in a few minutes, Anne told herself. First, she just wanted to rest her eyes...

* * *

On Monday, Anne drove along the highway with her windows open. The warm breeze caressed her face and hair while the clear blue sky promised a beautiful day ahead. It reminded her of the sermon Reverend Tom had given at church yesterday morning about being good stewards of the land. She still remembered the Bible verse he'd read: *"He is the Maker of heaven and earth, the sea, and everything in them — he remains faithful forever"* (Psalm 146:6, NIV).

As she drove along the rolling hills, she thought about the story in Edie's manuscript. She'd fallen asleep last night before she could read more, but the words she had read still haunted her. Now she was on her way to see Red and, hopefully, find out the truth about that wedding photograph.

If Red was a hermit, he might not be thrilled to see a stranger show up at his door. Especially a stranger asking questions. She'd baked a batch of blueberry muffins last evening, not wanting to show up empty-handed. Hopefully, that goodwill gesture would be enough to persuade him to open up to her.

Anne glanced down at the directions Alex had given her; then she made the turn at the next corner. Her tires rumbled along the gravel road, kicking up a plume of dust behind her car. She closed the windows to keep the dust from finding its way inside, and then she switched on the air-conditioner.

A few miles later, Anne turned onto another road, this one with more dirt than gravel. She had to drive slowly to avoid the deep ruts made after the last rain. Or maybe they were always there and the county just did minimum maintenance since few people lived out this way. She hadn't passed a house in over three miles.

Trees shaded the country road, blocking out the sun. *If a person wanted to be a hermit,* she thought to herself, *this would be the perfect place to do it.* As she reached the crest of the next hill, she saw a small farmstead in the distance. The house appeared gray from a distance, and as she neared it, she realized the paint had worn off and the wood had weathered to a dull gray color. But the house looked sturdily built and, to her surprise, there was a border of beautiful red rose bushes all around it.

A few yards away from the house was a tin shed, and she could see some pigs chasing each other inside the fence.

"This must be it," she said out loud, pulling into the long, dirt driveway.

A rusty tractor stood at the end of the drive, one tire flattened. The chicken coop a few feet away was full of white chickens, which began to raise a ruckus as she climbed out of her car.

Anne felt as if she'd just stepped into an episode of the television show *Green Acres*. But despite the rundown conditions of the place, there was something cozy about it. Maybe it was the well-kept roses or the fact that the animals looked well-fed and healthy, including the playful golden Labrador retriever who came up to greet her, his pink tongue lolling out of his mouth.

"Hello, there," Anne said, reaching down to pet him. He looked up at her then licked her hand. "Aren't you a cutie?"

The squeak of a screen door opening made her look toward the house. She saw a man standing on the porch, wearing a pair of denim overalls and a yellow shirt. His dark red hair explained his nickname, and he wore a pair of silver-framed glasses and carried a cane.

Anne walked over to greet him, the dog loping along beside her. "Hello," she called out to him. "You must be Red. I'm Anne Gibson." Too late, she realized that she'd forgotten the muffins in the car. But she didn't want to turn around now, afraid that he might go back inside and not come out again. "My friend Alex Ochs told me where to find you."

"Why did you want to find me?" Red asked her, looking a little suspicious.

Anne had spent the better part of yesterday afternoon preparing to answer that question, as well as others he might have. "I'm hoping you can help me. I'm trying to solve a family mystery."

He narrowed his bright blue eyes. "And who's your family?"

"Well, I was born in Blue Hill, and my maiden name is Summers. My parents are Dale and Charlene Summers, and my grandparents were Marvin and Elizabeth Summers and Wallace and Rose Everly."

"Don't know 'em," Red said. "Sorry."

"Then maybe you can help me find someone in your family." Anne stepped up on the porch. "I'm looking for James Roland. He graduated from Blue Hill High School in 1946."

Red didn't say anything for a long moment; then he asked, "Is he in trouble?"

The fact that he used the present tense when referring to James made her heart skip a beat. Red not only knew James, he might very well know where to find him.

"No, not at all," Anne replied with a smile. "Do you know him?"

Red hesitated then opened the screen door. "Maybe you'd better come inside." Then he looked down at the dog. "You too, Charlie."

"Is that his name?" Anne asked as the dog walked inside the house ahead of her.

"Yep." Red held the door open for her then followed her inside.

After seeing the outside of the house, Anne had prepared herself for the worst, but she was pleasantly surprised. The furniture was dated but very clean and well-maintained. As they entered the living room, she saw a beige throw rug covering the center of the wide-plank wood floor and a matching sofa and recliner. A large TV screen filled one corner, and a vase of fresh-cut red roses adorned the coffee table.

"Your roses are beautiful," Anne said, walking over to sniff them. "Have you been growing them for a long time?"

"Ever since I started using this cane," he said, tapping it lightly on the floor.

The dog walked between the recliner and the sofa then settled onto a large dog pillow on the floor.

"You can have the sofa," Red said, taking a seat in the recliner.

As she sat down, Anne noticed there wasn't a speck of dust on the coffee table or anywhere else in the room. Red might be a hermit, but he was a neat and tidy hermit. He also seemed like a nice man, although not one to make small talk. So she decided to avoid annoying him with idle chitchat.

"What can you tell me about James?" Anne began, coming straight to the point.

His hand dangled from the arm of the recliner, just far enough to scratch Charlie behind the ears. "What do you want to know?"

She noticed his tendency to answer a question by asking a question. It let him continue the conversation without having to give out too much information. "Everything."

"I'm eighty-four years old, so everything I know about James Roland might take quite a while to tell."

She gaped at him. "You can't be eighty-four!" There wasn't one gray hair on his head. And he moved with the quickness of a man half his age.

"I surely can," he replied. "I was born on October 24, 1929, also known as Black Thursday. That was the day the stock market began to crash."

Anne still couldn't believe it, but she had no reason to disbelieve him. She quickly did the math in her head. "That would make you close to the same age as James."

"That's right. And he was born on Black Thursday too."

Anne stared at him. "You're...twins?"

"No," Red told her. "I'm James."

She blinked, wondering if she'd misunderstood him. "You're *James Roland*?"

He chuckled. "That's right. I would have told you sooner, but I wanted to make sure you weren't trying to sell me something."

Red's discovery that she wasn't attempting to part him from his money seemed to make him more talkative. But Anne's mind was reeling with this newest revelation. "So that means you knew my great-aunt, Edie Summers?"

"That's right."

She took a deep breath. "Can you tell me what happened between the two of you?"

His brow furrowed. "What do you mean?"

"I found the wedding picture," she said, pulling the photocopy out of her purse. She held it out to him, realizing that the black-and-white photo wouldn't have shown his red hair or blue eyes. That was probably the reason that she didn't see the resemblance when she first saw him. Even now, it was hard to match the young man in the photograph with the elderly man seated before her now.

"That's not me," Red said bluntly, handing the picture back to her.

"But it has to be," Anne countered. "You're James Roland and you graduated from Blue Hill High School in 1946. I even read in an old newspaper that you enlisted in the army right after graduation."

"That was my plan." He sighed. "I wanted to get out of the sticks, as I called this place back then, and go see the world. But before I could leave I broke my back in a fall from a hay wagon. It took me years to recover and learn to walk again with this cane. That's when I started growing roses, so I wouldn't go crazy cooped up here for so long with nothing to do."

Anne was still trying to make sense of it all. Had she been following the wrong clue all along? "That means you didn't marry my aunt."

"No, ma'am," he said. "I've been a bachelor all my life, just like Charlie here. I only went to Blue Hill High for a couple of months before graduation. My grandmother lived there and was sickly, so she needed some help around the place. My folks sent me there to do some repair work on her house."

"I see," Anne said, still a little perplexed.

"I do remember Edie though," he continued. "She seemed like a nice gal and had a pretty smile. I always took her as kind of a daydreamer."

Just like me, Anne thought to herself. Only she knew that Aunt Edie hadn't imagined "Harry" in her manuscript. There was photographic evidence that she'd married someone—and most likely someone with the initials J.R. But apparently, that someone wasn't James Roland.

She still wanted to know more. "Did you have a pair of gold cuff links made in 1950 with the initials J.R. engraved on them?"

He considered the question for a long moment then shook his head. "The only thing I was doing in 1950 was tending to my new rose bushes outside. That's about as far as I could get out the door without a lot of pain."

"So that means you weren't working on a harvest crew with Walter Ochs either?"

"The last harvest crew I worked on was in 1946, and I've never met anyone named Walter Ochs."

Anne considered the possibility that he could be deceiving her, but for what purpose?

"Here, I'll show you," Red said, taking her silence for doubt. He used his cane as leverage to push himself out of the recliner; then he walked out of the room.

Anne looked at Charlie. "What do I do now?"

The dog reacted to her question by wagging his tail. Cute, but not exactly helpful.

A few minutes later, Red returned with some photographs clutched in his free hand. He handed them to her. "That's me when I was about twenty years old," he said. "Now compare those pictures to the one with Edie and her husband."

Anne took the old photographs from him. She saw a young man who looked nothing like Aunt Edie's mystery groom. The shape of their eyes was different, as well as their hairlines and noses.

She'd found James Roland, but she'd also just come to another dead end. Now it made sense that Red didn't resemble the man in the picture.

But that didn't make her feel any better. Anne thought she'd been so close to solving this mystery, and now the identity of Aunt Edie's husband seemed more elusive than ever.

Chapter Twenty-Three

The sky didn't look quite so blue when Anne left the Roland farm. She tried not to feel dejected and did enjoy seeing Red's face light up when she presented him with the muffins. He went so far as to thank her for her visit. But even the dog's good-bye kiss—a lick of her hand—didn't make her feel better.

"Cheer up," Anne told herself as she drove back to Blue Hill. "You'll find Aunt Edie's husband if God wants you to find him. And if you don't find him, then life will go on. It's a beautiful day, so don't waste it by wallowing in disappointment."

The pep talk helped a little, and she decided to listen to some of her favorite hymns to make herself feel better. She put a CD into the player and music soon filled the car. She began to hum along.

By the time she turned into her driveway, Anne had finished listening to the CD and found herself refreshed and ready to begin the search all over again. But first she needed to prepare for Ben and Liddie's first day of school tomorrow. Butterflies fluttered in her stomach at the thought of taking them to school in the morning. Most of the time, she'd have them walk together, but tomorrow was special and she wanted to be there.

She walked into the house, surprised to find the first floor empty. She set her purse on the foyer table then thought she heard movement on the ceiling above her and something that sounded like an animal's roar.

As Anne climbed the stairs, she heard Alex's deep voice—though it didn't quite sound like Alex. When she reached the second floor landing, she saw that the door to the Children's Room was ajar and the light was on inside. Then she heard Alex say, "Oh, please don't go—we'll eat you up—we love you so!"

She smiled, recognizing a line from one of her favorite books, Maurice Sendak's *Where the Wild Things Are*. Anne moved closer to the door, not wanting Alex or the kids to see her and interrupt the story. She needed to purchase more copies of the book for the library, certain that it would be checked out often.

Then something tickled her nose. Anne tried to stop the sneeze that followed, but it was impossible. "*Achoo!*"

"Mom?" Ben called out. "Is that you?"

"Yes, it's me," Anne said cheerfully, pushing the door open and walking into the room. "I didn't mean to interrupt. Go on with your story."

"Maybe another time," Alex said, setting the book on the table in front of him then rising from his chair. "I have another stop to make on the way home tonight, so I'd better get going."

Ben turned to Anne. "Mom, Ryan asked if I could stay overnight at his house on Friday. Is it okay?"

She glanced up at Alex. "Is that all right with you?"

"It's fine," he said. "I'll make sure the boys stay out of trouble."

"Please," Ben implored.

She smiled. "Yes, you may stay overnight with Ryan. You two will probably have a lot to talk about with school starting tomorrow."

Ryan groaned. "Don't remind me."

She laughed as Alex headed for the door, motioning for Ryan to follow him. "That's why we've got to run some errands. We've been putting off buying school supplies until the last minute. I don't think Mr. Layton will like it if you show up to class empty-handed."

Then Alex looked over at Anne. "Any luck today?"

"I'm afraid not," she replied, "but it was nice meeting Red. I guess I'm back to square one."

He shrugged. "At least you gave it a shot."

After Alex and Ryan left, Anne helped Ben and Liddie set out their clothes for school. Then they checked their backpacks to make sure they had all the supplies on the list.

"I think we're ready," Ben said at last.

Anne just wished *she* was ready.

* * *

Later that evening, Anne listened to Ben's prayers and tucked him into bed then walked into Liddie's room. Liddie was already kneeling in front of her bed, zipping and unzipping her backpack.

"Let's put this up until tomorrow," Anne suggested, taking the backpack off the bed and placing it on top of the dresser. Liddie had been practically bouncing off the walls during supper. Anne was afraid her daughter was so excited that she might not get any sleep tonight.

Liddie squeezed her eyes closed, her hands clasped in front of her. "God, please help me not get lost at school tomorrow. And don't let there be any mean boys in my class. And please let there be peanut butter sandwiches for lunch. Amen."

"Do you want to thank God for anything?" Anne asked gently.

"Oh yeah," Liddie said, squeezing her eyes shut again. "Thank you for Alex. He makes lots of silly voices when he reads. Amen."

Anne smiled, especially since Alex didn't seem like the silly voices type. "Did you have fun today?"

"Yes, but I'm so excited for school tomorrow!" She started jumping up and down. "I want school to start right now!"

Anne laughed. "Remember this moment, Liddie. Because about eight years from now, I'm not sure you'll be quite this excited about school."

"Yes, I will," Liddie assured her. "I like my teacher and my classroom and all the toys there." Then she looked around. "Can I put Cleopatra in my backpack too?"

"No," Anne said firmly. "I think Cleopatra needs to stay home with me tomorrow."

"Oh." For a moment, Liddie's lip quivered. Then her mouth curved into a smile. "Maybe I'll take Cleopatra for show-and-tell! Miss Reed told me that we're going to have show-and-tell every week."

"We'll see," Anne said, not ready to commit to anything until she heard from Miss Reed herself. At the open house, the kindergarten teacher had promised to keep the parents informed with a newsletter about the happenings in the kindergarten class.

Liddie scrambled under the covers, and Anne pulled them up around her shoulders. She lightly brushed Liddie's hair off her forehead then leaned down to kiss her. "Sweet dreams, Liddie."

"Don't forget to wake me up in time for school tomorrow," Liddie said.

"I won't." Anne loved seeing her so excited, but it was time to settle down for bed. "Now remember, the sooner you go to sleep, the sooner tomorrow will be here."

"Okay, Mommy," Liddie said then closed her eyes.

Anne decided to hope for the best as she turned off the light and walked out of the bedroom.

Then she made her way to her own room. Aunt Edie's manuscript was waiting there for her, and Anne was determined to finish it tonight. She sat down on the edge of the bed and picked up where she'd left off.

Ruth had arrived early for their rendezvous then dreamed of their wedding while she waited for Harry to arrive. But now he was late. She tried not to think the worst, certain that he was coming. They'd planned this moment for so long and loved each other far too much to go back now.

Walking out of her home had been the hardest thing she'd ever done. She prayed that her family would forgive her and that she might be able to see them again someday.

Something rustled the grass behind her, and Ruth turned to see Harry approaching her. The moonlight shone on his hair and face, and as he moved closer to her, she could see the love shining in his eyes. "Are you ready?" he asked.

"Yes," Ruth replied, without any doubt or hesitation. Then she reached for his hand.

And she knew, in that moment, that her life would never be the same again.

Anne turned the page, surprised to find the next one blank. She flipped to the page after that one, only to find it blank too. Several more blank pages followed until she reached the last one, which had the words *The End* written on it, along with Aunt Edie's name and the year 1954.

* * *

The next morning, Anne herded Ben and Liddie out the door of the house, eager to take some pictures before she drove them to school.

"Do you both have everything you need?" Anne asked them for the third time that morning.

"Yes," Ben replied, slinging his backpack over his shoulder. "Do we have to take pictures? I don't want to be late."

"We won't be late." Anne looked around for a good photo spot. "I promise." Then she waved them toward the backyard. "I want you to stand in front of the lilac bushes. That will make a pretty backdrop."

Ben and Liddie walked over to the bushes and turned to face her.

Anne held up her camera. "Say cheese pizza," she directed them, naming one of their favorite take-out foods.

"Cheese pizza," they echoed in unison, both with big smiles on their faces.

Anne snapped the picture then looked down at the viewing screen. It was a good shot but a little blurry. "Let's try one more."

"Hurry up, Mom," Ben prodded.

She held up the camera. "Say..."

"Cheese pizza!" they shouted.

Anne took another picture and checked out the viewing screen again. This one was perfect. Her two beautiful children were smiling at the camera, and Liddie was holding her big brother's hand.

New house. New school. New memories.

"I've got it," she told them, waving her camera in the air. "Let's get in the car."

The kids scrambled toward the Impala, with Ben and Liddie settling into the backseat. Anne sat in the driver's seat, waiting until they'd both secured their seat belts. Then she backed out of the driveway. Once she knew the children felt comfortable with the route, she would let them walk when the weather was nice. But today, she wanted to spend as much time with them as she could before school began.

The drive went by in a flash, and Anne knew that soon she'd have to say good-bye to both of them. For the first time in nine years, she wouldn't have a child at home with her. Sentimental tears stung her eyes, but she blinked them back. She wanted to stay upbeat for the kids, fearing they might worry if they saw her cry.

"Here we are," Anne announced as she pulled into the school parking lot. "Who's ready for school?"

"Me," Liddie said, opening her door.

"Me too," Ben said, although he sounded a little apprehensive. For a boy who had been so concerned about arriving late, he was now moving awfully slow.

"Everything all right, Ben?" she asked, as they both sat in the car while Liddie stood beside the car.

"My stomach feels funny," Ben said at last. "Do you think I'm getting sick?"

Anne smiled, ready to reassure him. "Those are called butterflies in your stomach. It means you're about to do something new and you don't know what to expect, so you're a little nervous. Everybody gets butterflies in their stomach once in a while. I'm sure they'll go away as soon as you get settled in your classroom."

"Okay," Ben said, popping his car door open. But he didn't look convinced.

Anne sent up a silent prayer for them as she got out of the car. Then she flashed a smile. "Let's go."

Soon she joined the parade of other parents accompanying their children into Blue Hill Elementary School. Liddie clung tightly to her hand, looking in awe at everything and everyone around her.

Ben marched forward, his gaze straight ahead. She wanted to reach for his hand but knew that would embarrass him. They walked through the open doors and into the busy hallway. Kids were zipping by in both directions, many of them shouting greetings to each other.

"Ben!" a boy's voice called out.

Anne looked over to see Ryan a few yards down the hallway. "There's Ryan."

Ben followed her gaze; then he smiled as he took off in Ryan's direction. "See you later, Mom!"

Anne started after him but forced herself to stop. No matter how much she wanted to protect him, he needed to learn to do things on his own. But that didn't mean she couldn't watch him.

She saw Ben and Ryan meet up then turn in the direction of Mr. Layton's classroom. She started to follow, pulling Liddie along with her.

"Hey, Mommy," Liddie protested, tugging on her hand. "My room is that way."

"I know, dear," Anne told her, trying not to lose sight of the boys in the crowded hallway. "We'll go there in a minute."

Anne slowed her step as the boys reached Mr. Layton's room. They chattered excitedly as they opened the door then disappeared inside. She smiled to herself, relieved that Ben's butterflies had apparently vanished.

Then she looked down at her daughter. "Now it's your turn."

They headed for the kindergarten room, which was filled with parents when Anne and Liddie arrived. Some of the mothers were fussing over their children, fixing their hair and straightening their clothes. Most of the fathers took a more hands-off approach, chatting with the other fathers around them and taking in the room. Once in a while, one of them would lean down and whisper something in their child's ear.

Oh, how she wished Eric could be here to share this moment with her.

Miss Reed cheerfully greeted the parents and students, but when the morning bell rang, she clapped her hands to get everyone's attention. "All right, class. It's time to take your seats. I have a nametag on each desk. If you need help reading it, you can ask me or someone else in the room to help you."

Liddie bounced up on her toes then pointed to a desk in the middle of the classroom. "That's mine! I see my name!"

Anne knelt down beside her. "Can I have a hug before I go?"

Liddie reached over to hug her neck. "Bye, Mommy. I love you."

"I love you too, sweetie." Her voice cracked, but she managed a smile. When she let go of Liddie, her daughter turned and hurried to her desk, looking at it with something like awe.

Anne stepped back closer to the door, unable to leave just yet. She watched as another little girl in the desk next to Liddie started to talk to her. They compared backpacks and then Liddie unzipped hers to show the girl something inside.

When all the children were seated at their desks, Miss Reed smiled at the remaining parents and said, "You're welcome to stay here as long as you like. When you're ready to leave, please do so quietly, so the classroom isn't disturbed. I'm sure your children will have plenty to tell you when they get home from school today."

Some of the parents left right away, but Anne lingered with a few other mothers and fathers until the class had recited the Pledge of Allegiance and Miss Reed started explaining the class rules. Then she slipped quietly out the door and into the hallway.

She stood there silently for a long moment, a lump in her throat. How was it possible to be happy and sad at the same time? Then she took a deep breath and walked out of the school and into the August sunshine.

As Anne drove back to the house, she started to make a mental list of the supper she planned tonight. She wanted to make something special to celebrate the first day of school. But she forgot all about her supper plans when she pulled into the driveway and saw Wendy Pyle standing on her front porch.

CHAPTER TWENTY-FOUR

"Hi, there," Wendy greeted her as Anne walked up to the front door. She held a covered basket in one hand and her purse in the other.

"Hi, Wendy," Anne replied. "This is a nice surprise." She'd been meaning to talk to Wendy ever since the incident at library camp last Friday. She still felt awful about lashing out at her when Liddie went missing, but she didn't feel that her initial apology on that day had gone far enough. Her uncharacteristic reaction was a combination of panic about her daughter's safety and pent-up frustration at Wendy's take-charge attitude. Still, she'd never meant to hurt the woman's feelings.

"I thought this might be a tough day for you," Wendy said, holding up the basket. "So I brought you something to make you feel better."

Anne lifted the blue-and-white checked napkin to peek inside. "Chocolate?"

Wendy smiled. "That's right. It's the best medicine when you're feeling a little blue. I made brownies, chocolate crinkle cookies, German chocolate cupcakes, and chocolate marshmallow fudge, just to cover all the bases."

Anne laughed. "It sounds delicious. But I can't eat all of this by myself. Why don't you come in for a cup of coffee and we can sample everything in the basket?"

Wendy hesitated. "I don't want to be a bother..."

"Nonsense," Anne said sincerely, feeling a twinge of regret that Wendy might feel unwelcome at her house. "I'd love the company. It's going to be awfully quiet in this big house without the kids here."

"All right," Wendy said, "I guess I can stay for a few minutes."

They walked inside the foyer, where Anne turned and said, "Would you like a sneak peek at the library rooms? The furniture arrived last Saturday."

"I'd love one!" She set down her purse and basket on the foyer table, and Anne led her into the History Room.

"Oh my," Wendy said, looking around her. "This is so charming. I love the vintage look of the furniture. It feels like I've stepped back into the past."

"Well, that's good, because this is the History Room. I've got a few books on the shelves and more on the way. I can't wait until those bookcases are brimming."

Anne led her into the Fiction Room next and told her about her plan for a book-of-the-month display and letting patrons participate in it. "I want people to see something new in this room every time they come here. I think it will help keep things fresh and interesting and should be a lot of fun for me too."

"That's a fantastic idea," Wendy said, "Maybe you could hold a contest and the winner could choose the book of the month."

Anne started to say something, but Wendy cut her off.

"I could run it for you if you're too busy. We could have so much fun! We could even offer prizes of some sort for the winners—like a free book or something. In fact, you could hold all kinds of fun contests at the library—something to keep people coming back for more."

Not for the first time, Anne noticed Wendy's tendency to use the word *we* whenever she proffered a new idea. This time Anne didn't rush to agree to it, like she'd done in the past. This time she smiled and said, "Let me think about it."

"Great," Wendy said as she peeked into the other room. "This must be the checkout area.

"It is," Anne said, as they left the Fiction Room. "I love that there's a fireplace in this room as well."

"It is a lovely house," Wendy said. "I can't imagine a more perfect place for a library."

Anne used the spiral staircase at the back of the house as a shortcut to take Wendy to the second floor. Then she led her down the hallway, showing the Nonfiction Room first. "The rooms are all so different," Wendy said, looking around at the solid oak furniture and the modular furniture. "I love how you're using a combination of different styles. There's something for everyone."

"Thanks," Anne said. "I've never done much decorating, but this has been so much fun. And it's nice to hear a second opinion."

Anne saved the Children's Room for last. Wendy didn't say anything for a long moment as she stood in the center of the room, just soaking it all in. Then she turned to Anne. "How come that wall isn't yellow?" she asked, pointing to the wall with only a coat of primer on it.

"I'm planning to put chalkboard paint on it this afternoon," she replied. "Then the kids can draw on it as much as they want. I've already ordered a hefty supply of colored sidewalk chalk and, I have to admit, I'm excited to try it myself." Then she turned to Wendy. "But first I want to try one of those German chocolate cupcakes.

* * *

Twenty minutes later, Anne was indulging in her second cupcake. She and Wendy sat in the new kitchen on the second floor, the basket of chocolate goodies sitting on the table between them.

"This is so good," Anne said, licking a crumb off her finger. "Did you really make all of this yourself?"

"I did," Wendy said, taking a sip of her coffee. "With seven kids, we can't afford to buy a lot of prepackaged food, so I do a lot of cooking, baking, and freezing whenever I find a good sale at the market."

"I want to do more home cooking," Anne said, anxious to put her new kitchen to good use. She loved the stainless steel appliances, dark maple cupboards, and the creamy granite countertops.

"You'll have more time now that the kids are in school," Wendy popped a piece of fudge in her mouth. "And I'm sure it will help not to have library campers making a mess of your house."

That reminded Anne that she wanted to apologize again for her harsh words the other day. They had been a weight on her heart that she'd been trying to ignore, but she knew that the longer she waited, the heavier that weight would become."

"Wendy," she began, praying for the right words, "I want to tell you again that I'm so sorry for the things I said to you last Friday. I was scared when Liddie went missing and I..."

Wendy held up one hand. "You don't have to apologize, Anne. You were right—I should have been watching her more closely. I wanted so badly for library camp to be a success, but look what happened: Ryan broke his arm, your floors were almost ruined by rain and mud—twice! And then I lost track of Liddie."

"It's not your fault," Anne countered. "I told you that I would help with library camp, but I was too busy chasing after the mystery groom in that wedding portrait. I should have helped you more. One person can't keep track of that many kids, not even Superwoman."

"Superwoman?" Wendy echoed then laughed. "Please don't tell me that I have anything in common with Superwoman."

"Of course you do," Anne said, surprised by Wendy's modesty. "You ran the library camp and came up with some fantastic ideas. On top of that, you run a household with seven kids and always seem so cheerful. Sometimes, I get exhausted just with my two."

"Well, I have some help," Wendy said gently. "I can't even imagine how tough it must be to be a single mom."

"It's not easy," Anne admitted. "And sometimes I bite off more than I can chew." She hesitated, wondering just how honest she should be. But she felt God nudging her to continue the conversation. "I realize now that I should have made it clear when I didn't want to do something—like help make those costumes. I've never been good at saying no, and you were so—"

"Oh, honey," Wendy said with a sigh. "You've got to understand. I was the youngest of eleven children. I had to learn to talk as fast as possible if I didn't want to be drowned out by the older kids."

"Eleven?" Anne said, trying to imagine it.

Wendy nodded. "I guess that habit has carried over into adulthood, but please just put your foot down if I try to drag you into one of my harebrained schemes! I'll never hold it against you." She chuckled. "In fact, Chad does it all the time, so I'm quite used to hearing the word *no*. When I don't hear it, I just assume the other person is on board."

"I'll try," Anne told her, "but it's never been easy for me to say that word. I guess I just need some practice."

Wendy laughed. "Well, you should get plenty of it around me. In fact, we'll give it a try right now. Do you want me to run a contest for folks to choose the book of the month?"

"No," Anne said then felt a twinge of guilt. "I mean, not yet, anyway I want to get the library up and running for a while before I start having contests or any extras."

Wendy gave her a nod of approval. "See, you can say no. And you did it in such a nice way that I'll probably bug you about it again sometime in the next few months."

"I love the ideas," Anne said, not wanting to discourage her. "I just need to learn not to take on too much at one time."

"That's something we all need to learn," Wendy said. "And when we do get overwhelmed, we turn to chocolate. It works wonders." She pushed the basket toward Anne. "You have to try one of the cookies. It's my aunt's recipe."

"This time I can't say no." Anne smiled as she took a cookie from the basket.

"And speaking of aunts," Wendy said, grabbing a cookie for herself. "Are you any closer to finding out who Edie married?"

Anne dunked half of her cookie into her coffee cup. "I'm afraid not. In fact, I seem to be at a dead end. I'm not ready to give up, though. I know he's out there somewhere, dead or alive, I just need to keep looking." Then she told Wendy about the manuscript, asking her to keep it just between them for now.

"I won't breathe a word," Wendy promised. "But if you think the story was about Edie and her groom, then how does it end? That might give you the answer right there."

"That's what I thought," Anne told her. "It ended with Ruth and Harry about to elope. The last line read: 'And she knew, in that moment, that her life would never be the same again.'"

"Wow. That leaves a lot to the imagination."

"It sure does." Anne took another bite of her cookie, the chocolate melting in her mouth. "These cookies are amazing. I'd love to have the recipe."

"I'll be happy to give it to you. I can also bake some for the library's grand opening if you'd like too."

"That would be a big help," Anne said. "I haven't scheduled it yet, but I do want to hold a small reception for my friends to have a sneak peek at the library."

Wendy glanced at her watch. "Oh my! Look at the time. Chad's coming home for lunch, and I need to get back and put it in the oven."

"Thank you so much for coming over," Anne said, "and for the basket of chocolate. I feel so much better than I did when I left the school."

"That's what friends are for," Wendy said. She gave her a wave as she headed out of the kitchen.

A few moments later, Anne heard the front door close and she was alone in the house.

Friends. She'd been praying so long and hard for God to provide good friends for her children. He must have realized that she needed a friend too.

"Thank You, Lord," she prayed, this time letting the tears fall, "for my friend, Wendy."

* * *

Anne had eaten too much chocolate to even think about making something for lunch. She was heading upstairs to the Children's Room when the phone rang.

"Hello?" she answered.

"Is this Anne?" a man's voice asked.

"Yes it is," she replied, noting that his voice sounded familiar.

"This is Walter Ochs."

"Oh, hello, Walter," she said, smiling into the phone. "How are you?"

"I'm just fine. I hope I haven't caught you at a bad time. I just wanted to let you know that I finally remembered something."

She froze, her heart skipping a beat. "You remembered J.R.'s name?"

His sigh carried across the line. "No, not that, I'm afraid. Try as I might, it just won't come to me. I remembered that the fella told me that he and his girl were going to take a trip together."

"Oh," Anne said, tamping down her disappointment. At least this was something new. Maybe the mystery groom had told Walter where he and Edie planned to elope. "Where?"

"Pittsburgh," Walter said. "I remember he'd gone to the barber that morning before coming to work and had a new haircut and shave and everything. The boys sure ribbed him about it."

Anne took a moment to process the information. It wasn't much, but it was a new lead. "Thank you, Walter. I really appreciate it."

"I'm happy to help," he said then chatted with her a few more minutes before ending the call.

"Pittsburgh," Anne murmured to herself as she continued on her way to the third floor. Something about it niggled at her, but she couldn't figure out why.

She entered the Children's Room to paint the chalkboard wall. Alex had already applied blue painter's tape to the wall to frame the chalkboard. Once she let the chalkboard paint cure for three days, he was going to frame it with a natural wood trim board that matched the rest of the furniture in the room. Anne planned to do some stenciling work on the outside borders of the chalkboard just to add more interest and color to the room.

Anne opened the can of chalkboard paint and gave it a good stir then poured some into the paint tray that Alex had left for her.

He'd put down a tarp to protect the floor and moved furniture out of the way. She applied paint to the roller and then began. It rolled on smoothly, moving easily over the primer.

Thirty minutes later, Anne stepped back to peruse her handiwork. The paint was still wet, but the coat looked nice and even, with no bubbles. She couldn't wait to see how it looked in three days when it was done curing.

She cleaned up her work area then went to turn out the light when she saw a book lying on one of the tables. She moved closer and realized it was the book Alex had been reading to the kids when she'd arrived home from Red's farm on Saturday.

She picked it up, smiling at the monsters on the cover. Then she looked at the chalkboard wall. Could she stencil the characters in the book onto the border of the chalkboard? That would be fun and pay tribute to the best gift Aunt Edie had given her as a child.

The more she thought about it, the more Anne loved the idea. She hurried into her room and started up her laptop. Then she did a search for paint stencils. It took her a while, but she finally found some stencil patterns by an artist who did his own original drawings of characters in the book. They weren't an exact match, of course, but close enough to capture the spirit and whimsy of the story.

Anne placed an order and put a rush on the shipping, hoping she could have the stencils painted on the wall before the grand opening. She turned off the laptop then picked up the book in front of her. She opened the cover, remembering the hours of enjoyment she'd gotten from this book as a child. In an instant, she was reading it again, the familiar story giving her both pleasure and comfort. She turned to the last page with a satisfied sigh.

Then she saw something unusual.

There was a small envelope taped to the inside of the back cover. The name *Anne* was typed on the front of the envelope. For a moment, she wondered why Alex hadn't said anything about it. Then she remembered that she'd interrupted them when he was in the middle of reading the book, and he hadn't finished it.

Curious, she carefully peeled the small envelope from the back cover and opened it, pulling out the folded letter inside.

My dearest Anne,

I knew you would find this wonderful book and, once you found it, you would read it again. I didn't want to leave this message to you in my last will and testament. I wanted it to be just between us.

You have been like a daughter to me. You will never know how much love and wonder you brought into my life. It's a life I've loved, and I thank God every day for all of my blessings. You are one of those blessings, Anne, the best one. Always know that my love will be with you and that you are a special woman.

I have given you my dream of turning this house into a library for Blue Hill. My prayer is that my dream becomes your dream too. I trust in your good judgment to do what is best, and I know that you will always follow your heart.

I pray that you and your precious children find as much happiness in this house as I did.

All my love,
Aunt Edie

A tear slipped from Anne's cheek onto the letter. She held it to her heart, wishing she could hug Aunt Edie just one more time. She was so honored by her aunt's faith in her, and that dream to open the library truly had become Anne's dream as well.

She carefully folded the letter again and slipped it back into the envelope, intending to keep it forever. Maybe she could buy a pretty hatbox like the one Aunt Edie kept in the attic to store her letters and special mementos.

Anne stopped in her tracks. Aunt Edie had stored some receipts from Kaufmann's department store in that hatbox. Kaufmann's was located in Pittsburgh. Was it possible that those *receipts* were special? Anne had barely glanced at them at the time, but now...

She hurried up to the attic, carefully making her way through the maze of boxes until she reached the hatbox. Taking a deep breath, Anne opened it and found the Kaufmann's envelope inside. She reached in and pulled out the small handful of receipts. Aunt Edie had a charge account there, so her signature was at the bottom of each receipt.

Anne began to slowly page through each receipt, studying each one. The date on each of them was very faded, but she could just make out the year: *1950*. "Shoes, a suitcase, a dress..." She stopped, pulling the receipt from the pile to look at it more closely. It didn't say wedding gown, but at the bottom Aunt Edie had signed her name *Edie Summers*. Then below it, in parenthesis, she'd written: *the future Mrs. Joseph Riley*.

Anne had found J.R.

The doorbell rang as she rose to her feet. She wanted time to think, but she was expecting a book delivery, so she made her way downstairs.

But when she opened the door, she saw Mildred Farley standing there.

"Hello, Anne," Mildred said. "There's someone I want you to meet."

CHAPTER TWENTY-FIVE

"W ho is it?" Anne asked her.

Mildred stepped aside and a tall man moved into view on the doorstep. He was elderly, with snowy white hair and deep, rich blue eyes with small flecks of gold.

"Hello, Mrs. Gibson," he said, holding out his hand. "My name is..."

"Joseph Riley?" Anne said, recognizing him from the wedding photograph.

He smiled. "That's right. But my friends call me Joe."

Anne stood there in shock for a moment, unable to believe that the J.R. she'd been searching for was now standing on her doorstep. She glanced over at Mildred, who stood with her white leather purse pressed against the waistband of her navy blue dress. Then she held out her hand. "Please call me Anne. "

He smiled as she shook her hand. "It's nice to finally meet you, Anne."

She had a million questions for him, but standing on the front porch in the hot sun was no place to ask them. She opened the door wider. "Please come in."

As they walked inside the house, Anne remembered Mildred's statement that Edie's secret wasn't hers to tell. Mildred must have decided to contact Joe to let him decide if Anne should know the truth.

Anne led them into the History Room and motioned toward a small sitting area in the corner. "Please have a seat." A low, round table sat between the four wing chairs, making it the perfect conversation space. "May I get you something to drink?"

"Perhaps some water," Joe said. "It's been a long trip."

"Of course," Anne said then looked over at Mildred.

"Nothing for me, dear," Mildred said, easing into one of the chairs.

Anne headed into the old kitchen, her head still spinning. She couldn't believe that the mystery groom was in her house. That she was finally going to learn the truth about that wedding portrait.

The wedding portrait.

Inspired, she hurried up the back stairs to the third floor and headed for the hidden room. Once inside, she carefully lifted the framed wedding portrait from the wall and carried it downstairs to the kitchen. She poured a glass of ice water for Joe then carried both the portrait and the glass into the History Room.

Joe was now seated next to Mildred. Anne handed the glass to him then took a seat across from them. She held the portrait in front of her, looking down at it. "I found this about two weeks ago. I never knew Aunt Edie had married or who she had married. Not until today, anyway."

Mildred leaned forward, compassion etched on her face. "I know you wanted me to tell you, Anne, but as I had said before, it wasn't my secret to tell. Edie had made me promise to never tell anyone—and I'm not one to break my promises."

"So she sent me a letter," Joseph interjected. "And told me about you and the marvelous work you've been doing to turn Edie's house into a library for Blue Hill. That's when I knew I had to meet you. I asked Mildred not to say anything until I could speak to you myself."

"And that was very difficult," Mildred admitted.

"I understand." Anne carefully set the portrait next to her, propping it against her chair. Then she turned to Joe. "I have so many questions for you."

He smiled. "I'm sure you do. You may ask me anything."

Now that Anne had the opportunity, she wasn't sure where to start. Then she remembered the end of the story in Edie's manuscript and decided to begin there. "Did you and my aunt elope?"

"No," he said with a sigh. "We had planned to elope, right down to the last detail. She was going to leave her parents' house and meet me in the meadow, near the barn." He looked over at Mildred. "You were the only one she told."

Mildred nodded, then met Anne's gaze. "You have to understand that eloping like that would have been quite scandalous. Joe wasn't raised in Blue Hill and had only lived here a short time when he met Edie."

"I'd been something of a drifter," Joe continued. "Moving from town to town, looking for work. My parents died in a fire when I was fourteen, so I had to take care of myself. It wasn't easy, but I managed."

Anne couldn't imagine a boy of fourteen having to fend for himself in this world. But those were different times, better in some ways and worse in others. It made her heart hurt to think of this man alone in the world at such a young age.

"Then you met Aunt Edie," Anne said. "You took a job helping with the apple harvest on Grandpa Summers' farm."

He nodded. "I did. Edie was the first person in town to show me kindness. There was something about her smile..." His voice trailed off, and for a moment he was lost in thought. Then he gathered himself. "I never thought she would be interested in me. I had no real job, no family, and no prospects. But we connected right away." He chuckled. "I think I fell in love with her the moment I burned my mouth on her blueberry pie, strange as that sounds."

Anne leaned forward, fascinated to hear how similar Joe's story sounded to the one in her great-aunt's manuscript. It truly had been like a diary, she thought to herself. Only Anne still didn't know how it ended.

"Her father didn't trust me," Joe said, "and I guess I can't blame him. A drifter comes to town and starts flirting with his only daughter—what father wouldn't be protective?"

"But Edie was headstrong," Mildred added, a twinkle in her eye. "She always followed her heart."

"And I thought I was the luckiest man in the world," Joe said wistfully. "To have a pretty girl like Edie believe in me was stunning enough, but when she told me she loved me, well, I just about fell out of an apple tree the first time it happened."

Mildred laughed. "Edie told me about that day. She figured you were a captive audience and couldn't run away when she declared her love."

"The last thing I wanted to do was run away," Joe confided, a shadow crossing his face. "I wanted to marry her."

"So what happened?" Anne asked him.

He sucked in a deep breath. "Her brother Davey intercepted me at my boardinghouse on the very night that Edie and I were planning to elope. And he'd brought the police with him."

Mildred turned to Anne. "Davey accused Joe of stealing some of the apples from the harvest and selling them. So instead of getting married…"

"I ended up in jail."

"Edie waited for him in the meadow for three hours," Mildred said softly. "She never realized that Davey had found the wedding photograph she'd left for her parents—the same photograph you have now, along with a letter, and intercepted Joe before he could meet her."

"So the photograph was taken before you were married?" Anne said.

He nodded. "It broke her heart that her family wouldn't be at our wedding. So we had the portrait taken in Pittsburgh a few weeks before we planned to elope. I think she hoped they'd be more accepting if they saw us in our wedding clothes."

"A wedding that never took place," Anne said softly. Her heart ached for her dear aunt, waiting in the moonlight for the man she loved—a man who never appeared. She must have been heartbroken.

"Davey and her father came to the jail the next morning," Joe continued. "They said they had enough evidence of theft against me to get a conviction. I tried to tell them it wasn't true, but they wouldn't listen. I know now that they were bluffing—trying to use the fear of imprisonment as leverage to convince me to leave town." His voice wobbled a bit. "And I'm ashamed to say it worked."

"So you left Blue Hill?"

He nodded. "They told me I could go to jail or go join the army. I guess Edie's father figured his daughter might be safer if I was halfway across the world somewhere."

"And did you get a chance to tell her?" Anne asked softly, but in her heart she already knew the answer.

A muscle flexed in his jaw. "No. I had to leave town before dawn. Her brother Davey gave me a ride to the recruiting station in Deshler. He stood glued to my side until he saw me enlist with his own two eyes."

Anne leaned back in her chair, trying to take it all in. She remembered her great-uncle Davey as a frail, elderly man and couldn't picture him forcing anyone to do anything. She should have known better. The two young sweethearts had been separated by an overprotective father and brother, leaving Aunt Edie to await a bridegroom who never arrived...

Anne thought about the receipt she'd just seen upstairs. "How were you both able to go all the way to Pittsburgh together without her parents knowing about it?"

"I'd taken off work early that day," Joe explained, "claiming I was sick."

"And I was the alibi for Edie," Mildred confessed. "We told her folks that the two of us were going to Pittsburgh to do some shopping for my upcoming wedding. I drove and we picked up Joe on our way out of town. When we got to Pittsburgh, Edie bought a wedding dress with the money she'd saved up, and Joe rented a suit."

Anne turned to him. "And you wore the cuff links—the ones engraved with your initials."

He smiled. "That was a little tricky. I wanted to look sharp for the wedding, but I didn't want to arouse any suspicion by ordering them for myself—you know how people in a small town can talk. And what did a drifter need with cuff links?"

"So you had Walter Ochs buy them, using the money that he owed you?"

Joe arched a brow. "How did you…" His voice trailed off as he looked over at Mildred with a wry smile. "You were right. She is a sharp cookie."

Anne smiled. "I just did a little digging when I found those cuff links and realized they were the same ones in the wedding portrait." Then another thought occurred to her. "If you left town before the wedding, why did I find your cuff links in her house over sixty years later?"

"I gave them to her for safe-keeping after we had our portrait taken in Pittsburgh." His expression softened. "I guess she's been keeping them safe for me all these years."

"So did she ever find out what happened?" Anne asked him. "Did you ever see her again?"

"Not for a long time," Joe said, and then he looked at Mildred. "You know the rest of the story better than I do. You're the one who helped Edie through it."

Mildred sighed. "Edie was devastated. She didn't understand how Joe could just leave without a word. At first, she thought he'd been in an accident—maybe even lost his memory. She searched all the hospitals and convalescent homes in the area, but he wasn't in any of them."

"I wrote to Edie," Joe said, "every time I got the chance. But she never wrote me back."

"That's because she never received the letters," Mildred said grimly. "She found out later, much later, that her parents had been watching the mail and intercepting the letters from Joe."

"Four years later, I finished my tour of duty and called her from Boston," Joe said, "but her father told me that she'd married and now had a family of her own. I couldn't blame her—and I knew I needed to move on with my own life." His shoulders drooped. "So I found work in Boston. Later I discovered through a friend of Edie's family that she'd never married. But by then, I was married to a wonderful woman."

Now the last line of Aunt Edie's manuscript made a little more sense to Anne. Her life had never been the same without Joe in it. But in the story, the two of them had eloped and lived happily ever after.

Only the blank pages had never been filled.

"My wife passed away about eight years ago," Joe continued. "One day, I was browsing the Internet on my new computer, and

I decided to look up old friends, Edie among them. I found out she was still living in Blue Hill and was listed in the phone directory by her maiden name. I called her, and we met for coffee in some little town that was half the distance for both of us." He smiled. "She was still the same. Happy and fun, with that same incredible smile."

Mildred turned to Joe. "Edie told me all about that day. She said the friendship the two of you rekindled was as strong as the love you'd shared all those years ago."

"It sure was," he said wistfully. "Edie was one of the finest women I've ever known. I mourned when I heard that she'd passed away and wanted so badly to attend her funeral, but some health problems prevented me from making the trip."

Anne breathed a soft sigh, so grateful that her aunt had reconnected with the love of her life sixty years later and finally learned what had really happened to him all those years ago.

She turned to Mildred. "When Aunt Edie discovered what Grandpa Summers and Uncle Davey had done, was she upset?"

"No," Mildred said with a note of bewilderment in her voice. "She told me that her life—and Joe's life—turned out the way they were supposed to be. That God had brought Joe into her life for a purpose and, when that purpose was fulfilled, had sent them each on their path."

Joe nodded his agreement. "Neither one of us had any regrets about our lives. We loved each other deeply once, and for that I shall always be truly thankful."

His words made Anne realize that she felt the same about Eric. They'd loved each other so much—and losing him was the hardest thing she'd ever experienced. But she'd do it all over again in a heartbeat rather than to have never loved him at all. All of God's gifts were precious, no matter how fleeting.

Joe reached into his back pocket and drew out his wallet. "There's something I want to show you." He opened the wallet and slid out a photograph then handed it to Anne. "This is the Edie that I've always known and loved."

Anne looked down at the photograph. It was a picture of Edie as a young woman, standing in a field of daisies with her face turned up to the sun. Her long, dark hair hung in ringlets over her shoulders, and the smile on her face was both lovely and playful.

The photo had captured her aunt's spirit in a way that was timeless. "It's beautiful," Anne breathed.

"My wife always thought so too," he said with a chuckle, placing the photo back in the wallet. "She wasn't the jealous type and knew that Edie had been an important part of my life."

He rose to his feet. "Thank you for seeing me today. Edie told me all about you when we met for coffee. You were very special to her."

"Thank you," Anne said, her voice tight. "It means so much to me to see this window into my aunt's life. She was very special to me too." Then Anne realized that he shouldn't leave empty-handed. "I should give you back the cuff links," she said, starting toward the stairs.

"No, keep them," Joe said, reaching for her arm. "Edie told me that you have a son. My wife and I never had any children. If you don't mind, I'd like your son to have the cuff links someday, as a symbol of the love that I shared with his great-great-aunt."

Touched by the gesture, Anne leaned up and lightly kissed his cheek. "Thank you. That's very generous."

"It's my pleasure." He patted her hand then turned to Mildred. "And thank you for bringing me here. It was well worth it."

"I'm so glad that I could be of service," Mildred said. "That secret was the longest—and hardest—one that I've ever had to keep!"

Anne laughed. "You were a true friend."

They chatted with Anne as she walked them to the door then took their leave. She watched them drive away, content that Aunt Edie's story finally had a real ending. Then she retrieved the wedding portrait from the History Room and put it back on the wall in the hidden room where she'd first found it.

Anne stood there for a long moment, staring at her lovely great-aunt and the mystery groom she now knew as Joe Riley. He'd won Aunt Edie's heart and stolen a piece of Anne's heart as well.

An hour later, Anne picked Ben and Liddie up after their first day of school. Anne waited while they situated themselves and buckled their seat belts. Then, before she pulled away from the curb, she glanced into the backseat.

"Well, how was it?" Anne asked them.

"I love kindergarten," Liddie said. "Can I go back tomorrow?"

"You sure can," Anne said, laughing. Then she turned to her son.

"And how about you?"

"I had a great day!" Ben said.

Ann reached out to give him a high five. "Me too. I think we're going to like living in Blue Hill. In fact, I think we're all going to love it!"

CHAPTER TWENTY-SIX

One week later

W hat time is it?" Anne asked, feeling a little frantic.

Wendy glanced at her watch. "Six o'clock. Don't worry. We've still got an hour before everyone arrives."

Anne put the finishing touches on the vegetable platter then set it in the refrigerator. The small reception she'd planned was scheduled to begin at seven. She would hold a grand opening for the library later, but tonight she wanted to thank all those who had been so instrumental in putting the library together with her.

Ben and Liddie were spending time at the Pyle residence with Chad and his children. They'd all head over here when it was time for the reception to start.

And so would her new friends in town.

Mildred bustled into the kitchen carrying a grocery bag. "I picked up paper plates and cups. The market was hopping, and I heard people talking about the new library. They can't wait for it to open."

"I just hope tonight is a success." Anne nibbled her lower lip. "Do you think we have enough food?"

"We have plenty," Wendy assured her as she poured some seasoned crackers into a basket. "I made three dozen of those chocolate crinkle cookies and just as many oatmeal cookies. Plus, we've got all this caramel popcorn that Mildred made—that will go a long way."

Anne nodded, doing some mental calculations. She'd purchased some blocks of cheese and plenty of crackers to go along with the sweet offerings. "I guess we can always make more popcorn," she said at last. "I bought five pounds of it from the high school choir's fundraiser."

Wendy chuckled. "That should last us awhile." Then she looked up at Anne. "The coffee is brewing, and I have lemonade in the fridge. What else would you like me to do?"

Anne considered the question. Both Wendy and Mildred had been a blessing to her as she'd prepared for the reception. They'd helped her record and shelve all the new books that had arrived, made food for today, and even pitched in to get the library in tip-top shape on both the first and second floors.

Anne smiled, feeling calmer now. "Shall we take one last walk though to make sure everything is ready?"

"Good idea," Wendy said, waving Anne toward the stairs that led to the Fiction Room. "Lead the way."

When Anne walked into the Fiction Room, her gaze went straight to the book-of-the-month display. She'd chosen *The Adventures of Sherlock Holmes*, by Sir Arthur Conan Doyle, one of Aunt Edie's favorite authors. To get in the spirit of the chosen book, she'd decorated the display table with old maps, a violin like the one played by the brilliant detective, as well as other assorted items and a photograph of the character as portrayed by Basil Rathbone.

"It looks great," Wendy said, following her gaze.

Anne and her friends walked through each library room, straightening a chair here and there or wiping a smudge on a window. Platters of Wendy's homemade cookies adorned each table, along with a big bowl of Mildred's caramel popcorn.

When they reached the Nonfiction Room on the first floor, Anne pointed out the quotes she'd chosen to go on the wall. "This one is my favorite," she said, pointing to the quote by John Burroughs, which was inscribed on the wall directly in front of them. *"I still find each day too short for all the thoughts I want to think, all the walks I want to take, all the books I want to read, and all the friends I want to see."*

"That describes my life perfectly," Wendy said.

The back doorbell jangled, interrupting their tour. Anne checked her watch, noting that it was only six-thirty.

"Looks like we might have some early birds," Mildred said as all three of them made their way to the back entrance.

Anne was surprised to see a delivery man standing at the door and holding a rectangular package about the size of a large cutting board.

"Is that for me?" Anne asked him.

The delivery man checked the routing ticket. "It sure is, Mrs. Gibson. Will you sign for it, please?"

Wendy took the package out of his hands as Anne signed her name. After the delivery man left, Anne set the package on a small table and tore off the brown paper wrap.

"Oh my," Mildred said, staring at the framed picture in front of them.

Anne was speechless, barely aware of Wendy bending down to retrieve a small card that had fallen out the package when it had been opened. "Here you go," she said, handing it to Anne.

Anne opened the card then began to read it out loud:

Dear Anne,

Thank you for the invitation to the sneak peek of the new Blue Hill library. I know this is a special night for you, and I truly wish I could be there. In my place, I hope you'll accept this gift. I know Edie would love to be there as well, although I'm certain she's there in spirit. I wanted to give you something to honor her memory and bring happiness to your library just like your aunt brought happiness and love into my life.

Sincerely,

Joseph Riley

Anne stared at the picture. It was the same one that Joe had shown her the day he'd come to visit. Only he'd had it enlarged and copied onto a canvas, so it looked more like a painting than a photograph. She looked at her great-aunt, laughing in a field of daisies, and knew just where she wanted to display it.

"Follow me," she told the women then headed for the check-out area.

Alex had hung a clock there about a week before. Anne took it down then hung the picture of Aunt Edie in its place. Anne wanted to give her a place of honor in the library—one that everyone would see.

Tears shimmered in Mildred's eyes as she gazed at the photograph. "Now I feel like she's here too."

"She is," Anne said softly. "She's always in our hearts."

The front door opened and the sound of children's voices filled the foyer.

"That sounds like my brood," Wendy said, heading in that direction.

More people followed the Pyles inside the house, including Reverend Tom and his wife, Hank and Heidi Kepple and their two boys, Coraline Watson, and even Walter Ochs, accompanied by Alex and Ryan.

Anne saw Ben and Liddie coming toward her, each with a big smile on their face. "Are you ready for a party?"

"Yes!" Liddie exclaimed.

"I am too," Ben said. "Ryan just got here, and we're going to show the other kids around the library together."

"That's awesome," Anne said then breathed a silent prayer of thanks as she gathered her children close to her, feeling as if this day—and their lives—were finally coming together.

About the Author

Emily Thomas is the pen name for a team of writers who have come together to create the series Secrets of the Blue Hill Library. *Nowhere to Be Found* was written by Kristin Eckhardt. Kristin is the author of more than thirty-five books, including sixteen for Guideposts. She has won two national awards for her writing, and her first book was made into a TV movie. Kristin and her husband live in central Nebraska and have three children. Kristin enjoys quilting, traveling, and spending time with family.

A CONVERSATION WITH THE AUTHOR

Q. *What elements of your own life have found their way into* Nowhere to Be Found?

A. One of my favorite parts of writing fiction is using personal stories from my own life and family. In *Nowhere to Be Found*, the pastor tells Anne about his first date with his wife. This story is based on my grandpa's first date with my grandma. Grandpa always chuckled whenever he recounted that story. Telling his story let me share an important piece of my family history with my readers.

Q. *In what ways are you like Anne Gibson?*

A. Anne's family is very important to her, as evidenced in her relationship with her adorable children, her memories of her husband, and her early life with Aunt Edie. I've been blessed to have a close, loving family to share times of happiness and times of sorrow. I believe that blessing has given me an inner strength that I also see in Anne.

Q. *Anne's great-aunt Edie was a strong woman and a major influence in Anne's life. Who has influenced you?*

A. Writing about Aunt Edie evokes fond memories of my own great-aunt Fern. One of twelve children, Aunt Fern lived her entire life in a small town in Iowa. After her fiancé was killed in World War I, she remained single for the rest of her life. She liked to take "mystery bus tours" where the passengers didn't know their destination until they arrived, and she always enjoyed a good joke.

My sister and I used to spend a week every summer with my great-grandmother and great-aunt Fern. They lived together and Aunt Fern did all of the cooking and cleaning. And she always had a huge garden in the backyard. She wore simple cotton dresses and sensible shoes and had an infectious laugh. Even with all her household duties, she always made certain my sister and I were well-entertained during our visits. Aunt Fern never liked anyone making a fuss over her, but she was a wonderful woman in so many ways.

Q. *A number of different authors write stories for the Secrets of the Blue Hill Library series. What are the challenges in collaborative writing?*

A. I love writing a series with other authors. With the help of a wonderful editor, we create a small-town community full of warm, delightful characters. The most challenging part of the process is making certain that the community and those characters flow seamlessly from one book to the next. Good communication is the key to making it all come together. We e-mail each other whenever we have a question or a new idea about the series. This contact not only helps us write our stories but allows us to form friendships with each other.

RECIPES FROM THE LIBRARY GUILD

Oreo Truffles

16 ounce package Oreo sandwich cookies
8 ounce package cream cheese (softened)
16 ounces semisweet chocolate, melted

Mix Oreo cookies and cream cheese in a blender or food processor until well blended. Form mixture into one-inch balls and place on waxed paper. Melt the chocolate. Dip each ball into the melted chocolate and then place it on wax paper. You may also melt white chocolate and drizzle it on the top of each truffle for a decorative touch. Refrigerate until ready to eat.

FROM THE GUIDEPOSTS ARCHIVES

*"The Little Red Library" originally appeared in
the February 1991 issue of* Guideposts *magazine.*

Growing up in the Arkansas hills, Robbie Tilley Branscum loved to read, but she was frustrated because she couldn't get enough books. She read and reread everything in the little one-room school she attended while living with her grandparents on their sharecropper farm in Searcy County. Her father had died when Branscum was quite young, and her mother left to find work cleaning houses in town.

Then when she was thirteen, her mother remarried and returned to take her to Colorado. That was the end of schooling for Branscum, who worked in a theater taking tickets and selling popcorn.

In Colorado their house was next to a red-brick building that fascinated Branscum. She used to peer in the windows at the large room where a woman sat among shelves of books, and Branscum would think how unfair it was that one lady had all those books. Finally the woman went outside and invited her in. Branscum had never heard of a public library before.

Thus began a life of reading book after book, starting with the works of Zane Grey "because he wrote about Colorado," Branscum said, "and that's where I was." She went on to greater tomes: Dickens, Shakespeare, *War and Peace.*

After marrying at a young age and moving to California, Branscum began to write. Her first byline was in a Southern Baptist newspaper in Fresno, which took her on as a regular contributor, although there was no pay. Then, starting in 1971, Branscum wrote her first novel, *Me and Jim Luke,* and, before her passing in 1997, she had published twenty titles with major publishing houses, winning several prestigious literary awards along the way.

Robbie Branscum never forgot her debt to public libraries. Whenever she could, she made herself available to speak at and on behalf of libraries, encouraging others to continue their education by reading.

Read on for a sneak peek of another exciting book
in Secrets of the Blue Hill Library!

Shadows of the Past

R eady or not, here I come." Anne Gibson removed her hands
from over her eyes as she yelled. She smiled as she took off in
the direction of her bedroom. Her children loved hiding in Anne's
closet every time they played hide-and-seek.

She opened the door to her bedroom, decorated much like her
bedroom had been in New York. She lifted her voice. "Ben? Liddie?
Are you in here?" She went through the motions even though she
knew they weren't on the third floor any longer.

Anne had grown up playing in the eight-sided room in the
cupola at the front of the house, around the spiral staircase, and in
all the little nooks and crannies that had long ago opened the
floodgates of her youthful imagination. This house held many of
her favorite hiding places as a child.

Giggles sounded from the second floor.

Anne shut the door with a resounding click. The giggling
stopped. "Where, oh where, are my Ben and Liddie?"

Muffled giggles answered.

With a smile on her face, Anne moved to the grand staircase
with its hand-carved mahogany banister. The top stair creaked in
response. Anne always loved the grand Queen Anne Victorian

house with its white clapboard and slate blue shingles and the winding path down to the base of the hill. Now she lived in the house that perched atop Blue Hill, which she frequently visited as a child. The first floor and a portion of the second had recently been converted into a library, a legacy from her great-aunt Edie.

The afternoon breeze blew over the rolling hills and in through the open window of the second-floor landing.

"*Ah-choo!*" Her eyes watered from behind her large-framed glasses as she lifted a tissue to her nose. Late September brought bright, vivid colors to the leaves that adorned the beautiful old trees surrounding Blue Hill. And autumn brought seasonal allergies to Anne as well.

"God bless you." Five-year-old Liddie's singsong voice echoed down the hall.

"Thank you, honey." Anne pushed the tissue into her jeans pocket then headed toward the Fiction Room. The kids often hid in the Children's Room on the library's second floor, but lately they'd explored the Fiction Room. With the four walls each painted a different warm color, accented by white molding and trim, the room beckoned readers—and playing children—with its cozy aura.

Like fitting the genre to the reader, Anne had taken great pains with each room of the library, trying to reflect the book category each room housed. She was delighted with the final results of her fledgling attempts at interior decorating. Another gust of wind stirred the air and resurfaced the tantalizing aroma of the pot roast they'd had for dinner. Time to find Ben and Liddie and get them into bed. Wendy Pyle had agreed to help with the final indexing of the historical fiction books this evening, after she got her own kids tucked in and her husband situated in front of the television. It was nearly that time now.

Anne ducked into the Fiction Room. "Where is my Ben? Where is my Liddie?" Her daughter would probably be crouched behind the reupholstered wingback chair, her fist pressed against her mouth to squelch her squeal. Ben would either be hiding beside the armoire that held all the award-winning books or next to the shelves of newest releases.

Anne went for her daughter first. She jumped around the chair. "Liddie!"

But her daughter wasn't there. Giggles filtered up the stairwell from the first floor. Ah, so they'd somehow managed to sneak downstairs.

Anne crept down the stairs to the first floor and into the History Room. They hadn't hidden in here before; the dark walls and serious tone hadn't appealed to Ben or Liddie. Although there were still a few finishing touches to be done, it was Anne's favorite room so far. Maybe because she adored old record books and long-forgotten history.

"Where, oh where, is my little girl?" She inched around the dark leather, overstuffed chair. She jumped, popping her head over the top of the chair.

Liddie shrieked then leapt into her arms. "You found me, Mommy."

Anne buried her face in her daughter's neck, inhaling the baby-shampoo scent clinging to her. Little Liddie looked so much like her father, with her chocolate brown eyes, that it sometimes made Anne's heart ache. After three years, she still missed Eric something fierce.

"I'll always find you." She released Liddie, smoothing the legs of her pink pajamas. "Now, let's find that brother of yours."

Lately, Ben was having a bit of a hard time adjusting to small-town life. He missed New York, his friends. Her thoughtful nine-year-old hadn't yet connected with a Little League group in their new hometown, since they'd moved to town mid-season. Although, thankfully, he had befriended Alex's nephew, Ryan, whom Alex was raising following the death of his sister and brother-in-law.

"I think he's in the closet," Liddie whispered.

"Ah. Let's see."

She opened the closet door with a flourish and at the same time, yelled, "Found you!"

But Ben's round face didn't greet her with a smile. He wasn't to be found. "Ben?"

No response.

Anne swallowed the panic. This was Blue Hill, Pennsylvania, not exactly filled with crime. People left their doors unlocked here, for pity's sake. "Ben?"

Still no response.

She looked in the shadow behind the historical periodicals, but her son had gotten too tall to hide there without crouching. "Are you sure he came into the room with you?" she asked Liddie.

"Yes, Mommy." Her curls barely brushed the top of her shoulders as she nodded.

So where was he? Had he left the room after helping hide his sister?

Anne stepped into the hall and lifted her voice. "Ben? Hide-and-seek time is over. Come on out. You got me this time."

No response.

Anne's heart thumped wildly in her chest. "Ben, come out." She hardened her tone. "Now. It's time for bed."

Crash! The sound came from back in the History Room.

She spun in time to see a loaded book cart clatter over onto its side. Volume upon volume of books—plus Ben on top—skidded across the polished wood floor.

"Mom!"

She ran to him and helped him to his feet. "Are you okay?"

He nodded. "I'm sorry, Mom."

"Stay in the hall, Liddie," Anne said. "What happened, Ben?" She stepped over several leather-bound books.

"I was hiding against the wall, behind the book cart. I heard you coming, so I pressed against the side of the cart..."

Anne raised an eyebrow.

"I didn't mean to bump it, didn't even know I had, really." Ben frowned, reminding Anne of how much more of a loner he'd become since moving to Blue Hill. Back in New York, he'd been a smiling, popular boy. But now that school was back in session, he would surely make more friends.

Anne pressed her lips together. On one hand, she wanted to gather him in her arms and tell him everything was okay; another part of her knew he needed to stand on his own, so to speak.

He straightened and focused his hazel eyes, much like Anne's own, on her. "I'm sorry, Mom. I'll help pick everything up and put it all back the way you had it." His gaze dropped to the books and boards littering the floor. "I didn't mean to break it, honest."

"It's okay, sweetheart, I'll get it because I really need you to help your sister." Again she fought the urge to hold him. "Take Liddie and brush your teeth; then climb into your beds. I'll be up in a minute to listen to your prayers."

He turned, holding his hand out to his little sister. "Okay."

"Make sure Liddie uses toothpaste this time," she said.

Turning to the mess on the floor, she grabbed the first book and lifted it gently. Anne ran a finger down the front of the old copy of *Poor Richard's Almanack*. Its cover felt rough to her touch, taking her back to her childhood when she'd spent many summer days lazing on the creaky porch, immersed in a book right alongside her aunt. She loved the feel and smell of books, even the old dusty ones—always had. And she missed Aunt Edie. Although, since moving back to Blue Hill, Anne was discovering a number of details about her beloved aunt that she hadn't known before.

"Mom, we're ready!"

"Coming." She climbed the stairs, suddenly more tired than she'd been before. The renovations seemed to be a never-ending project, and the constant demands exhausted her. Not for the first time she wondered if could she do this. *Really* do this?

Yes, she could.

Even with losing Eric and then getting laid off from the New York Public Library system, Anne counted her blessings. God had it all worked out according to His will. Like this bequest from Aunt Edie—the timing was perfect for their little family to start over in her hometown. God had a good plan for her and for her children. She just needed to remember to trust Him all the time and in all things.

She'd barely finished tucking in the kids, reading Liddie yet one more bedtime story, and listening to their precious prayers when the front bell chimed. Anne rushed down to the first floor and opened the door.

"Sorry. Jacob and Ethan both had to have twenty glasses of water before bed." Wendy grinned as she stepped over the threshold. Her chin-length, bobbed hair was held off her face by a blue band that accented her big, blue eyes. To look at her, no one would guess she had seven children. How she found the time to read as much as she did, Anne couldn't guess, but the woman went through books almost as quickly as Anne herself.

"Come on in. I just got my two down for bed."

Wendy shut the door behind her. "I'm glad you decided to go with the Victorian doors. These ones you picked out are much more in keeping with the original architecture of the house."

Which was exactly why Anne had vetoed her first instinct to have strong security doors installed and went with those designed more for the 1896 house. Having grown up in Blue Hill, she knew the town was safe, even the quaint downtown area. She'd been away in the big city for years, following the career path Aunt Edie had encouraged her to take.

And now she was back in Blue Hill, turning Aunt Edie's house into a library. Everything always seemed to come back to Aunt Edie.

"So, what are we indexing tonight?"

Anne led the way up the stairs. "The rest of the historical fiction, after I clean up the mess."

"Mess?"

"Ben accidentally knocked over a book cart. Unfortunately, it was full," Anne said. She flipped on the History Room's light. The jumble of books sprawled across the floor was just as bad as she recalled. Maybe worse.

"Oh, my." Wendy nearly stepped on a book, sidestepped, then reached for it. "Is he settling in well at school? Christian is a year ahead of him, so they don't have recess together."

Anne pulled up the shelving cart and then knelt by the largest grouping on the floor. "He's really trying to fit in. It's hard for him, since he had so many close friends in New York."

"We'll just pray him through the adjustment period."

"Thanks." Anne smiled. "Becoming friends with Ryan has helped. And Christian inviting him over to play has helped, too."

"What about Liddie? How's she settling in?"

"She's informed me she can outrun any boy in her kindergarten class."

Wendy chuckled. "So my Justin tells me. You'll have to keep an eye on that one. She's quite spirited."

Now it was Anne's turn to laugh. "That's a rather polite way of saying she's precocious."

Wendy only smiled as she carefully picked up the books and placed them on the cart. "Did Alex mention what time he'd be by to check out the measurements for the new doorframe?"

Alex Ochs. They'd been best friends even before they were high school sweethearts. But Alex had been so hurt when she'd left him after graduation to go to college that even when she'd returned to Blue Hill several months ago, he'd been somewhat reserved toward her. Before long, though, their friendship had been restored. Anne was glad...she needed friends. She couldn't help that she'd met and fallen in love with her husband, Eric, when she'd been in college, no more than she could help when he'd died three years ago from a heart attack and she thought she'd never feel whole again. But now, tackling the renovation project seemed to have spurred her past the depression. She'd hired Alex as the contractor for the library renovations and being in his company on a regular basis again, well, he wasn't quite as aloof as he'd been just a few weeks ago.

Anne reached for two books lying on top of each other. "He said he wouldn't have time to get by until tomorrow midmorning, which is okay. It'll give me time to get the kids off to school."

"I know the town is more than ready for you to finish and open," said Wendy.

"Once these last shelves are inventoried, I'll be able to open the doors at least. All the rooms won't be as complete as I'd like them to be, but the adult fiction, the children's, and this historical area should be ready." Excitement pulsed through her veins as she reached for another book. Aunt Edie's vision was within reach. "And Alex says he's almost done with the Blue Hill History Room. We're on schedule for the grand opening this weekend."

"I got the postcard announcement. You've made great progress." Wendy pulled the cart toward her just as Anne reached for it.

The book Anne held slipped from her fingers and thudded to the wood floor. "Guess this one is determined not to be shelved." Anne grabbed the spine and lifted the book.

A yellow piece of paper drifted from between the pages.

Oh, no. A page must have ripped out. It felt almost as if Anne's own heart had been scratched. She opened the cover and tried to make out the name on the bookplate, but it had been torn and most was missing. What little remained was very faded. All she could make out of the writing was *Isa*, then the large part was slashed, then *es*.

The yellowed page landed closer to Wendy. She grabbed it. "What's this?" Her nose crinkled as she perused.

Anne carried the book to Wendy and looked over her shoulder as Wendy unfolded the yellowed paper. "A map?"

She turned the book in her hand to the cover and read the title. "*The Journals of Lewis and Clark*." She opened the cloth hardcover with no dust jacket to read the copyright date. "1953."

Wendy handed her the yellowed map. "Looks like a state map. A very old one. With some writing on it."

Anne studied the page. "A map of Pennsylvania." It did contain some scribbles, just in the corner. She couldn't make out the words, even though she squinted and pushed her glasses back to the bridge of her nose. She could make out the formal print. "By William Scull. 1775."

"That's from 1775?"

"I'm no expert by any means, but by the brittleness of the paper, I'd say it's an original, not a copy of a 1775 map." Anne's heart thudded. She'd have to get the map authenticated as well as appraised. There was so much to do....

"You know, when Chad and I moved to Blue Hill, the first person to befriend me was Coralline Watson. That woman loves to talk, especially about history."

"I've met her. She's sweet, but you're right, she does love to talk," said Anne.

"Among other things, Coraline told me all about was Blue Hill's now defunct Historical Society. Evidently, at least one town ruckus originated there." Wendy sank to the arm of the leather chair.

"Ruckus?" Anne asked. "What kind of ruckus? Why?"

"According to Coraline, the society claimed to have an original state map that was the actual one used by Lewis and Clark at the start of their expedition."

"What happened to it?" Anne asked.

"The way the story goes, it was stolen from the society about a hundred years ago. But I don't know for sure," said Wendy.

Stolen?

"Knowing Coraline's penchant for details, I'm betting her story is pretty accurate."

Anne stared at the map. "Do you think this could be it? The stolen map?"

Wendy shrugged. "I don't know. You'd have to get an expert to validate its age, I guess, then go from there."

Anne nodded. How did it get into this book and onto Aunt Edie's shelves? What if it *was* the original state map that Lewis and Clark had used? Then this was an important piece of American history, and she would have to decide what to do.

But first, she had to find out if the map was real.

A Note from the Editors

We hope you enjoy Secrets of the Blue Hill Library, created by the Books and Inspirational Media Division of Guideposts, a nonprofit organization that touches millions of lives every day through products and services that inspire, encourage, help you grow in your faith, and celebrate God's love in every aspect of your daily life.

Thank you for making a difference with your purchase of this book, which helps fund our many outreach programs to military personnel, prisons, hospitals, nursing homes, and educational institutions. To learn more, visit GuidepostsFoundation.org.

We also maintain many useful and uplifting online resources. Visit Guideposts.org to read true stories of hope and inspiration, access OurPrayer network, sign up for free newsletters, download free e-books, join our Facebook community, and follow our stimulating blogs.

To learn about other Guideposts publications, including the best-selling devotional Daily Guideposts, go to ShopGuideposts .org, call (800) 932-2145, or write to Guideposts, PO Box 5815, Harlan, Iowa 51593.